MURDER IN KEY WEST

a novel by

William Freeman

"mystery and erotica"

copyright 2003
ISBN 09675540-3-9

booksonnet.com
p.o.box 4522
st. augustine, fl
32085-4522

COVER DESIGN

BY

STARR EMERSON

Dedication: To my friend Old Phil

CHAPTER ONE

Harry Knight and his girlfriend Eve were on their way back to the boat from the health clinic when he saw the familiar yellow crime scene tape stretched across the jetty. After working nearly twenty years as a cop with NYPD Emergency Services, he had seen thousands of dead bodies. He had seen dead bums and he had seen dead millionaires. One was just as dead as the other. But this body on the jetty in Key West was different. It was special. It was his brother Billy.

Billy looked pretty much the same as he had the last time Harry had seen him ten years ago. His hair was still curly. And death had relieved all tension in his face, so he looked younger than he should. He looked like a kid with his eyes opened wide.

"Shark attack," someone in the forming crowd said.

It looked that way from a distance, because the legs were gone. But that had been Billy's choice, after the doctors told him that they would only be a source of problems for the rest of his life. He had figured that it would be easier to live without them. His shoulders and chest were broad and tan. He could probably outswim any shark. But that was Billy, he always made the best of a situation.

In the present situation, the best Billy could do was to look out through a third eye in the middle of his forehead, letting the world know that somewhere inside was the bullet that killed him. Other than that, you could see the family resemblance. Harry didn't see a wheelchair.

"Where is his wheelchair?" Harry said to Eve. "He had one that Workmen's Comp gave him, and he customized it. I've got pictures of him in marathons. I just wonder what happened to that chair. He was proud of it."

"He doesn't need it anymore" Eve said.

Two coroner's assistants had bagged the body and were bringing it up the rocks to an ambulance.

"This one is easy," one guy said, hefting the load.

"Yeah," said the other. "We only got half a man."

Eve grabbed Harry's arm. "They didn't mean it," she said.

"It's obvious they didn't know Billy." Harry smiled.

A police inspector in a short-sleeved shirt and open tie was moving along with the body-bag, taking notes on a small pad.

"He's my brother," Harry said to him, and he stopped.

6

"You sure?" the cop asked, looking at Harry's face and then over to the black plastic bag being placed inside the emergency vehicle.

"I'm sure," Harry said, and took out his wallet that showed a retired police I.D.

"An ex-New York cop," the Inspector said. "I guess you're going to tell me what happened."

"Twenty-two caliber, close enough to burn the skin around the entry wound," Harry said." No exit wound. It must have fragmented and done a lot of damage. And he saw it coming."

The cop looked at Harry for a full minute without speaking a word. He then stuck out his hand, and Harry shook it. It was a rough hand, almost as rough as Harry's. He probably owned a boat.

"Captain Art Adkins," the cop said, with the emphasis on "captain" to establish some sort of rank with the retired yankee cop. Harry ran into the same attitude when his boat was broken into in Coconut Grove, and he fingered two crack monsters that hung out at the dock. They didn't want his help, and Eve had gotten him back to sea and out of the maelstrom before he got upset. The thieves had only taken a portable television that didn't work, and an ounce of Jamaican weed that Eve had drying in her cabin. They left behind a crack pipe that Harry tossed overboard. He didn't want a paraphernalia rap if DEA stopped him, as they had twice already on his trip south to Miami. The police I.D. didn't always help, but it never hurt, especially when they

7

found the big .44 magnum he had the proper paperwork to posses.

"Did he have any enemies?" Detective Adkins asked. "Or was he married?"

"I hadn't seen him in ten years," Harry said. "He was a cop like me, but he got shot and lost his legs. I know he was on a pension and he rented out kayaks over at the beach. He wasn't there earlier so we were going to try and hook up for dinner tonight. I'm on the Peaceful Coexistence. It's the big catamaran straight out the channel. We dropped anchor last night but it was too late to go ashore. I wish I had gotten here a day sooner."

"A day late and a dollar short," Captain Adkins smiled. "The Peaceful Coexistence. Good name for a multi-hull. Me, I've got a little runabout called `Just Us'. Say it real fast and it sounds like justice, but it's not. It's a candy apple red Cigarette boat we seized in a drug operation. Got it cheap. It needed a lot of work, after sitting for two years until the case came up. Patience! And in the end, `Just Us' was mine."

"Just Us, against Them," Harry said.

The inspector laughed, and looked Harry over real good, for a reaction. But Harry just smiled and said nothing. This wasn't the time to talk boats.

"William Knight," the captain read from his notes. "Seems one of the officers knew him. Kayaks. Did he have any other family?"

"I'm it," Harry said. "We grew up in an orphanage after our parents were killed in a holdup. Billy won a prep

8

school scholarship for sports, and I went as part of the deal. Two years in the Army. I was a medic, and he was an M.P. in Germany when they were putting up the Wall. We did fifteen together on the NYPD before he got hurt."

"And it's been ten years since?" Adkins asked.

"I had to finish out my twenty," Harry said. "Our lives just took different paths."

"So you inherit the family fortune, any insurance policy, whatever Billy had of value." Captain Adkins was being efficient. Anything he got now was free.

"I'm the guy," Harry said. "It was just me and Billy all our lives. Until now. Now its just me. There is no `Just Us.'"

Harry said it fast enough so that the Cop got the point. There was a hand at Harry's elbow, and Eve was there. She had been hanging back in the crowd but now showed herself. Capt. Adkins gave her the once-over. She was a slim blonde with real short hair. She wore short shorts and a tank top. Her body was lean and muscular. She had great legs and small breasts. She wore sandals and was tan all the way down to her toes.

"She's with me," Harry said. "She's my crew."

"So this is the kind of benefit retirement brings," Art Adkins sighed. "Me, I'm going for thirty. I still like catching the bad guys."

"Some of them get away with what they do," Eve said.

"They just don't get convicted," Captain Art Adkins looked up in the sky. "But they really don't get away with nothing. They just think they do 'till Judgment Day."

9

"Did the cop that knew Billy say where he lived?" Harry asked.

"You don't have his address?" Adkins acted surprised.

"We always used his P.O. Box," Harry said.

"He lived in the garage apartment on an estate off of Duval Street. You can't miss it. It's the biggest lot in the city, and it has a steel fence around it." The Captain pointed in the direction he was speaking about. "It's owned by a retired business man who made a lot of money in health care products. He's from up north."

"Everybody here is from some place up north," Eve said, looking out to sea.

"I guess you're right," Adkins said. "We are about as far south as you can go. But everybody doesn't come down here on the day his brother is shot dead. Stay away from his place until we can go over it for clues. You understand, don't you? And don't leave town. Come by the station so we can get a statement from you."

"Is he a suspect?" Eve asked.

"At this point," Adkins said, "everybody is a suspect."

The police Captain folded his notebook and put it in his hip pocket. He directed a couple of lab-coated technicians to the scene of the crime, and then closed the back door of the vehicle that took away Billy's body.

Harry stood there and watched until the van and the investigator were gone. Then he looked at the pile of granite boulders that formed the jetty. He didn't want to go out there right now. Suddenly the world had changed, from a bond of birth to the isolation of death.

10

He no longer had his older brother to depend on if something had gone wrong. The same way Billy had depended on him when something had gone wrong. Harry felt a great loss, but at the same time he felt a release. And the lessening of ties to the land gave him a greater freedom. Harry couldn't cry about Billy. It just wouldn't feel right.

"Let's go back to the boat," Eve said softly in his ear. Her breath was hot. She had his arm firmly in both hands and led him away from the scene of the crime. They walked through an empty lot, past a hotel and a restaurant, down to the end of Simonton Street, where the dinghys from the anchorage tied up at a small dock on a small beach just off the main channel. Theirs was a small boat that had been patched a number of times and didn't look like it was worth stealing, so they left it turned over with the oars underneath. When they righted it, a bum crawled out and offered them a cigarette and a beer from a six pack. They both refused, and slid the boat into the water. They looked back to see their recent tenant surrounded by the others that hung out at the beach, and before he could get away all the beer was gone and he and his cronies sipped and smoked, and watched Eve pull on the oars and steer the dinghy into the channel.

Harry loved to watch Eve row. It took his mind off of everything else in the world. He sat between her legs in the stern with his back to the transom on a plastic bench seat. She sat midship on another plastic seat just forward of the oarlocks. Her long legs stretched back to him, a foot braced on each side as she stroked. As she came forward

11

with the oars, her face came close to his, and he could taste her breath as she exhaled and pulled on the oars, leaning back into the bow. Her entire body stretched, and the muscles of her abdomen, chest and shoulders rippled. Her arms flexed. Her thighs bulged. Her bare feet rubbed against his bare legs. She moved fluidly without pause. She was part of the sea.

Harry adjusted an old cushion behind him and rested back against the boat. She continued to row, adjusting her strokes to the current and the wind, heading into it as she steered toward the catamaran. When she leaned forward, the tank top fell away from her chest and Harry could see her nipples. She was all nipples. Then she leaned back and he saw the contours of her shorts between her legs as the seam rode deep in the crease. The sun was straight up and she glowed. Her short blonde hair was a golden halo. But Harry already knew she was no angel. Eve kept pulling on the oars. Her breath deepened and her movements became more muscular when she and the sea disagreed and she had to pull the bow back on line for an oncoming swell. Then she extended her stroke and mounted the crest, and surfed the back of the wave. She smiled at him and didn't miss a stroke. It was just the way he taught her.

From the back, the catamaran squatted on the water, the space between the hulls growing larger as they approached. The deck and main cabin embraced the large pontoons and waved its tall mast in a light chop. There was an outdrive for an engine tilted up out of the water, and the back of each hull had a gangway molded into it for easy

12

boarding. But Eve was pulling hard and had maneuvered the dinghy up under the deck in the tunnel between the hulls. She had to lean way back and Harry had to lean way forward to pass beneath the deck to the net that was strung between the bows of the boat.

When Eve reached the underside of the net, she shipped the oars and grabbed on to the webbing. The current tried to push the dinghy backwards, but she kept it in place with her legs. Harry was bent all the way forward so his face rested on the fabric of her shorts, at her pubic mound. Each wave thrust her pelvis upward with the motion of the sea.   And it fell back with each trough. Again and again.

When she was satisfied, Eve released her grip on the net and drifted back beneath the deck between the hulls, until they came out the back, and she grabbed the stainless steel stern pulpit, stood up, took a line from the back of the dinghy and tied them off to a cleat on the port hull. Harry stayed out of the way and admired her athleticism, the curve of her hips and the shape of her buttocks. She hopped up on deck and steadied the dinghy for him as he came aboard. Then she let the dinghy fall away on its tether and they were home free.

Harry had told Eve that getting back to the boat after being ashore was like coming in off of a ledge. In the three months that they had been together on the boat, they seldom went ashore. He taught her about boat life, and she took to it. She learned fast, and had even plotted their trip to Key West from Miami. They had arrived just when she

13

said they would.

They both stood and watched the dinghy bounce and pull until it found the motion of the sea, the boat and the air moving together.

"Did you love your brother?" Eve asked.

"Billy?" Harry said. "Everybody loved Billy. He was a great guy. Sure I loved him...like a brother."

Harry walked around the deck checking the rigging, and enjoying his island of sanity. He and Billy had grown up on an island. Long Island. They had worked on an island, Manhattan. Harry felt at home, and this island could move. He watched Eve go below in the starboard hull where she had a private berth, head with shower and the galley. Harry lived in the port hull; private double berth, head with shower, and chart table and electronics. Although both hulls had their private companionway from the deck, they could be entered from the main salon in the center of the boat, where there was a large settee that lowered into a king size berth with a large hatch overhead. The two private berths also had hatches large enough to climb through to the deck.

It had a winged mast shaped like an airplane wing that made it possible to sail into the wind. There were also compartments that had been glassed over in both hulls, where two million dollars worth of heroin had been hidden when the boat was seized. Harry had waited two years to get her. Captain Art Adkins wasn't the only cop who knew how the system worked. Just Us against Them. Every cop knew that feeling at one time or another. Harry used to be

14

one of Us, but since he had been at sea, he was feeling more like one of Them.

Harry sat on the bow of the boat with his legs dangling over the side. He meditated on the water. In the time since Billy had been hurt, Harry had tried everything to make peace with himself. He looked into all the major religious philosophies, cults, Hinduism, Buddhism, Zen, Transcendentalism, Mind Control and Yoga. Though none embraced him, he was able to take what suited him to realize inner peace. At sea, his life was no longer in the hands of man, he was in the hands of God.

Eve had made a pot of espresso and brought it up to the large cockpit, aft of the main salon. She had taken off her clothes and pinned them to a line between the backstay and the shrouds. She had crawled into a large caftan in a bright print. It belonged to Harry, and was too large and flapped in the breeze.

Harry came back to the cockpit and sat in the chair by the wheel, while Eve lounged on a cushion in the shade of a bimini top and a dodger that gave privacy to them and protection from the wind.

"How much longer?" Harry asked.

"I don't know." Eve was concerned. "You know I like boat life. I want to stay, but I can't say how long. Why? Do you have plans?"

"That's not what I'm talking about," Harry said. "I meant until we get the results of the HIV tests."

"Oh my!" Eve said, and laughed. "I thought you were putting me under pressure to decide about staying. Two or three days. Don't worry. I'm not worried. These last three months must have been very frustrating for you. It has been for me. You were telling the truth when you said you hadn't had sex for three months before we met."

"Not with another person," Harry chuckled.

"Don't joke," Eve said.

"I swear," Harry said. "It hasn't been so bad. It's given me a goal."

"And when we accomplish that goal," Eve said "Are we going after Billy's killer?"

She had the coffee poured and held it suspended above his hand, while she waited for an answer. He finally reached up and took it. She still waited.

"Maybe he deserved it," Harry said.

"He certainly was a handsome guy." Eve sat back down. "And what a build. A hunk. Billy was a real hunk."

"He was training for the wheelchair Olympics," Harry said. "He wrote me about it once. We stayed in touch a couple times a year. Neither one of us was big on writing or telephones. Usually he sent post cards with pictures of girls in bikinis that Billy said he knew intimately. Billy always did like the ladies, and they liked him. He was a dancer and an athlete, and the best brother a guy could have."

"And you don't care why he was killed?" Eve asked.

"Well, maybe just a little," Harry said.

"Have you got any other plans?" Eve asked.

"Explain it to me again," Harry said. "After we get a negative result on the HIV test, we can have unsafe sex?"

16

"Uninhibited," Eve sighed, and smiled at him.

"I've got plans," Harry said, and winked at her.

"My husband divorced me rather than wait six months, after I caught him with a friend of mine," Eve said.

"Is that the man you're running away from?" Harry asked.

"Yes," Eve said, and looked into her cup. "I knew who he fucked and that wasn't so bad, but I also knew who she fucked and that scared the hell out of me."

"And this all happened three months before we met," Harry said.

"Maybe more," Eve said, "For my own peace of mind, I decided to spend my six months celibate."

"Two or three more days," Harry said and finished his coffee. He watched her as she ran her fingers through her short hair. Her eyes were as grey as the sea gets just before a storm. Other than boat talk and the foods they shared in common, this was the longest conversation they had about themselves in three months. There was sex talk too, but it was more biological than erotic; menstrual cycles and the things that went with it. Sperm and its ramifications. Children. Adult talk about adult subjects.

"Billy told the cops that we were twins after the folks got killed," Harry said. "We both saw the bodies. Billy kept his arm around my shoulder and we didn't cry. I can barely remember a time when we were a family. Billy was a year older. Same month two days apart. He knew where the folks kept the birth certificates because we needed them to get in to school. Billy doctored the date so we were

17

twins and the State wouldn't separate us. Then Billy got drafted in our senior year of high school, so we joined up together."

"So, you managed to stay together," Eve said.

"No," Harry said, "That was when they split us apart. They didn't want brothers to be killed together. I think it was the Sullivan Brothers, seven brothers killed on a Navy ship during World War II. It was some kind of rule, but we were men by then and we could make it on our own."

"But when you got out, you got back together again on the Police Force." Eve remembered everything the first time.

"That's right," Harry said. "But we didn't work much together after we were rookies. You see, Billy and me and three other cops were supposed to guard the outfield gate at Shea Stadium when the Beatles played there. We were supposed to control the situation with a thousand fans trying to get in free. We had barricades and two squad cars blocking it and we had a radio in case we needed additional help. Do you know what a thousand gate crashers looks like to five cops with night sticks? Inside was what, forty or fifty thousand screaming lunatics. So Billy is talking to this one kid up at the barricade and they're laughing. Billy asks the kid if he'd pay ten bucks to get inside. The kid says yeah. Billy says, `this one got a ticket. Let him in'. We did that a thousand times cause everybody's got ten bucks. When the brass calls in, we say the situation is under control. Two grand each and we keep the peace like we're supposed to."

18

"And the other cops went along?" Eve said.

"They were guys with time on the force," Harry said. "This was hazard pay."

"And they never said anything?" Eve asked.

"No," Harry laughed. "Everybody knew. Word always gets around about what really happened. But what they showed on television was a thousand crazed fans running onto the outfield grass and the reporter said they had overpowered a police force unprepared for such a popular group."

"So, they found out it was Billy's idea?" Eve said.

"Anybody that knew Billy knew it was his idea," Harry said. "So they split us up after that. Since I had medic training, I worked mostly Emergency Services. We were 911 before there was a 911. I was in lower Manhattan and Billy was a street cop on the upper West side where Harlem begins."

"You went your separate ways?" Eve asked.

"We still got together for the Super Bowl when the Dallas Cowgirls were playing. Billy was crazy about their uniforms. We watched mostly for the girls. Two more days?" Harry said.

"Sensual pleasure is a reason for existence," Eve said. "Some guys get off watching the men. Let's go watch the sunset."

"It's high noon," Harry said but he knew what she meant. It was one of those unspoken things between them that enabled them to get along so well together.

Harry followed her back to the stern. The bright

caftan wrapped around her by the wind and shoved at the shape of her naked body. Sitting side by side on the transom, they could lean back against the cowling of the cockpit. They were hanging so that there was no boat behind them and they could see anybody coming out of the channel.

Eve put her arm around Harry's neck and kissed him on the cheek. She pressed her tongue in his ear and he laughed. She smiled as she covered his lap with the excess material of the caftan. Harry leaned back and smiled. They had seen the sunset before. With her hand under the cover of the caftan, Eve unbuckled his belt and unzipped his fly. Her hand was cool as she found him and freed him so that a tent formed under the caftan. He was hard. She knew what aroused him especially when there was something he didn't want to think about. She stroked him and stroked him, kissed him around his ear and eyes. She pressed her teeth in his neck hard enough to hold him. She unbuttoned his shirt and kissed his chest. She bit his nipples and kept watch for approaching boats. At the last moment she pulled away the caftan and Harry ejaculated into the water. He sat up and caught his breath. She flicked the last drops of semen from his penis into the sea.

"So long, junior," she said.

"You know," he said rezipping himself. "I could always do this kind of thing myself."

"If that's what you like," Eve said.

He turned now so that she could lean across him and he could hug her. He held on as if she were a dream and he

20

didn't want to wake up. She rubbed the back of his neck. He inhaled her hair and then her breath as they kissed once more.

"I think we got it in the dinghy," Eve laughed. "The wind must have caught it."

He looked back at the rubber boat bouncing on the water. It was about twelve feet away. It was possible. A bucket of salt water would wash away his progeny, his offspring, as millions of struggling sperm became basic to the ecosystem; food for brine shrimp that lived in the growth that built up on the hull.

"Where life begins and ends," Harry said. "So long, juniors and sisters."

"Only juniors," Eve said. "You need a woman for the Y chromosome. You've only got X 's."

"Well, I'll clean up the guys when I go back in." Harry said.

"To give your statement?" Eve said.

"I want to talk to Captain Art Adkins again," Harry said. "I just want to ask a few questions, maybe look around Billy's place," Harry said, getting up and pulling the dinghy toward the boat.

"There's no such thing as an ex-cop," Eve said.

"Or an ex-wife," Harry said. "Billy was married once."

"Before he got hurt?" Eve said.

"No," Harry said. "After. I got a card about a year ago he was getting divorced."

"You didn't tell the Inspector." Eve said.

21

"Why should I do his job" Harry said. "I'm just a private citizen who knows how the Just Us system works. I think I'm better off not having to consider local politics. To them Billy is bad for tourists."

"So, you're going to ask around and find out if he had any enemies or a wife?" Eve asked.

"Murder is usually committed by someone you know," Harry said.

CHAPTER TWO

Alone. When Harry Knight was alone in the dinghy
pulling on the oars, he could breathe again; watching Eve
go below as he moved away from the boat. She had occupied his mind. They had been together constantly since she
had come on the boat, except for a stop for fuel and water
in Big Pine Key and the time it took her to pack before they
left Miami. They did have the privacy of their separate
berths but most nights she slept with him next to her and
the days were spent together on deck. For Eve, it had been
three months of learning from how to tie a bowline to how
Harry liked his margaritas. He never had to tell her twice.
And he had learned how to please a woman. This woman.
Eve.

The wake of a passing lobster boat tossed him off
course and he automatically corrected with a hard pull on
the left oar. He had rowed the dinghy so often, that its

23

movement came without thought. He was part of it, the ancient guidance system in this age of systems and components. He preferred being a deck monkey, a boat wanderer, a man without a country. But he loved his country. Its strength and humanity had enabled him to retire to the sea after having served with loyalty, as a public servant; protecting the lives and the property of its people. He loved the job. He loved the role of the hero. He loved the people he worked with. And now he was happy just to be with a woman he had to admit that he loved.

Usually when Harry was forced to row ashore, it was because of "the list", that endless number of things that had to be done to stay afloat, to stay alive disconnected from the land.

Repairs and provisions had been replaced by thoughts of Eve, the way she smiled, the way she massaged his neck, the feel of her lips on his eyelids. He liked it much better this way, though a lot less work got done. And she kept his mind off of Billy for three months, even though that was their destination. The process of getting there had far exceeded any thought of what awaited them when they arrived.

Harry had been anchored alone off of Miami at *No Name Harbor* when Billy called him on the ship to shore radio. It had been five years since they had last spoken but it could have been five minutes. Theirs was a brotherly bond that went beyond the limits of time. They had stayed in touch by mail from time to time. They had a great childhood. Harry could tell you stories from now until

Christmas about Billy. And, the time when they were cops was a three volume set. Then the years when they were apart and just couldn't make a connection between Harry's vacation time and Billy's rehab schedule. They were on separate paths but still bound by a brotherly love. Billy wanted Harry to come down and help him with something he couldn't discuss over the open airwaves. There was no urgency. Billy just wanted to be sure that Harry was coming. Take your time. Enjoy the sail. Harry had been planning on going to Key West eventually.

At the time, Harry hadn't touched land in over a month. He had loaded up with beer and traded with the lobster boats for perishables and "shorts"; tails that were too small to be legal so they had to be eaten or dumped before they returned to port where the Marine Patrol waited at the fish dock. They also had vegetables and fruit if they were heading out. Any beer they had, had been finished by the crew the first night.

If it rained Harry didn't need water. With a hundred gallons holding he could shower every day and boil it for tea and drinking. With seawater he cooked pasta, rice, beans, anything that wouldn't spoil. He always trolled so he had fish. He dove the reef and was good with a speargun.

It had been a month alone; dive a little, read a little, sketch a little, study the charts, drink a little Spanish brandy, smoke a little weed, read *Penthouse* and masturbate for a love life. The last time he had been with a woman was ninety seven days ago, but who was counting.

25

There were no major problems with the boat. The weather was hot. Life was good.

There was still a list; preventive maintenance, the seepage in the port hull, the leak around the main hatch. Then with Billy's call the list got longer. Harry had to go somewhere. The boat had to be sea worthy. As the Coast Guard's new motto read, "A lack of planning on your part does not constitute an emergency on our part." It was the government's way of saying "Fuck You." They were in the drug business. They were sea cops. Harry wasn't worried about needing help and it felt good to be protected from the bad guys.

Near the boatyard where he provisioned and bought parts was an outdoor restaurant. He would go there for a beer and a bucket of steamed shrimp when he was ashore. It had a few tables shaded with umbrellas and the smell of fried food made you hungry for french fries. The wait-resses were friendly and the service was slow, but that was the way Harry liked it.

He was sipping his second beer, waiting for the food, when Eve walked in. She wore a pair of white short shorts that hung on her hips. She wore a blue shirt tied across her chest leaving her midriff bare exposing her naval. There was a white vest over the shirt where she stored things in the pockets. Her legs were shapely, long and tan. He thought she could do something with that short blonde hair but he still wanted to run his hand through it.

When she caught him staring at her, Harry turned back to his beer. He looked up again and she was smiling at

26

him. He had to say something.

"If you had a pair of white boots," Harry said, "You could play for the Dallas Cowgirls."

She walked over to his table and sat down. The waitress came at the same time with his french fries and shrimp. They waited for her to leave.

"My treat," Harry said and offered the attractive blonde his food.

"I'm looking for a boat captain," she said and got a bottle of catsup from another table and made a small red pool in the middle of the plate.

"What makes you think I'm a sailor?" Harry said. "Does it show?"

Harry could feel those stone grey eyes reading him. She looked at his faded blue shirt and frayed khaki shorts and his non-skid sandals. His hair hadn't been cut in a long time and probably combed as recently.

"It shows," she said dipping a french fry. "At least you shaved."

"I never know when I'm going to meet a good woman," Harry said.

"How about a bad woman?"

"What kind of boat are you looking for?" Harry said. He peeled a shrimp and offered it to her. She accepted it and licked her lips.

"I want to go sailing."

"Well, I'm not in the charter business," Harry said and watched her hold the little pink shrimp by the tail in front of her mouth.

"I wasn't thinking about business, I was thinking about pleasure" and she ate the shrimp.

"I'm going down to Key West to see my brother Billy," Harry said. "Do you want to crew?"

"I don't do crew," she said and wiped her mouth with a paper napkin. "But I give great passenger."

"I don't know," Harry had to laugh. He was really enjoying this woman.

The last woman on his boat had only stayed one night and that was ninety seven days ago, but who was counting.

She stood up and put her hands on her hips. Her belly button was about level with his nose. She looked down at him.

"You can always go alone," she said.

Harry didn't find out her name, Eve West, until he picked her up at the dock the next morning. She traveled light, two small duffel bags and a leather shoulder bag that could also be worn as a back pack. She wanted to row. So he let her. He was surprised at how well she did things for the first time. She was athletic and well coordinated, strong and rhythmic and only splashed him twice on the way out. He gave her a few pointers and she heeded his word.

Harry gave Eve the starboard berth and he took the port hull with its seepage. She stayed out of his way while he readied the boat to depart. But she watched everything. She was right next to him if he needed an extra hand. As long as she wasn't crew, he couldn't order her around. He said nothing and took advantage of her quiet assistance.

It was balmy and breezy on deck that night and she had a bottle of tequila and a nickel bag of Colombian gold. They just sat together as the sky turned from blue to red to purple to starry. She said very little. There were no questions about each others' respective history. There was great comfort in the quiet broken occasionally by laughter. Harry fell asleep on deck and when he woke up to go pee, she was next to him. He got a light blanket to protect them from the morning dew and they slept together for the first time. In the morning after coffee, they set sail. After three months of sailing, a shakedown cruise in the Bahamas and a visit to each of the keys, they arrived in Key West and Harry couldn't imagine being without Eve.

Billy had said not to hurry.

Harry tied up the dinghy at a restaurant along the waterfront where he'd buy a drink to pay for parking, then he would walk over to the police station and talk to Captain Art Adkins. He bought a beer and gave a kid at the bar a five dollar tip and told him to keep an eye on his boat. Harry wanted to stay away from the dinghy dock at Simonton Street. He might be going back after dark and he knew what happened in places like that when people had a few beers and a few smokes and maybe a rock. He was a retired gentleman and he didn't feel like hanging with bums. Maybe he was elitist, but then at sea, those things were never a consideration. He walked out into the street.

He looked in a newspaper rack to see what day it was. It was Saturday and Billy had not made the front page of the afternoon edition. Harry was sure it was in there. Maybe on the local page where the tourists wouldn't notice it.

It was Saturday, one of the Sabbaths. Harry made it a point not to work on Holy days, Friday, Saturday, Sunday and sometimes Monday. He was a good captain and it was his boat and he could do anything he damn well pleased or not do anything at all. He didn't take orders from anyone.

"Turn around real slow," the man said.

Harry had stooped down to read the headline. He pivoted and stood up. He did it slowly. The man had a gun.

"Jesus Christ," the man said. "I thought you was Billy. I heard you was dead. I saw the body."

"I'm his brother," Harry said.

"The cop?"

"Retired," Harry said.

Harry had seen this guy before. Only the names had changed and now they were all a lot older. The long hair, the beard, the thousand yard stare still in their eyes and the military clothing, fatigue pants, camouflage tee shirt and sandals made from tire treads with inner tube straps. He knew the next question before it was asked. "Were you in Nam, brother?" the guy said. He lowered what looked like an M-16 rifle to point at the ground. "No," Harry said. "Germany."

"I knew you did time," the guy said. "Name's Frisky. My real name was too hard to pronounce when I went in so they shortened it to Frisky. Billy was my best friend."

30

Frisky raised the rifle again, pulled the trigger and a jet of water hit Harry in the chest.

"It looks real to me," Harry laughed.

"It's a game we play for the `rush'," Frisky said. "Some old vets live around here. You'll see guys with AK-47s too. That's Charlie. We try to shoot each other. It's like the war. You always have to be alert. It brings back the `rush'."

"So, who keeps score?" Harry said.

"We only keep track of the individual kill." Frisky said. "There's no overall strategy. It's just an ongoing battle day to day. No end in sight. Like the war."

"And the same when the other guy hits you?" Harry asked.

"Then, that day, Charlie wins," Frisky said. "But then, there's always tomorrow. That's what makes it a game. I been playing for years. Sometimes, I feel guilty that I didn't die with my buddies in Nam."

"Who killed Billy?" Harry asked. This was getting maudlin. He had heard enough "my Buddy in Nam" stories over the last thirty years. He didn't need any more. Let them all wrestle with their own demons real or imagined. But keep it to yourself.

"Probably some babe," Frisky said. He didn't seem to notice that the subject had changed. "I wish it had been me they shot. Blew his brains out."

"Any babe in particular?" Harry asked.

"Maybe the twins," Frisky said. He pulled a joint from behind his ear, lit it and offered it to Harry who

31

refused. "Yeah, the twins. I know they sacrificed a cat once for a ritual. They do these weird things on their boat, the Gemini. They're strange."

Harry felt like he was hearing it from an expert. He could see the look on the D.A's face when they brought this guy in as a witness. After a while, they found out that half these guys had never been to Viet Nam. And most had served their time in a jail. They were living a lie.

"I need to go identify the body," Harry said. It was time to move on. The Berlin Wall was gone. Kentucky Fried Chicken was in Moscow and everything he wore had probably been made in Red China. It was time to move on.

"Bummer," Frisky said. "I got a couple of downers if you like. Take them. I get them from the VA. I could go with you."

"No thanks, there are some times when it's better to be alone. And straight. Keep the faith, brother."

Harry walked away without looking back. He got directions from a pretty girl hustling condos from a booth outside a hotel and headed for the police station not far from there. It wasn't a very large island.

If he took the side streets, it looked like there were fewer tourists and no hucksters. So Harry followed his own path. He had a good sense of direction and it was cooler off the beaten path. There were a few lookers taking in the old Victorian mansions that the salvage barons built before the railroad came through bringing law and order to the wild south. Hurricanes had wiped out the railroad but the mansions survived. And salvagers again were cleaning up

32

since the Coast Guard refused to provide aid if there was a commercial salvor in the vicinity. Harry had heard on the VHF 'may days' and 'pom pom' requesting assistance after going aground or loosing a mast. Taking on water was only a hazard if you didn't have a pump.

He had followed the calls from the security of his twin hulled boat. He knew the catamaran would never sink even if it capsized. It was a life raft and he sat out the storms in a safe harbor. He never wanted to fight the wind and the sea. And what if the weather was bad? Well, when the weather was bad he didn't go out. And if the weather got bad while he was out, he survived. There was a French saying, "There are no good sailors; there are old sailors."

The police station was a low grey building set among tropical vegetation. There were a few big oaks and benches where people were smoking cigarettes. Butts were strewn all over the ground. Two women smiled at Harry as he walked by. He headed for the back of the building where there was a sign for the Morgue.

Harry wondered if this was what he wanted to do for the rest of his life; try and solve a murder so personal he could never remain objective or fair let alone just. He thought of Eve back on the boat. Well, it was another two days before lift off. It would keep his mind off of the possibility, as improbable as it would be that one of their tests would turn out positive.

Captain Art Adkins was outside with a big cigar and smiled as Harry approached.

"I guess we won't be able to show `flight as evidence

of guilt'," Captain Adkins said.

"You'll need an I.D. of the body by a family member," Harry said. "Let's get it over with."

Adkins placed his cigar on a ledge where he could retrieve it later. Harry followed him through the doors where the Detective was met by a white gowned attendant who took them through the doors of cold storage using a card with hole in the face to access the electrically controlled entrance. Compared to New York, it was nothing. They didn't have enough freezers to hold what Harry had delivered in one hot summer night. Adkins watched Harry as the locker door was opened and the tray with Billy was slid out. The attendant uncovered his face.

Harry felt like he was looking down into the water and his reflection was asleep. There was no doubting the family resemblance.

There was a rush of sadness that passed through him and his eyes teared. But Harry looked at Billy and the memories of a lifetime passed before his eyes as they say your life does in that last second before death.

Harry had to smile. That was the effect Billy had on people. He made them smile. He left them a little happier if it meant bending the rules. He was a good cop. He was a great person. He was a memory.

"It's him," Harry said.

"It could be you," Captain Art Adkins said. "I mean the way you two look alike. Only you are much taller."

The attendant covered the corpse and shoved Billy back in the locker. He wouldn't have liked that, Harry

34

thought. Billy came to Florida for the warm weather. Captain Art Adkins led Harry outside where he recovered his cigar.

"Ybor City," Adkins said holding up the cigar. "That's where all the good ones come from. Not Cuba. All the Cubans are here. All the good Cuban cigar makers are in Ybor City. They've taken over the lobster business. I hablo español just to get this job. What's the country coming to?"

"Just us, against them," Harry said.

"Ain't it the truth," Art Adkins said. He had assumed a friendly air that didn't fool Harry.

"Do you want me to sign an identification form?" He didn't want to waste time with small talk.

"You don't have to, his wife did it earlier. You didn't know your brother had a wife?"

"I thought they were divorced about a year ago," Harry said.

"Well, what do you know! She had a Marriage License," Adkins puffed the cigar. "We finished with his place and released it as a crime scene. They gave her the key."

"Did they find anything at Billy's place?" Harry asked and found an upwind position away from the smoke.

"Before I tell you what I know," Captain Art Adkins said. "I want your story and I want you to sign it."

"Three months ago, I got a call from Billy on the VHF marine radio. `Come on down,' he said. He said he needed some help with something but didn't get into details. He

35

said there was no hurry. I provisioned, picked up crew and got here last night. We looked for Billy this morning at the beach and found him at the jetty."

"That's it?" Art Adkins said.

"Type it up," Harry said. "I'll sign it."

"And this Mrs. William Knight," Adkins went on, "You don't know who she is?"

"Never met the woman," Harry said. "Billy never wrote much. Only thing I remember was her name. Velda?"

"Velda," Art Adkins started to choke on the cigar smoke. He caught his breath and grabbed on to a tree. He wiped his eyes. "Holy shit! Billy was married to Velda?"

"I take it you know the lady," Harry said a little disturbed by Adkins reaction. He hadn't expected anything but Adkins face was red as he wiped his mouth. If he had a heart attack, Harry knew he wouldn't give him CPR.

"You have got to be kidding," Adkins said shaking his head. "Billy was married to Velda!"

"What's the joke?" Harry said. "Who's Velda?"

"She's a crazy old gal that hangs out at the sunset dock selling fudge. Chocolate only, calls herself Mrs. Brown. She used to be a pretty hot number from what I hear. Came down from up north like the rest of you damn yankees. She's still a good looker if you catch her in the right light if you know what I mean. She's a lot tamer since she took the cure a few years back. She used to get drunk and beat up guys who tried to fool around with her. Charged her with assault and battery a couple of times but she beat the

36

rap. Came in dressed like Grandma Moses. Broke the jury's heart. Also it has been reported that there is hash in her brownies but my undercover boys keep eating the evidence. She also has a Private Investigators license. She carries a gun."

"Sounds like your ordinary citizen to me," Harry said.

"I've known worse criminals. She's local color. The tourists love her. We live and let live here, Harry. It's the southern style. But when one of our own is killed we take it real serious. Billy was one of us."

"Billy was my brother," Harry said.

"Then you should have got here a little sooner," Captain Art Adkins said. "So tell me, retired cop, what's life like living on the idle?"

"I don't read the newspapers. I don't have a television and never turn on the AM/FM radio," Harry said. "I come ashore as little as possible. I avoid people. My check is deposited automatically to my VISA account. Life is good."

"You ever get bored?" Adkins asked.

"Yeah," Harry said. "Lots of times. But after twenty years working the big city, you know I really like it. No responsibility to anyone. But when you're standing in a hole in the water, your senses are more acute. You may not live longer, but it seems longer."

"That sounds pretty good if your only goal is to live longer," Adkins scratched his head. "Me, I'm the kind of guy that needs a reason to live longer. And right now that reason is to find out who murdered Billy."

"That's why they make shirts in different colors," Harry said. "To each his own."

"But sometimes," Adkins looked Harry straight in the eye. "One size fits all."

Adkins took a page from the back of his notebook and drew a little map for Harry with Billy's address.

"Thank you," Harry said and put the paper in one of his pockets. Adkins went off and left him alone at the back entrance to the morgue. He knew there would be an autopsy and a coroner's inquest before he saw Billy again. He was glad he got to see him first. It didn't matter, but to Harry it seemed important. It just wasn't the proper goodbye, not for Billy.

Billy had a garage apartment behind a big stucco house off of SimontonStreet. There was a driveway entrance through an iron gate opening in an eight foot high block wall. Ruts had been worn in the drive by the narrow wheels of Billy's wheel chair, as well as the usual tire tracks that led to a circular drive in front of the house. The backyard had a big magnolia tree and a sizable oak. Beyond that was the screened swimming pool and patio. Hibiscus blossoms, large red and sensual skirted the property rising above the wall. There was a coconut palm and a mango tree next to the garage. The original garage door had been replaced by a sliding glass door. It was slightly open. Inside, Harry could see a low table, a futon mattress and a couple of bean bag chairs. There were a couple of floor lamps but they were not turned on. The kitchen to the right was at a child's level, sink and stove close to the ground. There was a small refrigerator and a microwave oven in the corner. Harry couldn't see to his left because the angle brought only a reflection in the glass. On the door was a sign, a shoe with a line through it. Harry smiled. Billy always had been neat.

Harry took off his shoes and left them outside. He stepped inside and noticed the lushness of the carpet over a double pad that he sank into. There was a whistle by his left ear and he kept sinking and then he was swimming up though the water and his head slammed into the bottom of the boat. The back of his head pulsed with pain. Harry let himself sink back away from the pain trying to find relief in oblivion.

"Why did you kill Billy?" her voice entered the deep.

She held a blue steel .45 automatic that looked the size of a ham in her small brown hand. It was the first thing Harry saw when he regained consciousness. Each beat of his heart sent the pain from the back of his head to the front of his eyes and it made it hard to focus. It took him a second to remember the deep plush carpet where he lay and thought of how comfortable it must have been for....Billy!

"I'm a P.I., private investigator," her voice came from the gun. "You can check with the cops if you have to. I've had to defend myself before. So, I warn you. You wouldn't be the first man I killed. No funny business. Do you hear me?"

"Loud and clear," Harry said and looked at the woman behind the gun seated on one of the beanbags.

She was dressed like an earth mama, granny boots,

gypsy skirt in a brown print. A long sleeved tan blouse buttoned up to the neck. He hadn't yet been able to focus on her face.

Harry realized that he was not quite back yet. He had been knocked out before and knew it could have been for seconds or for days. He rolled onto his side but still couldn't lift his head above the pain. He felt behind his ear. It stung but there was no blood. She must have wrapped the gun in something when she hit him. She knew what she was doing.

"Why did you kill Billy?" she repeated as if he hadn't heard her the first time.

Her hair was black with streaks of silver that were twisted into a bun at the back of her head pulled away from her deep tanned face. Her dark brown eyes didn't blink. The gun rested on one of her thighs where the brown skirt had crept up and he could see that one of her legs was shapely and he guessed that the other one undercover was part of a matched set. The skirt fit tightly at the hips and she had a flat belly. She was busty and firm beneath the blouse that was shear enough to show that she was braless.

"Who in the world do you think you are!" Harry was getting steamed. The doctor who had interviewed him for the police said that Harry had an aggressive reaction to pain. He highly recommended Harry for the job. What the hell did he know. The pain behind his ear exploded as he tried to get up and fell back into the plushness.

"I'm Velda," she said. "Billy's wife."

"Well, I'm his brother," Harry said. "What do you

40

think you're doing?"

"The family is always the first suspect," Velda said.

"No," Harry said. "The first suspect is always the spouse. Or the ex-spouse."

"So you know about the divorce," Velda said. "Billy must have told you. He was the only one who knew. We had to go to Georgia."

"So that explains the postcard from Stone Mountain," Harry said.

"And Billy made it to the top in his chair," Velda said. "He took the foot path too. What a guy! I had to help him once when he got stuck in a crevice, but what the hell, I was just saving time. Billy would have done it eventually."

"Why the hell did you slug me?" Harry could feel the aggression building and he was able to sit up but the pain was now a motivation rather than a hinderance.

"I slugged you to let you know that I would if I had to," Velda said and pointed the gun away from Harry but didn't put it down. "Now you know who you're dealing with. Don't let the granny act fool you."

"You made your point," Harry said and stopped looking for something to use as a weapon.

"So, are you going to give me some answers?" Velda said. "Or do I have to shoot you in the foot?"

"What do you want to know?" Harry said. He sat up cross legged in a modified lotus position with his hands resting empty and open on his thighs. He exhaled and inhaled to restore himself to the moment.

"Billy used to do that," Velda laughed, "but he

usually had a joint in his hand. He used to hold it up to my
lips while I massaged his shoulders from behind. Not even
my first ex-husband had shoulders like that. You look like
Billy but you don't have his charisma."

"He had a years head start," Harry said. He blew out
again and became calm. He turned to Velda who was
leaning forward with the gun in both hands. She meant
business.

"You haven't seen your brother in ten years," Velda
had a tone that assured him she knew her facts. This
wasn't a cat and mouse game like Captain Art Adkins
employed to make his work more entertaining. "You
haven't talked to him in five. And the first day you show
up, he winds up with a bullet in his brain." Her dark eyes
were as intense as lasers. "Why?"

"Fuck you," Harry said with the same clarity that
Velda used to pose the question. "What are you, some kind
of one woman vigilante? If you want to talk to me about
my brother, talk to me about Billy. This hard ass bullshit
doesn't work with me. You want to shoot me. Shoot me."

"You didn't say that you didn't do it," Velda said.

"If I killed somebody," Harry said, "Lying wouldn't
be out of the question."

"You sound just like Billy," Velda said and put the
gun in her lap. She leaned back in the beanbag chair and
stretched out her legs. One was just a shapely as the other.
He knew Billy would have liked her. Billy was a leg man.

Harry looked around the room at floor level. He had
fallen toward the kitchen and he could see the low shelves

42

where food was stored and dishes stacked. Slowly he
turned and reached out for a bottle of brandy that was
within an arms length to his right. He grabbed the bottle
and he could hear the beans rustle and the click of a metal
safety. He didn't care whether she was putting it on or off.
He pulled the cork out of the bottle with his teeth and took
a big slug. When he put his head back, the pain sent his
arm a message to throw the bottle at her, but fortunately his
inner self overruled his instinct and he took a second
swallow. It burned all the way down. It felt good. When
he turned back to Velda, the gun was on the bean bag and
she was on her knees next to it looking through a cloth
brown sack for something. It turned out to be a compact
with a mirror and a lipstick.

Harry watched how she opened her mouth and then
pursed her lips as she applied a white frosting to her tan
face. Harry thought of ginger bread. She checked back
over her shoulder to see where the gun was and then
crawled over to where Harry sat. She looked at him with
those dark brown eyes and he thought of chocolate chip
cookies.

"Oh, fudge," Velda said and grabbed the bottle out of
his hand. She drank long and hard. She wiped her mouth
with her hand and held on to the bottle. She rested on her
side and became lost in thought.

"Billy told me last year that you two were divorced,"
Harry said. "So, why the act?"

"I was his wife, the only one he ever had," Velda took
another drink. "Wife. I liked the title. It's like Governor or

43

General. You retain the title even when somebody replaces you."

"Billy wanted to marry someone else?" Harry took the bottle back from her but not without an effort.

"That's the story of my life," Velda said and watched to see how much he drank. "Men leaving me for younger women. My first ex left me for a young bleached blonde with a tit job who fucked him like a dog. But he was some guy. He ruined me for any other man and then he dumped me. Went out one day for a pack of cancer sticks and never came back. Son of a bitch!"

"Was Billy like that?" Harry asked and gave her back the bottle.

"No," Velda said. "Billy was a mensch, a gentleman, a sport to the end."

"He always was," Harry said "And he always liked women, young and..."

"Not so young," Velda cut in. "It wasn't a marriage the way you think. We didn't do it for love. We already had that. We did it for money."

"Money?" Harry said. "Billy never did anything for money alone. There had to be a kick in it."

"There was a kick alright," Velda laughed and shook with delight. She let out a sigh and held the bottle to her belly. Then she came back down. "It was for the benefits."

"Billy's pension," Harry said.

"With full health coverage for him and his family," Velda said. "It was important at the time."

Some of the pain was dull now due to the alcohol and

44

Harry could watch Velda unwind with the same drug. She was close to him now and he could smell her vanilla perfume. He liked it.

"I had some health problems when I first came down here," Velda didn't look at him. "After my first ex dumped me, I crawled into a bottle for...for...a long time. When Billy picked me up off of the sidewalk outside of Captain Tony's joint, I was half dead. I wished I was dead. Booze, drugs, cigarettes and a broken heart had me on the ropes. Then Billy stepped in. He cared enough to stop the fight. He threw in the towel for me because there was no one else in my corner."

"When Billy walked a beat," Harry said, "he used to carry suckers for the kids and biscuits for the dogs."

"And a bone for the ladies," Velda laughed the forced laugh of a woman trying to cope.

Harry reached for the bottle but this time she put it on the floor next to the bean bag with the gun on it. There wasn't much left. They had both taken big drinks on an empty stomach and he presumed she was getting as drunk as he was.

"So Billy pulled your ass out of the gutter," Harry said and looked at the swell of her hips and the trimness of her waist. It was worth saving.

"Billy had this plan," Velda remembered. "If I married him, his health plan would pay for me to go someplace like Betty Ford to get well."

"But you had to be married a year," Harry said.

"That was no problem for Billy," Velda said. "He

45

back dated the license a year and sent them a copy. How close do they look. That Billy was a rascal."

"So, you took the cure," Harry said.
"What happened?"

"It worked," Velda said. "I gave up cigarettes after forty years."

"Congratulations," Harry said.

"I got it under control with Billy's help," Velda said. "I was able to update my P.I. license and work again. I wasn't working full time like I did in New York back when my first ex and I turned the city upside down in a P.I. practice we had in Manhattan. We were the best at the time. Forget it. The past is as dead as Billy. I work part time for a couple of law firms in Miami on retainer. Mostly divorce cases. Key West is a great place for an affair tryst."

Velda looked him straight in the eye, took a swig that emptied the bottle and created a broad smile.

"Take a picture with Mrs. Brown, the cookie lady," she said with charm. "Now let Mrs. Brown take one of you two together. It's a polaroid. Take it with you. My gift. I'll just throw the negative away in the trash. Oh, fudge, Y'all come back."

"Quite an act," Harry smiled.

"It's no act," Velda said. "I love selling cookies out there on the dock every sunset. I do pretty good. And I handle runaway cases too. Too many of them. Lost kids growing up to be lost adults. Billy always had a couple working for him at the beach with the kayaks. They liked

46

Billy. Everybody liked Billy."

"Then why would someone want to kill him?" Harry said.

"Love or money," Velda said. "It makes the world go round. That's why people kill one another. Love or money."

"All Billy had was his pension and the business," Harry said. "What's it worth? Love? Women?"

"Men too," Velda said. "Everybody loved Billy."

"Was Billy gay?" Harry asked. It occurred to him. He had to ask. He didn't care about the answer, just the information.

"Hell, no" Velda said. "But all the gay boys had a crush on him. They liked the idea that Billy was always on his knees. Even then he was more man than anybody I ever met, except maybe my first ex. He outgrew me. I was too old fashioned."

The alcohol had taken the hard edge off of her and even her features softened. She smiled. She was very pretty. She'd be a heart stopper all the way to the grave. She sat up and turned on him, pushing him back into the carpet. She got on top of him and began kissing him, big wet kisses, soft full lips and her tongue filled his mouth. He tasted brandy. She kissed him hungrily and he let himself be devoured. She put a hand between his legs and felt his erection. "Some things run in the family," she breathed in his ear. "I want you to fuck me just like Billy did. I want you to drive me past the point of self control. I want to lose myself in passion."

"Everybody should have a goal," Harry said.

47

Their faces were close together and he could see the clarity of her skin, an unblemished face with soulful eyes. He rubbed his hand across her forehead and eased her brow, touched her cheek with the back of his fingers and felt the soft hair at her neck. He kissed her and tasted the metallic flavor of heat. He hugged her and let her rest on his chest.

"Right place, wrong time," Harry said and held her.

"It's another girl, right?" Velda pushed herself up. "It's another woman. Just like Billy. You're just like Billy."

"It's this HIV thing," Harry said. "The rules of engagement have changed for us."

Velda got off of him and was on her knees putting the gun in her bag. She stood up and straightened herself. She threw a couple of keys at Harry.

"The front door and his post office box," Velda said.

"There's a lot more I want to ask you about Billy," Harry said.

"Right time, wrong place," Velda said. Her eyes never made contact with his. She checked her lipstick in the compact mirror and headed for the door.

"I..." Harry started.

"Shit," Velda said. "I was a virgin until I was thirty. I saved myself for my first ex all the way through the free love of the sixties. Oh, I had a few good years. I'm not complaining. Billy and me, the time of my life. But today I get rejected by an ex-New York cop on the floor of my dead ex-husband's apartment. What ever happened to the mercy fuck?" Harry laughed with her and started to get up.

48

"When she dumps you for a younger, richer, smarter guy, come down to the sunset dock," Velda said. "I'll be selling cookies. I'll save one with your name on it." She was gone before Harry could stand up.

CHAPTER THREE

When Harry rowed the dinghy up to the stern of his boat, Eve was waiting there to take the line. She wore a red thong bikini that showed everything but her nipples and her pubic hair. She bent down and tied him off then leaned out and kissed him as he stood to come aboard. He steadied himself as her mouth swallowed his. When she stopped, its force separated them and he drifted backwards. She towed him back in. Her smile was tempting and her laugh devilish. "You've been drinking," she detected.

"You've been smoking," Harry said and pulled himself aboard. He let out the sigh of relief at being back on the boat and stood for a moment to appreciate his blessing.

Eve stood next to him.

"I've been thinking about you," she whispered in his ear.

"Two more days," Harry said.

"A day and a half," said Eve.

Harry showered in his cabin and rid himself of the land. He brushed his teeth and felt his face but didn't think he needed to shave.

When Harry went into the main salon, he found that she had lowered the table of the settee to make the large king-size berth. She spread a table cloth over it, where she set out a picnic dinner. There was cheese, sardines, bread, Dijon mustard and a sliced onion. She also had fresh basil from plants she had gotten when they were in Marathon. She kept them by the porthole in the galley and put then on deck in the cockpit to get sun. A bottle of red wine was open in a corner against the bulkhead. They both laid down naked on opposite sides of the food. She poured the wine in plastic cups.

"After dinner, I'll give you a good massage," Eve said. "I know you must have had a rough day."

"You couldn't guess the half of it," Harry said.

"Did you have to see the body?" Eve asked.

"That was the easy part," Harry said.

While they ate, Harry told her about his conversation with Captain Art Adkins and his run in with Velda. She understood their suspicions.

"Its the easy solution," Eve said. "If you don't think so, you're denying the obvious. But that's no reason to pistol whip you."

Eve smiled slightly and tried to hide it from Harry.

"Is it funny?" Harry asked.

"Just one of my fantasies, but not with you."

"Then I don't want to hear about it," Harry said.

That was the last thing they said before Harry fell asleep during the massage.

In the morning, Harry liked to do his meditation on the bow of the boat. Sometimes he'd smoke a joint if he had it and have a cup of Cuban coffee next to him. When the wind, the tide and the world were right, the boat would hang to the west and he'd be able to watch the sunrise. When the weather was foul, he would sit in the cockpit protected by the dodger and canvas top, cocooned. It was the eye of the hurricane, calm and peaceful, while the rest of the world raged and Harry was not apart of it anymore.

Harry was calm. He was going nowhere. No hurry. He was on the idle. He was retired. For twenty years he had been at the edge of life and death, employed to keep victims on the side of life. Hurry up before he croaks! Hurry up, her water broke! Hurry up before the buzzard starts to circle and attract the television cameras.

Next call. Get them out quick! There's another jumper on the bridge. Go up and get him down before he becomes a "floater". And then he would hear the story of the victim, the relative, the jumper. And when the story came out about the cheating wife, the disloyal friends, the slave like existence to a job or an impossible dream, many times Harry thought, "if I was this guy, I'd go ahead and jump".

Harry had been a public servant. He had sacrificed the security of the center, for life on the edge. He had paid his dues, done his time and loved his job. But now it was time to see the side of life that wasn't a 911 call.

The purple clouds on the horizon were turning violet. An arc of brilliance across the top foretold the sun. It was another day.

Harry had passed through twenty years and it had passed through him. It was somewhere on the land in a memory bank, but out on the water, he felt free from the past and the future was a beautiful sunrise. He had patrolled that border between the light of human kindness and the shadow of death. Now, he wished to live only in the light. But Billy hid in the back of his mind and beckoned him to explore the darkness.

Eve came quietly and sat next to him. She handed him a lit joint and had another cup of coffee next to his empty cup. Harry took a hit and watched her as she stood completely naked before the sunrise, inhaling the dawn. Then she lowered her form into a perfect lotus, fair and fragrant, floating on the water.

It was good dope. The last of the grass that had been stolen. Eve had kept a bud separate from the bag to use as a buffer for when she ran out. He passed the remaining joint back to her. It was the only bad habit she had, if you were judging habits. As far as Harry was concerned, it was natural. It was Jamaican red and green, right off the boat for twenty five dollars an ounce. A bargain. It was $100 an ounce when it got to the street. But this was the Keys. By the time it got to New York, a reefer would be $5. Business. It was the way the world worked.

53

Harry closed his eyes as the sun exploded above the clouds and its warmth touched his skin. Life was delicious. His mouth watered and his stomach growled. He and Eve reached for the coffee at the same time. Their hands touched and they sat there silently, without looking, feeling each others presence and Harry thanked heaven for this woman. They coexisted completely without competition. They enjoyed the same pleasures, blended in the same space. One more day and they would consummate a romance. Velda's kisses had excited him in spite of his commitment to Eve and he wondered what would have happened if he had condoms with him. It was a choice he hadn't had to make.

Harry had put it off long enough. Billy was calling him from inside his conscience. He was calling him from the pockets of yesterday's clothes where Harry put the few items he had picked up at Billy's.

Harry and Eve went into the main salon together and she waited. One of the first things they discovered that they had in common was a clothing optional view of boat life. On such a small island modesty was the first convention to fall. The weather was wonderfully warm. They needed to dress only when they worked on deck because of the roughness of the nonskid surface that frayed their clothes. And Harry always wore shorts when he worked down below to keep his private parts out of the engine or the bilge. It was a basic way of life as free from restrictions as possible to the point where they were no longer a consideration.

54

"The police were there before me," Harry said.

"And Velda," Eve said.

Harry rubbed the back of his head. Eve reached across and touched the bump. It felt better. She had great healing hands. When Harry would hurt himself as always happens on a boat, the small dings, the big bruises, fortunately no compound fractures, Eve's hands would ease the pain. She now went through his pockets.

"Valium," Eve read the label on one of three bottles of pills that came out of the shirt.

"He had them stashed all around the place," Harry said. "All with prescription labels, some going back five years."

"The last time you talked to him before Miami," Eve said.

"I don't get the connection," Harry said.

Eve shrugged her slim shoulders and he could see the definition of her muscles. She looked further. She pulled out a wilted joint and smelled it.

"Good shit," Eve said. "The cops missed it."

"It was in the bathroom," Harry said. "Stuck in an old girlie magazine."

"*Playboy* or *Penthouse?*" Eve asked.

"*Penthouse*," Harry said and she smiled. "Billy was a leg man. He didn't care about big breasts."

Eve looked at her own small chest and pushed it out as far as she could. She posed seductively. Harry nodded. He viewed her from head to toe.

"Billy would have liked you," Harry said. "Billy

would have loved you. Billy would have done anything for you."

Harry couldn't resist touching her nipples and feeling her chest where the ribs joined the sternum. It was the bone that protected your heart. It was the place to make compressions in CPR.

"One more day," Harry said.

"Is it so important to you?" Eve asked, "That you be able to ejaculate inside me. That your sperm should invade my egg."

"I'll wear a rubber," Harry said. She laughed.

"Am I just a vessel?" Eve was high.

"I could go on living with you on this boat forever," Harry was high also, "without ever fucking you straight up. It's been on my mind a lot since we've been counting days. With you around it's hard to think of anything else."

"Well, I hope it's hard tomorrow night," Eve winked. "In the meantime, we need to finish up with Billy."

They emptied the rest of the pockets. There were a couple of credit cards, grocery receipts and medical records in brief. There was nothing that looked out of the ordinary. They were the remains of an American life.

"The cops got anything that looked like a clue," Harry said. "The place was clean. He paid his bills on time, lived within his means and kept a clean house."

"And needed pills to cope," Eve said, "With his wholesome existence."

"For the last five years," Harry said.

"Tell me what happened," Eve said and moved closer.

Eve had moved so that her head lay on Harry's belly and he rested back on the bunk looking up at the patch of blue the prisoners call the sky. He thought about it for a minute before he spoke. He was matter of fact.

"After Billy got shot," Harry said. "It broke my heart. Every time I looked at him."

Harry's face got heavy and his eyes teared and he cried as he talked. As he looked at a point in time, he closed his eyes. He let the sadness pass through him.

"Paralyzed from the waist down," Harry said. "Never to dance again. His legs were a nuisance prone to disease and infection. He could break one and not know. It took him six months to decide to have them amputated. By that time, he had dumped his electric wheel chair for one he could power with his arms. He said he was moving to Florida because it was flat and he could go forever. He said he still had bowel control and bladder function. His penis still worked. He just couldn't use his legs so he got rid of them with the help of his advising doctor. I was working full time cause of terrorist threats, bomb scares, the stuff of civilized men. I hear he got real good with the chair before he left. Workman's Comp, the Department and the Insurer gave him a lump of cash, a pension and free medical for the rest of his life, his wife and children up to the age of eighteen."

"Was he satisfied?" Eve asked and rubbed his chest and it eased the pressure.

"He said he was," Harry said.

"Did he blame anybody?" Eve asked.

"Not for a second," Harry said and he let her rub deeper. "That's what made it hurt so bad. He was so damn good natured about it. He had to get away because he saw what it was doing to me. It was my fault. We had nothing left to say to one another."

"What went wrong?" Eve asked.

"The nigger had a gun," Harry said.

Harry saw her flinch. They talked so little, he didn't know that words could hurt her. She sat up and looked hard at him. She moved away a little bit.

"I don't like that word," Eve said. "It's hateful."

"I won't use it," Harry said. "It was only a word."

"So, what happened?" Eve persisted.

"We were cops," Harry said. "I was emergency services. Back then, that meant we had the truck with more equipment than the car cops. We had ropes. We had ladders, Special rifles. All kinds of tools for cutting and digging. They didn't have all that computerized stuff back then. No SWAT team. No Bomb Squad. They only had us and our truck. We were 911 before there was a 911. On top of that we got called to pick up bodies out of the river. We called them `floaters'. Billy used to get these kosher hot dogs from a butcher on his beat. He used to boil them. When he tried to give me one I turned it down. I told him I didn't eat `floaters'."

Eve laughed but kept looking at him. He knew if he didn't answer she wouldn't care. But then maybe it was the beginning of the end.

"If you want to avoid the subject," Eve said. "I'll

understand. I was just curious. It isn't important."

"You have to understand who we were," Harry said. "Before we were orphaned, we lived on the living room floor, watching football on TV, the Cowgirls and fighting for fun. Our folks had a shop downstairs so we couldn't be too noisy. I remember Billy attacking in silence and I couldn't cry out. But we never hurt each other. Later when we got older, he compared it to making love with the girl's parents in the next room. Billy won most of the time, but I fought dirty, so we came out even."

"And you were there when he got shot?" Eve asked.

"I was there. It was my fault. The District Attorney has a whole written record of the incident if you want details. It's a big deal when a cop gets shot in the line of duty, especially when he's ruined for life. I testified. There was no indictment, no information. Just a report to the commissioner who wasn't concerned since the cop didn't die and the bad guy did. Billy got his pension. I kept fishing them out, bringing them down and delivering babies. Hundreds of them, all colors, all creeds. Emergency Service, 24 hours a day."

"And you never saw Billy again until yesterday?" Eve looked saddened.

"Not exactly," Harry said. "Five years ago, just before I retired, Billy came to New York to compete in the New York Marathon."

"And that was when you talked to him?" Eve said.

"I called him at the Plaza. He knew I was working the race, and he wanted to get some sleep so we planned to meet afterwards. My truck was parked on the East side of the park where the runners enter. When I saw the first wheel chair turn the corner, my heart stopped. But it wasn't Billy. He was the third one. I recognized the hair and his smile as he drove like a machine. My heart swelled with pride. And then a guy with legs passed him and I saw the emptiness beneath the chair. After all that I had seen in my job for twenty years, I never turned away until I saw my brother. I know he saw the truck. I don't know if he saw me. I called the hotel after and he said he hadn't been able to finish. Too many hills. He was worn out and said he'd see me in Florida."

CHAPTER FOUR

Harry and Eve came ashore at the Simonton Street beach. It was early and most of the derelicts hadn't crawled out yet. They had a quick Cuban coffee at a restaurant on Duval and then walked over to the police station.

Inside, the colors were pale green and what might have been beige before the mildew darkened it. The sergeant at the front desk pointed back through a maze to where Captain Art Adkins had his cubicle. They passed an old woman telling a detective what a good boy her grand-son was. The word "crack" reduced the conversation to a cry for help. Next cubicle: a redneck in a torn tee shirt listening to the definition of "assault". Onward past the girl trying to hide in the chair as she accounted a rape. Drug deal gone wrong was a skinny handcuffed, Latin, his clothes still dripping from his attempt to escape; flight is evidence of guilt.

Captain Art Adkins was ready for them around the next corner. He had two chairs set in front of his desk where papers, plastic baggies and a written list seemed to be organized for display. He was on the telephone. He put his hand over the mouthpiece and said "medical examiner" and resumed his conversation as they sat down.

"...one shot, death instantaneous, close range," Adkins was taking notes in his pad.
"Powder burns on the forehead. No other indication of offensive or defensive wounds. No sign of drugs other than a positive for THC. Speculation? Shot at close range by a friend or family member."

Captain Art Adkins looked up from the phone he placed on the hook and stared into Harry's eyes. There was a fax on his desk with a NYPD heading. He put it in front of Harry who didn't bother to read it.

"Twenty years of service," Adkins said, "With numerous citations and commendations."

"Retired five years ago," Adkins recited. "Only one blemish on an otherwise distinguished career. Ten years ago, suspension with pay for dereliction of duty resulting in the injury of a fellow officer. I need a court order for more details unless you want to save me some time."

"You said you're going for thirty," Harry said.
"You've got time if you want to waste it. Those records are sealed. Internal Police matters. You know how it works."

"I know how it works," Captain Adkins said. "It's hard to nail a bad cop, even an ex- cop. No offense."

62

"No offense taken," Harry said. "I met Velda."

"So, you met the spouse," Adkins said. "Isn't she a piece of work! She reminds me of a coral snake. So good to look at and so deadly."

Harry rubbed his head and winced. Adkins saw his pain and laughed. He took out a form.

"Do you want to file a complaint?" Adkins said. "You're not the first guy that old Velda had to knock around. Wait till you see her at the hearing. She'll break your heart next time, not your head. Be glad she didn't shoot you. She's a killer."

"What did you take from Billy's?" Eve asked.

Adkins raised his eyebrow when she spoke. She had been sitting back watching the two men. She leaned in next to Harry so she could see what was on the desk. Not just another pretty face.

"Not much," Adkins frowned. "Some catheters, syringes, prescription pain killers, downers. Everything legit. It didn't look like anything occurred there before he got it."

"No clue," Eve said. "Nothing out of the ordinary?"

Harry watched her work. She knew how to ask questions and she knew what to ask. She had Adkin's attention for a moment before he turned back to Harry.

"Not quite clueless," Adkins said. "The only thing out of the ordinary in Billy's otherwise normal life was a once in ten year visit from his brother Harry. You see, I knew Billy. He and I have been around this island for a while and eventually if you're here after tourist season year

63

after year. I notice. Especially if you drive a wheelchair like a skateboard and own a legitimate business. We Conchs all know each other. It's a small town when the tourists go home. Did you ever see that bumper sticker? `If it's tourist season, how come we can't shoot them?'"

"What about a guy named Frisky and the twins?" Harry asked. He didn't want to be folksy. He wanted to be to the point. "I know I didn't kill him, so it had to be someone else."

"You New York cops," Adkins leaned back and frowned. "You all think you're Sam Spade or Mike Hammer once you get south of Jersey and the cops in the sticks are all Inspector Clouseau with a drawl. We move slower because of the weather but we solve crimes. This isn't our first murder this year and it won't be the first one we solve. There's evidence. We drilled his safe deposit box at the bank."

"Did you get a court order?" Eve asked.

"Yes, we know how its done," Adkins was annoyed at her interruption of his assault on Harry.

"So, talk to me," Harry said.

"You're his beneficiary," Captain Art Adkins read from his list. "The kayak business was owned by his former wife, Velda Knight, aka Velda Brown, the cookie lady. He had no known descendants. You, Harry Knight, get all the rest since he's dead."

"Does that make him a suspect?" Eve asked.

"Who the hell are you," Adkins asked, "His lawyer?"

"Yes," Eve said. She went into the canvas bag she

64

carried and came up with a card that she tossed on the desk.

Adkins read the card. He put it in his shirt pocket. It looked official.

"Is Harry Knight a suspect?" Eve persisted.

"He had the best motive," Adkins said looking through some of the papers.

"What was that?" Eve asked.

"A half a million dollars," said Art Adkins, Key West Police Captain, as if he were a poker player calling a bluff holding a full house. "Here's a bank statement with both of your names on it. The signature cards at the bank have both of your signatures form ten years ago. We can do a handwriting comparison with you to confirm it or I can just ask the question. Is that your signature, Harry Knight? You can answer. Your attorney is present."

"Sure," Harry said before Eve could defend him. "When Billy got his settlement, he wanted my name on the account to avoid a hassle with lawyers in case he died."

"Did the medical examiner estimate a time of death?" Eve took control of the conversation. She could be forceful with a velvet glove. It was something Harry liked very much about her.

"Between three and six A.M.," Adkins had to be willing to give information if he was taking Harry's candor. "I believe you dropped anchor at sunset."

"And the cause of death?" Eve said.

"A .22 caliber slug, probably a magnum. It frag-mented when it entered the skull creating massive brain

65

damage. Somebody could have creased the bullet to make it hard to trace, and sure to kill. Somebody familiar with such things like an ex-cop."

"Are you going to release the body to Mr. Knight at this time?" Eve redirected him.

"Yes," Art Adkins said and ran his hand through his black hair. "Complete the paperwork."

"Then you really must not have any solid evidence against Mr. Knight," Eve said.

"How do you like that?" Art Adkins said. "You get a lawyer and all of a sudden you're Mr. Knight, Harry."

"I've had lawyers call me worse," Harry said.

"The tide was coming in that night, Mr. Knight," Art Adkins had a chart. "You could have drifted into the jetty while it was still dark. That time of night, no one up. You probably wouldn't hear the splash of an oar. The fishing boats would have gone out with the tide earlier. Everybody knew that Billy meditated at sunrise on that jetty. He was local color. Everybody knew him and liked him. A shot from a small caliber gun wouldn't be noticed with the water slapping against the rocks. And then slip back out when the sun would be in everybody's eyes."

"Or someone could have shot Billy and walked twenty yards back to a car," Harry said.

"We were together on the boat all night," Eve said.

"So you're not only his lawyer but also his alibi, I'd like to look at your boat, Harry," Art Adkins said.

"You'll need a signed search warrant," Eve said. "Harry, let's go. You don't have to say anything else to this man."

66

"Don't mind Art," Harry said. "He's just acting like a cop."

"And she's acting like a lawyer," Art Adkins said.

"We've all seen the same movies," Harry smiled. "Art, we have a saying where I come from: `You can't scare an old whore with a big dick'. So, if you have evidence that I committed a crime, indict me. If not, stop playing this good cop, bad cop routine until they give you a big enough budget so you don't have to play both parts."

Eve laughed out loud and Art Adkins messed his black hair and restrained a smile. He gave Billy's last effects with the bank statement on top to Harry. Harry and Eve walked out into the sunshine and breathed the free air. Harry smiled.

"I'm a rich man," Harry said. "Billy was a sport to the end."

"It's a possible motive," Eve said as they began to walk away from the official building without looking back.

"My name has been on that account for ten years," Harry said. "I could have drawn on it any time. I just didn't know how much was there."

"He can find evidence for his scenario," Eve said. "People can prove anything once they put their mind to it."

"We both know I was passed out in my bunk from that tequila and pot we had to celebrate our arrival and our getting the blood test." Harry was reconstructing the night to the best of his recollection. "Is it a conflict of interest to be a client's alibi?"

"That card was bullshit," Eve said stopping to look at

67

him. "I had them printed in Miami. I was a paralegal for a while, years ago. I just can't ask for a fee."

"What did you do, work for some slick defense lawyer?" Harry asked.

"No," Eve said. "I worked for the county for five years in the legal aid department."

"So, you were a part of the system too," Harry smiled. "Criminal justice is big business. That guy with the VCR under his arm, looking back over his shoulder as he flees the scene keeps a lot of people employed. Billy got to the point where he couldn't take it anymore. When he started, Billy wanted to be The Lone Ranger. Ride into town, do good and ride off into the sunset. Ten years later, he hated everybody. Ten years of domestic violence, rape, murder and stuff so grotesque you can't believe a human being could have committed the act. It wore him down. Burned him out. He wouldn't go for a psychological disability which was really what he had. And then the problem was solved. He was injured in the line of duty due to the improper actions of a fellow officer. The money was the cash part of the settlement. He just let it sit and grow, I guess. He lived off his pension. It surprises me to be accused of killing Billy. I'm the one who saved his life. Five hundred grand is a lot of money to me, but not enough to kill for."

"Is there any amount that is enough?" Eve asked.

"It depends on the party in question. Some people don't deserve to live. I'd do it for free."

Eve kept up with Harry as he walked at a quick pace dodging in and out of the slow moving tourists who were

68

getting into their day. Harry had a good sense of direction and turned a corner and was out of the flow. Eve was at his aide. She had great legs.

It didn't take Harry long to find the estate where in the back Billy had his garage apartment. The gate was open. There was a green *Jaguar* sedan in the driveway. As they passed the big house, Harry saw a head of white hair in an upstairs window. It followed them as they went through the door at the garage.

"This is nice," Eve said as she went inside and flopped down in a bean bag and stretched out her legs. She looked around. "A perfect little studio. A place for every-thing and everything in its place."

Harry went into the bathroom and looked under the sink and in the shower where the faucets were at knee level and the shower head hung down on a long stainless flexible hose. Harry got on his hands and knees and looked through the kitchen, a small chest of drawers and a closet where shorts and shirts were folded and stacked. He looked under them. He looked in corners.

"What are you looking for?" Eve asked. She had been patiently enjoying the ambience of Billy's home. Its low center of gravity was very relaxing.

"Bladder bags," Harry said. "The cop said there were catheters. Then there should be bladder bags. If he used them, he would have more than just one."

"You said he had control of his bladder and bowels." Eve sat up.

"That's what he told me," Harry said.

69

"Maybe his condition changed," Eve said, "From time to time?"

"It's possible," Harry said. He was on his knees in the kitchen when the door opened.

A big guy in a dark suit started to come in but stopped when he saw Harry, as if he had seen a ghost. He blinked a couple of times. It was bright outside and his eyes needed to adjust. He finally got it together.

"I thought you were Billy with one of his dames," the big guy laughed and stopped.

Eve sneezed. She found a tissue in her bag and wiped at her eyes. The big guy looked her over real good.

"Are you all right?" Harry asked Eve.

"I'm fine," Eve said and wiped her nose. "Did Billy have a cat?"

"Nah," the big guy laughed. "That's not the kind of pussy Billy liked."

Harry had stood up and was next to Eve. The guy didn't look so big now. Harry looked at him. He was beefy and his suit was cut so he could carry a gun under his left arm. But his jacket was buttoned so he wasn't a threat.

"The Don would like for you to come up to the house," the big guy said. "He has a few things that he thought you might like to have and he wants to know about the arrangements."

"What arrangements?" Eve asked and got up with a hand from Harry.

"About the body," the big guy said. "He wants to talk about Billy's body. Maybe donate it to science. The Don

70

was very fond of Billy."

They followed the big guy out into the sun and across the yard to the main house. Harry held back a little with Eve. He didn't whisper but the tone was confidential.

"The Don," Harry snorted. "He was a wheel in the Mafia way back when. He had a place on McDougal St. where he used runaway boys to attract the gay trade. It was a male whorehouse. We busted him when Billy was still a cop. Billy cuffed him and read him his rights. They liked to use Billy for things like that when there were cameras going to be around. He had that style. Billy tripped him going down the stairs. I think he broke his arm."

"Do you think he knew," Eve asked.

"We were a couple of uniforms on a public arrest with thirty other cops." Harry said. "It was crowded. It was an accident. But it was the worst thing that happened to the Don cause he beat the rap."

"He can hear you," Eve referred to the big guy.

"Let him hear me," Harry said. "I know these guys."

It was a two story Spanish style house with a red barrel tile roof. Ornate metal work protected the window at ground level. It wasn't as tacky as bars. But Harry knew it should have been bars for twenty years. There was the green *Jaguar* parked out front.

Inside, it was cool and dark. There were small rooms filled with antiques set on oriental rugs. The floors were hardwood and shined. The shades were pulled and over-head fans turned slowly. The only part of the pictures on the wall that could be seen were the gold frames.

71

The big guy took off his shoes at the door so Eve kicked off her deck shoes and Harry left his sandals there. They walked up a flight of stairs and out onto a screened veranda. There was a lot of white wicker furniture and a wet bar.

The Don was at the bar. He wore a green cashmere sweater and white linen slacks. He had a full head of white hair and his face was a deep Mediterranean tan. His smile was brilliant. His dentist did good work. He stuck out his hand to Harry and Eve shook it when Harry didn't.

"I forgot to bring my handcuffs," Harry said.

"You insult me!" the Don was indignant.

The big guy who was standing back moved up behind Harry. He was met with a sharp elbow to the solar plexus that froze him with his mouth open gasping for air. He managed to reach inside his coat for his gun but the Don raised his hand and frowned.

"Something might get broken," Harry said and watched as the Don exercised his left hand with a small ball.

The Don saw Harry looking at the ball.

"An old war wound," the Don said.

"I don't like this guy," Harry pointed to the big guy who had caught his breath and was back on guard.

"He wasn't going to hurt you," the Don said.

"I'm sorry," Harry said. "I didn't know. Where I come from a hood is a hood even in a good suit."

"It was self defense," Eve said.

"My lawyer," Harry said.

"Oh, please, not another lawyer," the Don said.

"Paralegal," Eve said. It eased the tension in the Don's face. He smiled at her. She demurred.

"Take a deep breath," the Don said to the big guy. "Then go roll a substantial joint of that new Jamaican sensi bud. And get our guests something to drink."

"Roll one for me too," Eve said.

"Water," Harry said, "From an unopened bottle."

"You're just like Billy," the Don said. "I let him change the garage apartment to suit himself. I always layed a bag on him when the good stuff came in. I lowered his rent. And he always gave me a hard time."

"Why did you let him live here?" Eve asked.

"That body," the Don rolled his eyes and smiled. "I loved to look at those big shoulders. That incredible chest. He was magnificent. It was like having a pit bull back there. I should have paid him. All Billy wanted to do was eat pussy back there. I said Billy `suck a cock once in a while. It's just a piece of meat'. He says `I'm a vegetarian'. I'm going to miss that guy."

Harry was looking back at the garage. The mango tree blocked a clear view. At least Billy had his privacy.

"He told me about you," the Don said to Harry. "He told me about the Indian too."

"White Rage?" Harry said.

"Quite a story," the Don said.

"Billy had a lot of stories," Harry smiled.

"Do you have any idea who killed him?" Eve asked.

"Everybody liked Billy," the Don said. "The gays, the

73

straights, the blacks, the freaks. He always had a smile and a good word for everyone. But he never gave me a tumble. Do you think it's because of my age?"

"You're a great looking guy," Harry said. "For your age."

"You're not fooling, are you?" the Don felt his cheeks and chin. "I hate aging, getting old and ugly, deformed. That's why I've gotten into the health care business with a line of products based upon the strongest living organism."

"What is that?" Eve asked the obvious question.

"Sperm," the Don said. "I market a line of health and beauty products that contain human sperm. Sperm-care."

"Is there a market for that?" Eve asked.

"Larger than you can imagine," the Don grinned. "Not only gays but women like them because they are high in protein, makes your hair and skin radiant. There is a cult in Hawaii that believes that the secret of longevity is the ingestion of sperm. There are scientific studies from Europe that back it up. Sperm is the wave of the future."

"I didn't think you could exploit them any younger than you did in New York," Harry sneered, "But now you get them before they even reach the womb."

The Don nodded to the big guy and he brought out a cooler the size of a six pack from behind the bar.

"Take it," the Don said. "It's Billy. Frozen. His sperm. I can keep it if you don't have a place to store it. I just thought that his brother should have it. Velda approves."

"Billy gave you his sperm?" Harry was skeptical.

74

"No," the Don said. "I got it from the twins."

"Have there been any strangers around lately," Eve seemed to have a line of questioning.

The Don looked over at the big guy who had just entered with two Jamaican spliffs the size of cigars on a silver tray. He shook his head negative to Eve's enquiry and offered the tray. She took a joint and put it in her bag.

"For later," Eve said.

"Be my guest," the Don said. He took the other joint and the big guy was ready with a lighter. The Don took a healthy hit and offered it to Harry.

Harry refused.

"Nothing unusual?" Eve persisted and also refused the reefer.

"No," the Don was irritated. "Just some kids. You know, the runaways he was always trying to help. He used to let them take out the kayaks for free. Billy said it was good for business to see people using them on the water. And he even let them keep what money they took in when he went up to Miami."

"Did he go often?" Eve asked.

"Once a month for about the last year," the Don said. "He went to see a therapist with Candy. Maybe he had problems no one knew about."

Harry was getting antsy looking at the cooler and listening to the Don give answers he would never trust. He had heard enough. He didn't want to hear this hood talk about Billy's problems.

"How long will this stuff keep?" Harry pointed to the

75

cooler.

"A couple of days in that container. It's packed in dry ice." the Don said. "His last living remains. We are associated with a fertility clinic. We'd be glad to give Billy immortality."

"He'll go with us," Harry said.

"Then body organs are out of the question, I suppose," the Don said and placed the joint back on the tray and let it smolder. He began to squeeze the ball again.

"Let's get out of here" Harry said to Eve. "This place is beginning to stink."

"Then take this too," the Don reached into his pocket and took out a bag of white powder. "I was able to get it before the police got here."

"How did you know Billy was dead before they got here?" Eve asked.

"The police called and told me that my tenant was dead." the Don smiled. "I donate to the Police Athletic League. It helps a newcomer make friends in a small town."

The Don was holding the plastic bag with his finger tips, dangling it in front of them. He had no takers. He tossed it on the tray that the big guy still held at the ready. Harry started moving toward the door.

"I would sure hate to get caught with that much coke in my pocket," Harry said.

The Don didn't say anything and walked them to the top of the stairs. Eve was in front of Harry and he looked back up at the Don who stood frowning squeezing the ball

76

in his left hand.

"Did you know that it was Billy who pushed you down the stairs on McDougal Street?" Harry said.

"Billy! Why, Billy always told me it was you."

Harry led Eve back over to Duval Street where they blended in with the tourists and local color that now filled the sidewalks while a stream of traffic flowed unbroken bumper to bumper. The restaurants were full; the boutiques, shops and vendors were all occupied. The bright colors of the crowd and environs clashed and complimented, moved and stood still. There was an ambient murmur like the sound of the sea in a rough chop, when a rogue wave would slam up under the deck between the hulls and the entire boat would shake.

The red four door Ford pulled to the curb just in front of Harry as he walked with Eve at his side. The back door swung open as the driver reached across. The camouflage seat covers let Harry guess. He was right when Frisky yelled "Get in."

Eve got in the backseat. She moved over behind the driver, but Harry closed the door and got in the front seat. Frisky gave her little notice. He shook Harry's hand like they were arm wrestling. It was better than a high five.

"I'm going to score a nickel bag," Frisky said. "Do you want a piece of it?"

Harry looked at Eve in the back seat and she nodded. He kept looking at her and she nodded again and blew him a kiss. He smiled at her.

"Sure," Harry said. "I have a couple of dollars on me.

I'll take a couple of buds."

Frisky started to laugh out loud.

"You aren't in anyway connected with a law enforcement agency?" Eve asked.

"Hell no," Frisky said. "I should be asking you two that. A couple of dollars for a couple of buds. Man! Where have you been? A nickel is fifty. A dime a hundred. This is Key West, man. Jamaican red and green sensi buds."

"I'll go half," Eve said. "Drop the infomercial."

"Do you ever use Sperm-care products," Harry asked.

"The Don's shit," Frisky made a face. "People already think I'm a dickhead. I don't have to smell like one."

They headed out into Duval Street traffic away from the waterfront. Harry sat with the cooler on the floor in front of him. Eve stretched her legs across the back seat and let the sun shine on her face for a moment and then got a cap from her bag for shade.

Outside the tourist town backdrop of tee shirts and straw hats moved by. Sunburns and halter tops walked with tattooed bikers arm in arm. Two guys. Two girls. Sometimes it was hard to tell. Maybe they didn't know themselves. Harry knew it took all kinds to make a world and this was a neutral turf where they could congregate and enjoy. Be yourself.

Frisky turned right through an arched entrance on a cobble stoned street. They were away from the crowd. There was a crab shack and a bar on one side. On the other

78

were a few shanties, old wood frame houses that all leaned
or slumped. All the faces were African.

"Did Billy do a lot of coke?" Eve asked.

"Hell no," Frisky said. "He was hyper anyway.
Sometimes he needed help coming down but never getting
up."

There was reggae music coming from the crab shack.
No one seemed to take notice as Frisky pulled to the curb.
Eve was looking at Harry.

"I'll bet if they found a sizable amount of coke, they
could do just about anything they wanted," Eve said to
Harry.

"They could get all kinds of search warrants," Harry
said. "When white powder enters a case, the jury votes
guilty."

"Well, we're only scoring a little weed," Frisky said
looking in the side mirror and reaching under the front seat.

A black kid on a bicycle pulled up even with the
window and stopped. Frisky pulled a machine pistol from
under the front seat and stuck the barrel under the black
kid's chin. The black kid didn't seem to notice, but Eve
was half way across the seat before Harry grabbed her arm
to let her know it was strange but all right.

"What you want?" the black kid said.

Frisky put the gun down and a drip could be seen from
the mouth of the barrel.

"Did you know it was fake?" Eve said to the kid.

"That's nothing," the kid said. "What you want?"

"A nickel bag," Frisky said and looked into the back

79

seat and waited for Eve to come up with the cash.

"Give me the money," the black kid said. "I don't have it on me. I have to get it from the guy in the bar. You pull on down to the end of the block when you see me go in the bar and you wait. I'll meet you there."

Harry didn't say a word. He looked at the brown faces, black faces, tan faces. He caught a glimpse of his own white face in the mirror. He knew he didn't belong here.

Eve gave Frisky twenty-five dollars. He put in his half and passed it out the window to the kid. They saw the kid ride his bike to the front of the bar and put it down on the ground between some men sipping wine from a brown bag. Harry noticed that it was a blue bike, no bar in the middle, a girl's bike. Frisky drove to the end of the block and parked. Nobody paid any attention to them. The car was at least ten years old and fit right in.

"That Billy was some kind of guy," Frisky said. "He was my buddy."

"Why did you pull that gun on the kid?" Eve said. Her tone was angry. "I thought it was real."

"The gun?" Frisky said. "That was nothing. Did he come out yet? That Billy got more women than any guy standing. Some got freaked, but they didn't count. There were plenty that did it just to see what it was like. Billy had a way."

"We'll never see that kid again," Eve was disgusted.

"Relax," Frisky said. "I've done this before."

"So, Billy had a love life," Harry said. He watched

Frisky looking in the side mirror and then turned around. Eve looked out the back window.

Harry could see the muscles in the back of Eve's neck stiffen as Frisky talked. Her bare shoulders showed the definition of good tone. The curve of her spine as she turned accentuated her hips and her legs tucked up under her. It was a position Harry enjoyed. He was glad that they were together.

"Billy showed me once," Frisky was intense. "If he stuck his finger up his ass and stimulated his prostrate, he could get these huge erections that he said lasted for hours. What a guy! Babes! Billy said he used to go up on them. Go up on them!"

Frisky started to laugh. Eve turned around and looked right at him. Her sterness caught him off guard and he was quiet. He looked at her kind of funny for a second but before he could speak, she stopped him.

"We've been ripped off," Eve said.

"No," Frisky said. "Just hold your pants on. Billy was impatient like that. If I showed up late to take him up to Miami to see that therapist, he'd flip out. A lot of good that bitch did him."

"Shut up, dickhead," Eve said. "You go in that bar and get him."

"Okay," Frisky gave in. He got out and walked to the front of the bar. The men all stopped what they were doing and turned to Frisky.

"I'm looking for the kid on the blue bike," Frisky said.

"You a cop?" someone said.

81

"No," Frisky said.

A muscular looking black guy in a tee shirt with the sleeves cut off stepped forward. He looked at Frisky and smiled. He stood next to the fallen blue bicycle.

"This is my bike," the black guy said.

"No," Frisky said. "I want the skinny kid who rode up on it."

"I said that's my bike," the black guy said and two of his companions picked up empty bottles from near a trash barrel and stood at his sides.

"Sorry," Frisky said and backed away to the car as they laughed. "My mistake."

"You better believe it," the black guy said and sat down. His friends threw the bottles at the trash can. One made it in, the other crashed on the ground.

"Why didn't you pull your gun on them?" Eve said as Frisky got back in the car and started it up. "Just drop us at the Simonton Street dock."

"I'll make it up to you," Frisky put the car in gear.

"Sure," Eve said. "Stay in touch. Write when you get work."

"I'll score for you," Frisky said. "You can count on me."

"I won't hold my breath," Eve said.

As they pulled around the corner of the block, Harry could see down the alley. He saw the black kid come out of the back of the bar and hop on a red bike. He rode parallel to them in the alley. Frisky drove slowly and silently.

"Is that him?" Harry asked as they passed a vacant lot

that gave full view of the alley.

Frisky took a quick glance and then concentrated on the road.

"No," Frisky said. "The one we want was on a blue bike."

"He could have changed bikes," Harry said.

"No," Frisky said. "It was one on a blue bike. How else are you going to tell them apart?"

"Asshole," Eve said from the back seat and didn't bother to look. Nobody spoke until they got out near the dock. Harry opened the back door for Eve and she thanked him. She leaned against Harry as he stood by the car.

"I swear I'll make it up to you," Frisky said and looked hard at Eve. She turned away. Harry held her by the shoulder.

"I'll make it good," Frisky said. "You know me..."

"Fuck off," Eve said without turning around to face him.

Harry stood holding Eve as he watched the red Ford pull away and turn at the alley. It was where the kid on the red bike would be coming out. He moved over into the shade of a large flowering mimosa tree. The fragrance was sweet and gentle. Eve put her arm around his waist and squeezed him. She was content to wait with him in the sweet fragrance of the delicate pink blossoms that covered the ground beneath them. In a few minutes, the black kid on the red bike came out of the alley.

"That's the kid," Eve said and stiffened.

"It sure is," Harry said.

83

The kid on the red bike rode up to them. He stopped without them moving. He was a skinny kid with a big smile. He wore a tee shirt and old dirty cutoffs. He was barefoot.

"You're Billy's brother?" the kid said to Harry. "You two look a lot a like."

"Yeah," Harry said without smiling. "Who are you?"

"I'm Bogart, I used to work for Billy at the kayak rentals when he went out of town."

"What about my nickle bag?" Eve asked.

"Frisky has it," Bogart said. "He ripped you off."

"So that's why it didn't bother you when he put that gun under your chin."

"Shit!" Bogart laughed. "That was nothing. I've seen a lot worse dealing with these assholes."

"It was a water gun," Harry said.

"No shit!" said Bogart. "It looked real to me."

"You have any idea who killed Billy?" Harry got right to the point.

"Everybody liked Billy," Bogart said. "Since Candy left, he's been his old self again."

"Why did she leave?" Eve became interested.

"Something that had to do with the twins," Bogart layed the bike down and stood with them. "They were all upset when they left."

"Where did they go?" Harry asked.

"They took off for the Far Tortugas the day Billy was killed," Bogart looked at the ground. "They picked up on all the negative vibrations so they packed up their love

84

potions and moved out for friendlier places."

"Love potions?" Harry asked.

"Yeah," Bogart said as if everyone knew. "They the ones sell all that aphrodisiac shit at the sunset dock. You know, down where Mrs. Brown sells cookies from her bike. She had something to do with it too maybe. Maybe because of the sperm."

"Sperm," Eve asked. "What has that got to do with it?"

"I don't know," Bogart said. "But you can ask Mrs. Brown, she knows all about it."

"And how do you know?" Harry looked in the kid's eyes. They were clear and focused. They looked right back at him for a second and then away.

"Never make eye contact," Bogart said. "That's what Billy told me. Never make eye contact with a cop. If you do, they'll pull you in on suspicion."

"Are you a suspect?" Harry asked.

"No way, José," Bogart said and lifted his bike up so that he could mount it. "You got that cop talk. You know, the way cops talk to people. Billy told me all about you. He taught me about the business of good guys and bad guys. I do my business and Mr. Cop he does his business. We stay out of each other's way. That's how we survive. Big fish, little fish. Same pond."

"Billy taught you how to deal with cops," Harry laughed. Bogart was serious. Eve was hanging on his every word. The black kid leaned on his bike.

"Did he teach you how to rip people off?" Eve said.

85

"I knew that before I ever knew Billy," Bogart said. "After that guy drowned off the jetty a while back, my mother told me to stick close to Billy. She looked up to him. He taught me about life. How to respect the person inside of you no matter what other people say. Especially if you're not white. He taught me about White Rage. He taught me about women and how to use condoms for safe sex. Take life as it comes. Inhale the light. Live for the moment but don't do anything that you know might hurt another person. Billy had it down. Billy knew."

"Did he ever use a bladder bag?" Harry asked. The question caught Bogart off guard and he stopped cold. He thought for a moment and then smiled at Harry.

"Cop talk," Bogart said. "The way some cops hit you with a question from the blind side. You good. Shit, Billy was on the water most of the day, in a kayak, snorkeling, fishing with a cane pole. With a weight belt, Billy could free dive sixty feet. The onliest time he ever used a bag was when he was going in a car for a long time. Sometimes he'd send me out to buy those big diapers too. That's the way it was. And now he's dead. That's the way it is. What you going to do with the kayaks?"

"They belong to Mrs. Brown," Harry said.

"That's the way it is," Bogart said. He looked at Eve.

She was looking up at the mimosa blossoms falling to the ground after a stiff breeze. "You still interested in some Jamaican red and green?"

"I'd rather quit than get ripped off again," she said.

"You can pay me later," Bogart said. "This is square

86

business. Don't be too hard on Frisky. Everybody has to get by and he ain't got much help no how."

"He's on my shit list," Eve said.

"That will work," Bogart laughed. "He's always trying to do something for everybody so they'll like him. He's still freaked from the war."

Harry looked at Bogart and Bogart looked back at him. Nobody said anything. The black kid swung a leg over the bike as if he was ready to leave, but Harry's look held him there.

"The cop look," Bogart said. "You good."

"So," Harry said and waited for an answer to the unspoken question.

"What kind of game was Billy running?" Bogart said. "You want to know. You're his brother. If he ain't told you, why should I."

"He's dead." Harry said.

Bogart thought about that for a second and agreed. They had both been in this position before. The cop and the kid. The cop with all the power of the state behind him and the kid alone except for his wits. It was an old game. They both knew how to play.

"When I first met Billy a few years back," Bogart measured his words, "He was tracking runaways for Mrs. Brown. They all seemed to wash up down at the beach. I mean, he did a little of this and a little of that, but no felonies. Billy was careful. He was cool. Then Candy came along and she took up all of his time. Billy said it was love. She was fine. Real fine. That's when I started working for him when they would go off together."

"When was the last time he went to Miami?" Harry asked.

"Was Velda upset with him being with Candy?" Eve asked.

"About three months ago, maybe more," Bogart was rocking back and forth on the pedals ready to ride. "Sometime after Candy split. Right before the guy drowned. You know I don't keep a calendar."

"What about Mrs. Brown?" Eve asked again.

"After Candy left," Bogart was careful. "Mrs. Brown stayed. She and Billy were tight. They were selling sperm to the Don."

"The Don," Eve said.

"You didn't hear it from me," Bogart said.

"Sperm from runaway kids," Harry said.

"That's right," Bogart said. "Billy would have a Penthouse magazine on his table when the kid came over to his place. If girls turned him on and he picked it up, we figured the kid was straight, not high risk. One hundred dollars a load. But Billy didn't take no cut. He gave it all to the kid and talked him into going back home."

"Just sperm," Harry said. "Nothing else?"

"Hey, man," Bogart said. "The Don is into all kinds of shit, but Billy only told me about the sperm. This is what I can tell you. You have to talk to other people. Talk to Frisky. He was the bag man when the twins thing went bad. He drove Billy to Miami. He used to pick the sperm up from Mrs. Brown and take it to the Don. It was a way to survive."

"Billy was in on this?" Harry asked.

"'Til about a month ago," Bogart said. "He quit cold. Said you were coming down to take over."

"Was Mrs. Brown upset that he quit?" Eve asked.

"What about the Don?" Harry asked. "Was he pissed?"

"He was only pissed that Billy never gave him no sperm," Bogart said. "I ain't saying nothing about Mrs. Brown. Have you seen the gun she carries? I hear she killed a couple of guys up north. And I know the big guy who is with the Don is an assassin from Detroit. That's what Frisky told me. Man, I gots to go. Lady, you still want to score that shit?"

"I'm cutting down," Eve said. "Frisky said he would make good."

"He will," Bogart said. "He's a little fucked up, but he can be okay. Depends on how many rocks he's smoked."

Harry looked at the kid and sifted through what he had said. There were a couple of questions he wanted to ask. He wished he could get this kid in the back of a patrol car and then talk to him in private. He bet Bogart knew that routine too. This was as much as the kid was good for right now. Truth. Lies. Ripoffs. Sperm. Harry bent down to pick up the cooler that was resting between him and Eve.

"You got a beer?" Bogart asked.

"No," Harry said.

"What's in the cooler?" Bogart was figuring it might be an angle. You could see the kid's eyes flick from side to side as he thought. He was ready for anything.

"Billy is in the cooler," Harry said dead straight.

Bogart wasn't ready for that. His mouth fell open because he knew Harry was telling the truth about his brother. They all stood for a moment in silence. Then the skinny black kid on the red bike rode off at top speed and never looked back.

CHAPTER FIVE

They found a restaurant off of the main drag where you could buy a fish sandwich for five dollars. A couple of beers and a twenty was shot. That was a lot of rice and beans, pasta and sauce. On a fixed income, Harry had to think about money when he was on land. At sea, money was worthless. The list for the boat was in his head and he preferred to think of it for the time being instead of Billy whose sperm was in a cooler next to him. There was a half inch stainless bolt that he needed for the port chainplate that held the shrouds. The old one had rusted through. Stainless steel was no match for the salt air and water. There was the gasket for the toilet in Eve's cabin. There was no hurry. She didn't seem to mind using a bucket. And he preferred a bucket. There were less moving parts. There were fewer things that could go wrong. He also needed to buy more underwater patching compound for the seepage in the port hull. Before Harry realized it, they had finished their late lunch without speaking. Eve picked up the check.

There was a marine supply store up on the main highway that led to the north. It was a couple of miles away, but he and Eve both liked to walk so they spent the rest of the afternoon talking about the boat. They passed a schoolyard full of kids who were playing tag. The teams were a mixture of colors and languages. English, Spanish, black, white, brown, boys and girls together. They were running, pushing and screaming.

"When I first became a cop, we did whatever we did for the good of the country. If we bent the rules, if we violated someone's rights, it was okay, because we could always rationalize it for the good of the country. The commies were our enemies and whatever we did was for democracy."

"You think that's changed?" Eve asked as they walked along the shoulder of the highway. There were no sidewalks. She jumped as a bicycle rider came up behind them and passed without a warning.

"They should make them have horns on those things." Eve said.

"For the good of the children," Harry said. "That's the rationalization now. Pass a law, restrict the choices an adult has for the good of the kids. Don't educate the people. Legislate them."

"It's better at sea," Eve said.

"It used to be," Harry said. "But now they come right

out there and get you. Coast Guard, Marine Patrol, DEA, Customs, State police, local police, FBI, CIA, Department of Environment, Arms Tobacco and Firearms, Army, Air Force, Navy and Marines. More law enforcement, less freedom."

"It looks different from the other side," Eve said. "But it's for the good of the children. Just ask any politician."

"There are no politicians at sea," Harry said. "And very few children."

"So you have something against children?" Eve said.

"They grow up," Harry said.

"So you have something against adults," Eve goaded him.

"Most of the ones I've known," he said and then he laughed. "I don't know what got me on that roll. There are some good ones out there."

"I hope I'm one of the good ones," Eve said.

"You are," Harry smiled and shifted the cooler from one hand to the other as they walked. "Good, bad or ugly, they all start out the same. Sperm."

"And an egg," Eve said. "It takes two to make a baby."

"It used to," Harry said. "Now they come in test tubes."

"Is that a bad thing?" Eve asked.

"I'm no judge," Harry said. "I'm just a witness."

"For the prosecution," Eve said.

"For the defense," Harry laughed. "For the defense of the children."

"You know," Eve shook her head. "I like it better when we don't talk."

Harry smiled at her and they kept walking. She grabbed his free hand and held it. It felt good to have her beside him. Harry didn't need to say that. He could tell that they both knew what was happening. It had been a long time since he had been in love. It felt so good.

The marine store was Harry's Disneyland. He could spend hours wandering the aisles looking at all the items man had invented to stay afloat and alive on the water. There was a new Global Positioning System that told you by satellite where you were any place on earth, the longitude and latitude within five miles. Most land could be seen at that distance. And if you were on the open ocean, five miles of water didn't matter. There were still radio directional systems that worked by finding stationary beacons on the shore. There was the old sextant that located your position by the sun and stars. There were charts for every harbor. There were lines, cables, anchors and chains to hold you in one place. There was the running gear and the rigging for when you wanted to move. There were sails and engines and that half inch bolt.

Harry paid the high price and they left.

"If it says `marine'" Harry told Eve, "It coats twice as much. Nobody living on a boat gets a free ride."

Eve took the bag with the bolt and put it in her bag. The cooler swung between them as they walked toward the dinghy dock. They couldn't forget Billy.

It was getting late and most of the light was gone from

the sky. They turned off of Duval and the glitter and the crowds were gone. There was the wail of a police siren in front of them. Another came up behind them and passed them. Then another came from another direction. It was drawing a lot of attention. A parade of people began to form behind them as they headed in the direction that the police cars were going. People passed them anxious to get to the scene of whatever was going on. It was a diversion, excitement. Harry slowed his pace. He knew there was trouble. He was in no hurry to find it. It seemed to be where he was going.

The entrance to the Simonton Street beach and dinghy dock was blocked by three police cars. The sirens in the background let Harry know that there were more on the way. By the time they reached the barrier, the crowd was five deep. Across the roofs of the cars, Harry could see what looked like the whole Key West police Department. A boat with a searchlight was swinging in toward the dock. This was big. A cop must have been shot.

"Somebody shot a cop," a man in the crowd said and drew a lot of attention from the others around him. The mobile television unit had arrived. Night had fallen fast but now the lights came on.

"A cop got shot," the word spread.

Harry's body reacted with the same sickening chill that it did for twenty years; that it did ten years ago. A path parted for him through the crowd as he approached the closest uniformed officer.

He could feel Eve's hand squeeze his and it felt so

95

good. They reached the first uniform and could see Captain Art Adkins running his fingers through his hair in the middle of a command meeting.

"What happened?" Harry asked the cop.

It was the way he said it that brought an answer. It was cop talk the way Billy taught it to Bogart. There was an implied respect and instant communication. It takes one to know one.

"Some asshole took a shot at Captain Art Adkins," the cop told Harry. "He said it came from the dock area or maybe a boat going out."

"Was he hit?" Eve asked.

"No," the cop said, "But he's mad as hell. He said he's going to find the person who did it, if he has to search every boat in the anchorage."

"That's not legal," Eve said.

The cop looked at her and then shot a questioning look at Harry. He should know what was happening. And who was this lawyer?

"Cops don't like to be shot at," Harry told Eve loud enough for the uniform to hear. "It gives the profession a bad name."

"They're going to search our boat," Eve said.

"I've got nothing to hide," Harry said.

"Everybody move on," the cop was yelling over the squad cars. "It's just police business. Go on back home."

The command meeting had broken up and the troops had been dispatched. Captain Art Adkins spotted Harry as he was checking out the crowd. He came over.

"Well. I guess it wasn't you," Art Adkins said and smiled.

"We want to go back to our boat," Eve said. "I'm tired."

"Sorry," Art Adkins said. "I know it's an inconvenience but we're doing this for your own protection. There's an armed man out there somewhere."

"Close call?" Harry said.

"Lousy shot," Art Adkins said. "Missed by a foot. I'll show you where it chipped the building. We're looking for the slug."

"I bet you will find one," Harry smiled.

"I'm sure of it," Captain Art Adkins said. "It's hard to find witnesses around here. Nobody heard anything."

"It's not a respectable crowd," Harry said. "Transient boat people and derelicts. People living on the edge of society. The kind of people who keep you in business."

"And you're one of them now," Art Adkins said.

"Now or later," Harry said. He shifted the cooler from one hand to the other. The cop noticed.

"You're a lot like your brother," Adkins mumbled. "You know we have an open container law around here."

"It's not beer," Harry said.

"Sure, sure," Art Adkins said. "Your brother Billy was like that. He got away with a lot of little shit."

"He was always lucky that way," Harry said.

"A little dope in public," Adkins began a list. "A few girls who he represented; always able to place a bet. If he liked you, he could get you anything. I talked to the cops

97

that work the beach. They all knew Billy. They all liked him but they say he had no respect for the law."

"So, why didn't you arrest him?" Eve asked.

"Ha!" Captain Art Adkins laughed. "Are you kidding! What cop is going to arrest an ex-cop with no legs? For smoking a joint in public? It's bad for the kids to see. That Billy could get away with murder."

"Don't overstate your case," Eve said.

"About four months ago," Captain Art Adkins was working. "A doctor from Miami died in a diving accident. He came up under his boat, hit his head on the motor and drowned. It was right off the jetty where Billy went every morning. No one saw anything. It was ruled an accident."

"For a second," Eve said. "I thought you were going to try and pin an unsolved crime on a dead man."

"I checked on that card you gave me," Captain Art Adkins now addressed Eve directly. "They said that they thought Evelyn West was in South America."

"We're closer than we've ever been," Eve smiled.

"They also said you had long brown hair," Art Adkins wasn't finished.

"I used to dye it," Eve said and looked at Art Adkins' black hair.

"My wife makes me use that Grecian formula," Art Adkins looked at the ground.

"A blonde isn't taken seriously," Eve said. "Being a brunette worked for me."

"So this is a whole new you," Art Adkins said.

"I haven't had any complaints," Eve said and grabbed

98

Harry by the arm. He leaned into her and tousled her short hair. Art Adkins turned away.

"We're still investigating Billy's murder," Art Adkins said. "What's the story on the police misconduct charge against you?"

"Talk to my lawyer," Harry said and hugged Eve.

Captain Art Adkins came close to Harry. He hesitated and shook his head. It wasn't something he wanted to talk about.

"You can pick up the body tomorrow," Art Adkins said. "What are you going to do with your brother?"

"I want to bury him at sea," Harry said.

"You'll need a permit," Captain Art Adkins said.

"From whom?" Eve asked.

"Wildlife and Fisheries. Health Department. Sanitation and dumping. EPA, Florida Marine patrol and a certified mortuary." Art Adkins paused. "Now, that's just off the top of my head. The county commission or city council might have to vote on it."

A plainclothes cop with a gun holstered on his hip came up to Adkins and took him away from Harry and Eve. They watched additional lights searching under the dock and along the shore. Eve leaned against Harry.

"This could take all night," Harry said.

"If I knew a judge..." Eve started.

"This time of night!" Harry laughed. "This time of night belongs to the cops, not the judges. Maybe tomorrow, a judge will laugh in your face, but tonight belongs to these guys. They are the law. Let's go find an undertaker.

99

They're always available."

They found a phone booth where the phonebook hadn't been ripped out. Some of the pages had been torn, but the funeral directory was complete. Harry dialed the first number in the book.

Harry called the *Abbot-Charles Funeral Home* and asked for Mr. Abbot. He got Mr. Charles who explained that Abbot was a name he added to Charles five years ago when Mr. Burton came to town. He was still the first name in the book.

"This is our guy," Harry told Eve.

Harry got directions and they began to walk.

"I've still got that spliff from the Don," Eve said.

"Save it for later after Mr. Charles," Harry said. "I don't want to get the giggles when I talk to him about Billy."

"What about Billy?" Eve said pointing to the cooler.

"This is just the kind of situation he would appreciate," Harry said.

They kept to the side streets away from the night life. Harry was becoming familiar with the whole island. There was no place they couldn't walk. There were also public buses. It was his kind of town. He could see why Billy liked it. And it was flat.

"When Billy was a cop," Harry told Eve, "He got this call to a disturbance at CBS. He told me this guy had sold a house to Bozo the Clown. And part of the deal was that when the guy's kid had a birthday, he could bring him down to the show. So the kid has a birthday and the guy takes him down to the studio where Bozo says he can't remember any such agreement. Honk. Honk. The guy tries to strangle Bozo and Billy had to haul him off. Billy told him: `What did you expect? You made a deal with Bozo the Clown.' Honk. Honk."

Eve laughed and held Harry around the waist as they walked through darkened houses set back in foliage, occasional lights and a barking dog.

"Billy let the guy go," Harry said. "Maybe the guy should have been smarter. But like Billy said: `If there was a law against stupidity, we'd all be serving time'."

"Maybe we are," Eve said.

"We were the law," Harry said. "Not the judges, not the politicians. Out on the street we were the law. And if sometimes we had to decide a persons' fate, we could let him go. Do you think society is any less for not having to process the case of Bozo verses Dumbo?"

"Billy liked helping people," Eve said.

"That was in the early days," Harry said, "Before he had seen the depth of human hell for fifteen years. He wanted out at the end when he got hit. He wanted out with a pension."

"After only fifteen years?" Eve said.

"They had started affirmative action, equal opportunity, sexual equality," Harry said. "The commander told Billy that the only way he would ever make Captain in the next ten years was if he bought a boat. His future was gone. He could pass all the tests but he was a white male at a time when that wasn't enough any more. Billy burned out."

"Why didn't he just quit and get another job?"
Eve asked.

"Billy was a rascal," Harry said. "He always liked to
bend the law a little bit."

"Did he ever take a bribe?" Eve asked.

"Street cops don't get offered bribes," Harry said.
"Maybe higher ups. We had other business. Nobody calls
the cops when everything is going good. When it got bad,
they called us and we were the law on the street. Billy
liked to lighten things up a bit sometimes to break the
tension. And then one too many acts of senseless violence
broke him. He gave up on humanity but he was still a good
cop. He just didn't laugh anymore."

"Lighten up," Eve said. "What kind of talk is this for
going to an undertaker?"

Harry laughed. He swung the cooler to the other hand
and shrugged his shoulders. Eve poked him in the ribs.

"He ain't heavy, he's my brother," Eve said.

"Are you sure you didn't smoke that joint?" Harry
said.

"Guys like the Don," Eve said. "Did Billy ever deal
with them?"

"What for!" Harry said. "Gangsters and thugs. They
have a big reputation in Hollywood, but on the street we
used to bounce them around all the time."

"You weren't scared," Eve held his hand and massaged where he had been carrying the cooler.

"Scared!" Harry said. "Of what! Thieves, pimps, drug
dealers, hustlers, extortionists. Scared of low lifes and

punks. We used to give them a hard time. Put them through the system. And in the old days, if the merchants on the beat said they knew a guy in the neighborhood who was causing a series of breakins, we'd wait in an alley."

There was a long silence. Eve let go of his hand. They continued to walk side by side.

"It was law enforcement," Harry said. "You'd say: `psst, come mere,' and when the guy turned his head, you'd whack him a couple of times so he knew it wasn't an accident. The next day there would be a side of ribs on the hood of the car when you came out of the coffee shop. Maybe a case of wine, a box of canned goods, a couple of sport shirts. And there were no more breakins."

"But what about mistakes?" Eve said.

"We didn't make mistakes. This wasn't something we did all the time. Maybe once in ten years. It just shows what it was like twenty years ago. Are the streets safer today?"

"Everything is different every day," Eve said.

"They could stop all of the crime in the city in one day if they wanted to," Harry said. "They know all the crooks. All you have to do is sit on the corner and watch for a while and you can see everything that's going on, legal and illegal. But crime is big business on both sides. But on the street Billy taught me we were the law. He said, 'Arrest everybody, let the lawyers sort it out'."

"And Billy wanted out," Eve said and took his hand again. He could feel her fingers move across the calluses. It was as if she were touching his soul.

103

"How many battered women did Billy see?" Harry said. "How many abused kids? How many beat up old people? That's what police work is. Domestic disputes, robberies, rapes, violence and murder. They don't call 911 to invite you to dinner."

"So, what did Billy do?" Eve asked.

"He had a plan," Harry said. "Women and minorities were taking over the Department. There were guys faking back injuries to get retirement disability. There were guys making psych claims. Billy didn't want to go that way. He figured the best way out was to forget everything."

"Forget everything?" Eve said. "Sometimes I wish I could."

"He was going to get hit in the head," Harry said. "He had been in enough fights to know he could take a punch. But this time he would go down and when he got back up he wouldn't remember anything. I was going to have to tell him his name."

"So you were in on it too?" Eve said.

"Sure," Harry said. "Billy was my brother."

"So what went wrong?" Eve asked.

"White Rage," Harry said. "The Indian. That's what Billy called him. White Rage."

"Was he going to fight an Indian?" Eve asked.

"No," Harry said. "Nothing like that. This was an act of fate. There is this Indian tribe in New York that does all the high iron work on the skyscrapers. It was Billy's beat. There was this Indian 100 stories up on a construction site and he can't move. He's laying out on a beam and the wind is too strong to get him down. Billy volunteered to go up in a helicopter and be lowered on to the girder. He was in great shape. He thought it would be something he hadn't done before. That was Billy. The wind was so bad that when he swung down onto the girder, he had to release his harness so that he wouldn't be pulled back off. He tied himself to the Indian while he held onto the girder with his legs. He ran a lot. His legs were strong. And they waited for the chopper to come around again. While they were waiting, Billy and the Indian talked. He asked the Indian why his people did all the high steel work. The Indian told him that the Europeans had come and taken over every-thing. They had taken over the land and the water. The only thing left was the sky."

"How did they get down?" Eve asked.

"Billy managed to shackle his harness to a long line that he grabbed as the helicopter held against the wind. The wind was so bad that they didn't want to wait to pull them aboard. So they carried them dangling on a line over to Central Park where there was an ambulance waiting. Billy said it was some ride. When they got to the ground, the Indian was dead."

"Oh, no!" Eve gasped.

"White Rage," Harry said. "That's what Billy called him. Billy said that when that Indian died, his white rage died, and he was no longer hateful or resentful or angry. He realized that somebody was always taking over from somebody else. That's life. Ask the amoeba. He'll tell you the damn paramecium are moving in everywhere. And

105

the paramecium are complaining about two celled animals coming into the pond."

"So, he changed his plan?" Eve said.

"Two days after White Rage died," Harry said. "Billy was shot. He figured it was payback for all the shit he had done in anger."

They were at the Funeral Home, a large old white house set back on a lush green lawn with plenty of room for parking in the rear. While Eve leafed through some casket albums, Harry bought Billy a cremation without fire. Without fire cost an extra three hundred dollars. The discreet Mr. Charles, who had no distinguishing characteristics, would wrap the body for burial at sea. It was not an unusual request in an old seaport town like Key West. The extra money would take care of any paperwork and fees. Harry paid with his VISA card. Harry signed a release allowing Mr. Charles to pick up Billy's body at the morgue. Billy would be ready to sail by tomorrow evening. It all went smoothly and they were finished just as Eve closed the book on urns.

They were back on the street again. It was very late and there was no traffic. They stopped under a banyan tree in the darkness.

"The Banyan tree is sacred for meditation," Harry said.

Eve found the big spliff the Don had given her and lit it. She took a toke and passed it to Harry. There were only insect sounds and the glow of the joint was the only light on the street. Harry took a long drag and leaned back in the notch of a low branch. Eve sat farther out on the limb.

"Why are we doing this outlaw burial at sea?" Eve asked.

"Because Billy would like it," Harry said and then coughed up the smoke.

"This is good stuff," Eve said. She wrapped the remaining joint in a leaf and put it away. "Mr. Charles said this wasn't his strangest request," Harry laughed. "Can you imagine?"

"Please," Eve giggled, "I don't want to waste this high on Mr. Charles."

"It felt good to pay him." Harry said. "And knowing I had the money. Not having to wait till the first of the month. No easy payment plan. Just like cash."

"I forgot about the money. What are you going to do with it?"

"There's fourteen acres on the Intercostal Waterway north of Daytona Beach. I'd like to build a wall around it."

"Sometimes I get the feeling that you don't like people."

"I like people. I just don't like what people do to other people."

"I do some things to you," Eve said and leaned back against him in the tree. "You seem to like that."

"I like everything about you. You're a woman of means and substance."

"I have an accountant in Miami who pays my bills," Eve said. "We live on the same plastic. My family left me some money. I want to see the world."

"And this is how you came across me?" Harry said.

"It wasn't a lot of money," Eve teased.

"Sweetheart, you could have had me for a nickel. I'd pay you."

"You do every time you kiss me."

"I keep finding out new things about you. I know what you like and don't like but not who you are."

"Does it matter?" Eve asked, getting comfortable with his arms around her against the coolness of the damp night air. "Should everybody know our histories or is a new friend a chance for a new life?"

"What time is it? You're starting to sound sleep deprived."

"It never gets too heavy with us," Eve said.

"That's why we're together. Just one of the reasons."

They climbed down from the tree and slowly, silently, sweetly walked back to the dinghy dock. Everyone was gone. No crowd, no police. No one sleeping under the hulls. They put the dinghy in the water.

Harry rowed while Eve dozed in the bow. It was still dark with no hint of dawn but the moon was in the western sky and he knew that it was late. Eve came alive as he pulled the dinghy up to the transom. She quickly sprang aboard, tied them off and was on her way to her cabin before Harry could come aboard.

"I'm exhausted," she said. She had the key to her side of the boat in her hand. They always locked it when they went ashore. The hatch gave when she touched it.

"Shit!" Eve yelled. "Someone broke in!"

108

Harry came to her quickly and held her back. It was dark and impossible to see inside. He pulled her back to the cockpit where he got a rusted tool box out from under the seat. Inside, under the wrenches, was a gun wrapped in an oily rag. Harry took it out, and wiped it with his shirt. It was a big stainless steel .44 Magnum revolver. Eve stayed by his side as he went back to her cabin.

There was a battery powered lantern that Harry got from a cubby hole next to the Captain's chair. The light showed everything from the companionway back. Her berth and head were empty but all the doors and hatches were open. They went forward on the deck to the large hatch above her bunk. With the light he could see back into the galley. It was clean. Harry stooped on the bow and listened to the boat for the familiar sounds. He shined the lantern through the salon ports and into his cabin. When he was satisfied that there was no one, he turned out the light and put down the gun.

Eve went into her cabin and turned on the light. Harry took one more look around on deck before he went below. He put the big silver revolver on the table next to his bunk. It was what every boat needed. It was a cannon. He didn't have much, so not much could be missing. The radio and electronics were all in order.

When Harry went back on deck, Eve was in the Captain's chair in a nightgown drinking from a bottle of water.

"Seems all right," Harry said. "Nothing missing on my side. What about you?"

"I carry my life in that canvas sack," Eve said. "Who do you think did it, the cops or the guy with the gun?"

"I don't know," Harry said and he didn't.

"I want to sleep in with you," Eve said. "Keep that gun handy."

Harry liked the fact that Eve wasn't afraid of guns. They had target practice with wine bottles when they were off Key Largo. She learned fast and knew how to squeeze the trigger. She was a good shot.

They went into his cabin. Harry undressed and Eve was already asleep on the bunk when he turned out the light. He crawled in next to her and drifted with the sea for a moment before he was asleep. A gentle breeze blew through the cabin door from the companionway which had been left open.

When Harry was awakened by the footsteps on deck, Eve was already sitting up. He reached behind her for the gun that wasn't there. In the open doorway of the cabin, silhouetted by the light of dawn coming through the companionway, was a hooded man in black. As he moved forward, the light from a porthole shined on a gray machine gun.

The roar of the magnum deafened them as the hooded figure was thrown back through the door and fell on the cabin floor. That close, he was hard to miss. She had aimed for the middle and hit it.

When Harry looked down at the wound, he knew the man was dead. The slug probably took out his heart and lungs. He hoped that it didn't break anything on the boat

110

when it exited.

Harry knew before he lifted the hood that it was Frisky. He took a quick look and replaced the mask. Frisky was dressed like a ninja and his Uzi was full of water. Maybe he should have died with his buddies in Nam.

"Frisky," Harry said out loud. "There's probably a nickel bag in his pocket."

Eve was doing breathing exercises to steady herself when he went back to her. She handed him the gun. He placed it back on the table. He moved onto the bunk next to her and put his arm around her. She was steady.

"That noise probably woke up everybody in the anchorage," Harry said. "I have to get on the radio. The police will be here soon. I'll close the door so you don't have to look at it. I'll go up through the hatch so nothing is disturbed. I'll say I shot him, because I would have and it will be easier that way. I know what to say. I know what they have to know to fill out a report. You say the noise woke you up."

"That sounds good," Eve said. "There is no doubt that after what happened to Captain Adkins tonight and the boat being broken into, that you were within your rights. They'll never indict you."

Harry made the call. 911.

111

CHAPTER SIX

Captain Art Adkins was the first one to step aboard when the police boat arrived. Harry arranged the fenders between the two boats while they tied up alongside. Two more uniformed police came aboard while one stayed at the helm. Another white hulled boat was steaming out the channel toward them. That would be the lab crew. Harry looked at the sky. It looked like rain.

Captain Art Adkins was looking through the companionway, making a sketch on his pad. The cabin door was open and the gun could be seen on the table. The door to the head was closed and water could be heard splashing about.

"She's taking a shower," Art Adkins said as he turned to face Harry. "It's pretty obvious what happened. The hooded stranger, the realistic looking gun."

"The shooter at the dock," Harry said.

"We never did find him," Art Adkins admitted.

"This one is easy," Harry said, "Accidental Homicide with reasonable expectation of self defense."

"I thought you were retired," Art Adkins said.

"I shot him," Harry said. "I'll sign a statement."

"Shouldn't you consult your lawyer?" Adkins said.

"Let's save time," Harry was direct. "You and I both know that there was no shooter at the dock last night. That was just your down home way of searching the anchorage without all kinds of warrants signed by judges. You broke into my boat. Look at the locks. You didn't find anything. You didn't even find my gun. There was nothing in plain sight. And if you did find something incriminating, it was an elephant in a matchbox."

"You know the law pretty good without a lawyer," Art Adkins said.

"I was the law for twenty years," Harry said.

"Let's say your theory is right, for the sake of argument. The shooting for which I have a slug for evidence never happened. Say I was playing a hunch in the murder case of a beloved local citizen. And we might have searched your boat that had already been broken into by the fleeing felon. Look at the locks. And in plain site, we found a .22 caliber pistol like the one used to kill Billy."

"I'd say you were going through my underwear," Eve said as she came up behind him through the cabin hatch. Her short hair was matted wet. She wore one of Harry's tee shirts and shorts with a draw string that hung from her hips.

"And you must have witnessed everything," Art

113

Adkins stood up to acknowledge her.

"The noise woke me," Eve said.

"No witnesses," Captain Art Adkins said.

"Just one," Harry said. "Me."

"And forget manslaughter," Eve said. "He intended to stop an intruder with a gun. Deadly force at this range can be anticipated by anyone who ever woke up to a sound in the night. Especially after the big scene at the dock where this very man may have shot at you with a real gun. No Grand Jury would ever indict, and police misconduct is always so unpleasant."

"Your boyfriend ought to know about police misconduct," Art Adkins turned back to Harry.

"Just follow the manual," Harry told him. "This one solves itself."

"And I want my gun returned too," Eve demanded.

The police personnel were already processing the scene. The lab people were down below. Pictures were being taken. Someone yelled up from down below.

"Hey, Captain, he's got a bag of white powder in his pocket and a quarter bag of that Jamaican red and green that's been all over the place."

"Another drug related homicide," Captain Art Adkins said.

"If that will make it easier," Harry said. "You know it's impossible to trace a fragmented .22 slug. That's why the assassins in New York use them. They crease the tip."

"If you found my gun, it was in my drawer," Eve said. "If you were looking for a suspect, that's not a place he

114

would be. You can't search for an elephant in a matchbox."

"You two should open an office," Art Adkins shook
his head and ran his fingers through his hair. The grey was
starting to show. "I hope there wasn't anything else missing. Did you have other valuables?"

"Only a pair of Chanel pumps and a Versace dress,"
Eve said. She looked at Harry. "I was saving it for a special
occasion."

"I guess it isn't today," Art Adkins looked down
inside where they were bagging the body. "You know the
routine, Harry. My boys will finish up here while we go to
the station to take your statements. Boy, I'm glad I don't
have to clean up this mess. That alone is a punishment in
itself."

Harry and Eve sat in the stern of the police boat as its
engines revved up and the bow came up out of the water.
Within the noise of the engines, she whispered in his ear.
He could hear.

"I think someone is trying to frame you," Eve said. "I
never owned a gun in my life."

Harry looked at those grey green eyes and nodded. He
made a note never to play poker with her. That was twice
she had bluffed the Captain. At some point she might get
called, but there was something in the way she handled
herself that made Harry believe that her life was a pat hand.
He had felt relief when he knew Billy was dead, because he
knew that there was no other person alive for him to care
about. Eve took his hand and he knew he was not alone

again. He cared for her. He would put his life on the line for her. He loved her.

The morning had passed into lunchtime, by the time Harry had signed his statement and had talked to two sets of detectives. After lunch was the interview with the State's Attorney. By the time he met Eve back on the street it was near sunset.

"I'll clean up the mess," Eve said. "It was my fault."

"Do you need any help?" Harry asked.

"No," Eve said. "This is something I have to do alone to clean up some bad karma."

"I understand. Sometimes alone is better. Hitch a ride back with somebody at the dinghy dock. I'll do the same later. There's somebody I want to talk to and I know where she is right now."

"Sunset dock," Eve said. "Velda. Mrs. Brown and her cookies. Be careful. You remember what happened last time, and I'm not talking about the knock on the head."

They kissed goodbye and Harry watched her walk east toward the anchorage. He turned and walked west into the sunset. The sky was already turning pink.

Mallory Square Dock faced west where each day the sun set. And each day at sunset, there was a bazaar, a street fair, a carnival to celebrate the end of another perfect day in paradise; and to watch for the green flash. Jugglers, vendors, musicians, tumblers, mimes and a variety of fortune tellers, massage therapists, a balloon artist. The crowd of locals and tourists strolled slowly along the

116

midway as clowns took pictures of children with a snake.

"Oh, fudge," the voice was loud and sharp above the din and got the crowds' attention and laughter. "Buy a cookie and Mrs. Brown will take your picture."

She had a polaroid camera around her neck as she rode her tricycle with the large basket on the back that read "FUDGE $2.00". Velda was dressed in her hippie outfit, high top shoes and a bright print Bali shirt over brown tights. She had on granny glasses and her hair was swirled into a bun of black and grey.

Velda saw him as she was taking a picture of a hesitant couple who gave in to the woman's demand for a keepsake. No one would know. Velda took the picture and watched the faces brighten with the images on the paper. She kept the negative in a pouch she wore around her waist.

Velda peddled over to Harry and he took two dollars out of his pocket. She gave him a piece of fudge wrapped in plastic. He could tell from the way she looked at him that she knew about Frisky. It was a small island. Word gets around.

"I want to talk to you," Velda said and saved Harry the trouble. "Meet me at this address. Here's the key. There's a bottle of hooch in the bottom left drawer of my desk. Don't drink it all."

She had taken a card and a key from her pouch and stuck it in his shirt pocket. He unwrapped the candy and tasted it. It was very good.

"This stuff is terrific," Harry said.

117

"Oh, fudge," Velda yelled and everybody laughed.

Velda's place was north of the sunset dock. He looked back over his shoulder just as the sun slipped below the horizon and a gasp went up from the crowd. However, there was not that mythic event, the Green Flash, that was supposed to occur with an instantaneous burst as the sun disappeared. It didn't matter. The crowd would be back again tomorrow and the party would continue. Harry headed north. He was following his path.

Harry's path led by a drug store where he stopped for a caffeine soda and a candy bar. He hadn't gotten much sleep lately and he needed a rush if he was going to deal with Velda. At the checkout counter was a display rack for condoms. Harry picked the pack with the prettiest girl on it.

This was to have been the night of nights. The health clinic was closed by the time they had finished with the police. Eve had never mentioned it and he pushed the thought aside. Tomorrow was another day and that wasn't going to change the results. It was just delaying the action.

There was a trash can in front of Velda's office where Harry deposited his litter. Her office was on the first floor of a two story building with a balcony upstairs. The key she had given him opened a wooden door between two opaque windows that were stenciled "Mrs. Browns Cookies, Inc." on one side and "International Search, Inc." on the other.

Once inside, Harry slipped on some mail that had been pushed through a slot in the door. He shoved it aside. He felt the wall on both sides of the door but couldn't find a switch. His eyes were adjusting to the ambient light and he made out a large wooden desk at the back of the room. However, when he closed the door, there was only blackness and he had to make his way to the desk by memory and touch. He had no trouble finding the lower left hand drawer and the bottle of whiskey. With a pocket lighter, he found the switch to a desk lamp that lit a green blotter. He sat back in a leather executive chair and put his feet up on the desk corner. He left his sandals on the floor. It had been a long walk at the end of a long day. His feet hurt and his legs were tired. The caffeine and the sugar hadn't given him a boost so he opened the bottle. It was a good brandy. He could tell by the smell.

There was a door half open to the side of what turned out to be a bathroom, Harry found a clean glass by the sink. He resumed his relaxation in the brown leather chair and poured himself two fingers of liquor. As the chair swiveled, he could reach the other desk drawers but they were all locked. The bottle was something Velda probably needed to get to in a hurry. She didn't want to have to mess with keys when she needed a drink. Behind him was a large filing cabinet with the lock at the top depressed for security next to a door with a dead bolt lock that took a key from both sides.

In front of Harry, in the darkened room, he could make out a sofa and a couple of chairs. Every once in a while, a car would pass on the street outside. The rays of light would move through the cracks around the door and bare

119

spots in the painted windows. Harry swallowed half of his drink.

The shade of the desk lamp kept him in darkness as he found comfort in the chair. He exhaled and blew out the tensions the day. He could feel ripples of exhaustion slowly building into waves. He closed his eyes and listened to the water. Someone upstairs was taking a shower.

The meditation took Harry to another place on another plane. His physical being was gone. He existed only in his mind. Soon that existence was gone. He was in the zone. There was only pleasure and passion. There was no pain.

The adrenaline kicked in with the sound of a woman's heels on a set of steps behind him. His eyes opened. He was alert to the sound of a key in the dead bolt lock. He swung around as the back door opened. What he had thought was an exterior door was a partitioned hallway with a bright overhead light that cast Velda halfway in shadow.

What Harry could see looked like dessert from the ground up. She had on a pair of chocolate colored pumps. Her bare legs were caramel colored. Her short brown leather skirt was so tight it would have shown a panty line if she had been wearing any. A cream colored blouse was open at the top revealing plenty of cleavage. There was no bra. Her dark hair was down straight to her shoulders with the streaks of grey looking like rays from a heavenly light.

"Make yourself comfortable," Velda said and kicked the door closed with her heel. She came over and sat on the desk with her legs crossed. The desk lamp gave a good view from her hip to her toes, but he couldn't see into her eyes. A tan hand at the end of a cream colored silk sleeve took the glass of brandy from Harry and put it back down empty.

"You live upstairs?" Harry said.

"It's an apartment. If you're looking for a place. I own a couple of buildings like this. I'd have rented to Billy but he needed something on the ground floor."

Harry tried to focus on what Velda was saying but the shot of brandy had reached his brain and everything was muddy.

"You look kind of bad," Velda said. "Is there something I can get you?"

"May I please have a shower?" Harry said.

"Sure," Velda laughed. "Boat people! You're all out of your minds. When was the last time you felt hot water?"

"I've been in hot water ever since I got to this town," Harry said and followed Velda out the back door.

Going up the steps behind Velda was like going into a candy store; the chocolate chip shoes, coffee legs. Truffles for hips. Topped in whipped cream. And there was the scent of vanilla as they surfaced into her apartment.

The apartment was dark, but Velda knew the way. She flipped on a switch that lighted a clean bathroom. There was still fog on the mirror and the bath mat was damp. The shower dripped and Harry smelled cinnamon. While Harry was under the hot water working up a lather with the scented soap, the bathroom door opened and closed. There was a mint shampoo on the ledge and he indulged. Harry washed well and long. When the hot water gave out, he rinsed off in cold.

On the commode, Harry found a fresh towel and a razor. He shaved using the lather from the shampoo. There was a toothbrush and baking soda that he used. He dried and wrapped himself in the towel. There was coconut oil in a jar above the sink. He rubbed it on his face and shoulders then wiped it from his hands on his hair.

"I put your dirty clothes in the washer," Velda called from the kitchen. "There's a robe on the couch. I hope you like silk."

It was a woman's robe but large enough to wrap around though a little snug in the shoulders. It was white silk. Harry savored his cleanliness. He luxuriated in silk. He felt like a goddess.

The living room was simple. A big brown couch sat in front of a fireplace with a duraflame log burning in it. There was a big square wooden end table with a lamp, a phone and a bucket of ice with a bottle of French Champagne and two glasses. From the kitchen came the aroma of meat, garlic and onions. He could hear the sizzling and the splatter.

Velda had on a white apron when she served him on one of those folding trays. Steak was topped with mushrooms, onions and garlic with spinach on the side.

Velda leaned forward and spread a kitchen towel across his chest. She tried to tuck it into the top of the robe but wound up catching her nails in the hair that grew down the center. She pulled away gently.

"Thank you," Harry said.

"You're welcome," Velda said and went back into the kitchen. She returned with a beer in a cold glass and a brandy snifter for herself.

"I'm speechless," Harry said.

"Sometimes I like to get a little homey," Velda said. She sat at the far end of the couch with her legs stretched out between them careful not to touch the white robe with her brown shoes.

"My ex," Velda said as Harry began to eat, "You know, the one who dumped me for the tit job. He used to like me to cook for him. That guy was a real old fashioned romantic. From the old school. After I fed him, we'd sit in front of the fire and he'd drink champagne out of my shoe. We'd get bombed together. Then he would fuck me like a dog and I loved it."

"Sounds like you're still carrying a torch," Harry said and kept eating.

"Not so much a torch," Velda laughed. "More like a child proof lighter. You know, I killed people to save that son of a bitch back when we were fighting the cold war against the commies. They were Fifth Column spies and saboteurs, the scum of the earth. I don't regret any of it. I took a beating for my trouble. I gave better than I got, because I'm still here and those red slime are dead. But you don't want to hear about my story and my guy. We just had this animal thing. He was a lousy drunk and a chauvinist pig. But I loved that man with a passion.

"So, how did a woman with your style and experience

123

wind up on the Sunset dock selling cookies?" Harry paused and sipped the cold beer. The food couldn't have been better if he had fixed it himself. And the company was amusing.

"I heard this was a good drinking town," Velda said and took a sip of her brandy. "I wanted to drink. I was a good Private Investigator and could always make a living working with the lawyers. I had a trade but I didn't like that either. I had a few bucks put away. Financially I was secure, but emotionally I was a wreck. I was a middle aged woman alone. I found out a lot about myself. And one thing I liked was to drink. I could hide inside that bottle until I couldn't remember his face."

"You don't look any worse for wear," Harry said. Looking up from the meal, the confection next to him looked delicious. She was staring at him and he went back to the steak.

"You sound like Billy," Velda said and looked deep into the amber brandy that she swirled in her glass.

"You should have seen me back then. I was on my ass. One night Captain Tony threw me out of his place for kicking some wise guy sailor in the nuts for grabbing my breast. What I got is mine. I was stewed to the gills and could barely get on my bicycle. I remember I was turning the corner in front of Sloppy Joe's when the next thing I know, I'm sitting in the lap of a good looking guy who's wiping my nose and telling me not to worry. It sounded good. I was comfortable where I was so I went to sleep. People tell me I was riding like the devil was on my tail

124

and Billy was showing off when I hit him broadside, did a header over the handlebars, and landed in his lap. I remember people yelling and clapping but I was inside a bottle and life was distorted."

"I'll bet Billy really enjoyed it," Harry said. "He liked to play to the crowd."

"He took me to his place," Velda said. "He'd been in that apartment for years. The Don gave him a break on the rent because Billy was from the old neighborhood. You know Billy. Let bygones be bygones. Live and let live. He thought the Don was retired. Anything else he didn't want to know. The Don liked him, but Billy kept it strictly on a landlord tenant basis. It never got personal in all those years. Who can figure why people change? Why did I change from a falling down drunk to a woman of substance?"

"Cookies," Harry said.

"Don't laugh," Velda kicked at him without touching. "That was the best idea Billy ever had. It bought this building and three more just like it, with good tenants on long term leases."

"Mrs. Brown's Cookies was Billy's idea," Harry smiled.

"It got me outside and gave me a direction," Velda said. "I meet a lot of nice people. It's like going to the circus every day. The circus was a big thing when I was a kid. Billy made me happy. I told you about our marriage, so I could get his benefits. Well, it was a lot more than that."

125

"Did you stay with Billy?" Harry asked. He was finishing up the steak and mixing the spinach in the juices. He watched Velda take a hard hit on the brandy.

"We always had our separate places," Velda said. "But we were a couple. We were a pair. Everybody knew. Billy and Velda. We got invited to parties. Are Billy and Velda going to be there? Sure. Then I'm going. I was his wife. It was legal. I was even faithful to Billy for those eight years."

"And what about Billy?" Harry asked.

"Billy was a rascal. Billy really liked women. He preferred their company. He liked to hang with them. He wasn't afraid to run down to the drug store and pick up a box of tampons. And he listened. Billy always had a girl around. But when he wanted love, Billy called me. That was until Candy showed up on his doorstep. Listen, if a woman wanted to spend time with Billy, I didn't care. He was a hell of a man. He had those incredible arms and shoulders. That chest! He could lift me by the cheeks of my ass and lower me onto him. I loved to guide him inside of me and watch the joy in his face when I would come. I never had to fake anything. Billy was a real ladies man."

"I taught him everything he knew," Harry said and winked at Velda who giggled.

Harry had finished eating and swallowed the last of the beer, then wiped his mouth with the linen napkin. He then set the food tray on the floor next to the end table. The bottle of champagne was in front of him and he took it from the ice. He turned off the table lamp. They were

126

alone in the glow of the artificial log.

Harry unwrapped and unwired the cork. He twisted it so it came out slowly and there was a soft pop. He could see Velda's eyes shining in the firelight. He slipped off one of her brown leather shoes and filled it with bubbles.

Velda sat up close to him. She took the shoe and held it up to his lips. Harry sipped from the side. She moved her face close to his and sipped from the other side. Their eyes were locked together. Velda took the heel of the shoe and tilted it back and the champagne ran into her mouth and down her cheeks.

"Wait here," she said, putting the shoe back on and standing. She leaned in front of him and bent over to pick up the food tray. Her breast under the silk blouse brushed against him and he smelled lavender. She went to the kitchen with the dirty dishes. He put the champagne back on ice.

The meal had made Harry feel heavy, but the champagne had lightened his outlook. He had expectations. He had been lucky most of his life. He was lucky to have had an older brother like Billy when he was a kid.

Velda came back into the room with a machine rolled cigarette in her hand and a lighter.

"This is krypto from California," she said as she handed him the joint. "Don't do too much or it will knock you on your ass."

Velda tried to work the safety feature on the lighter to no avail. Her hand wasn't too steady. He finally lit it himself and took a big hit. Velda laughed at him when he coughed it right up, burning his nose and throat.

"Don't waste it," Velda scolded him. "This isn't any of that cheap Jamaican that's going around. I have a nephew that sends this to me direct from Humbolt county. I'm his favorite auntie."

"I'll bet," Harry said.

"This stuff is hard to come by and expensive as hell," Velda took the joint from him. "I'll take a hit. We'll do a human bong. I'll blow it into you. That way it will last longer."

Velda took a long slow drag. She held it in. Then she leaned over Harry covering his mouth with hers she blew the smoke into his lungs as he inhaled. Her long hair with the rays of silver light surrounded his face while the flames from the fireplace danced through it. She lifted up and Harry felt himself levitate as he exhaled. The rush was like a volcano that blew the top off of his head.

It didn't take Harry long to realize that he was wasted, slumped back on his end of the couch. Velda had her legs in his lap with her head resting against a pillow. There was a distant look in her eyes. She was someplace else at the same time.

"I want more champagne," Velda pouted. She lifted her foot so he could take off her shoe. There was an adhesive sound as he removed it. "Oh, fudge, my toes are all sticky."

Velda lifted her foot in front of his mouth. Harry put her shoe down on the couch and took her ankle in his hand. She wiggled her toes.

"Billy used to suck on my toes and tell me I was as good as Princess Di," Velda said in a way that it seemed like a dare.

Velda touched her toes to Harry's lips. He stuck out his tongue and licked the tips. She pressed against his teeth and he opened his mouth for her to enter. She giggled and squirmed as he slowly moved his tongue over, under and between them.

Velda sighed and relaxed as Harry took her heel in his palm and ran his tongue the length of her inner arch. His mouth was dry so he took a swig from the bottle of champagne.

"Watch me," Velda said from deep in her throat.

Harry looked down the smooth tan leg to the dark valley underneath the leather skirt that had worked its way up around her hips. Her thighs opened and she took the brown shoe and pointed it into the black hair that adorned her vagina. Velda was masturbating. Her eyes were closed and her beautiful face showed her pleasure. Her mouth opened and her stomach contracted. Her bare foot raked Harry's chest and opened his robe down to his groin. Velda's orgasm came with a writhing moan before she collapsed back against the couch.

Velda was motionless for a moment. Then those big dark eyes snapped open and she let out a deep animal laugh. She lifted herself on her elbows and kicked Harry playfully in the ribs.

"I've always been a bit of an exhibitionist," Velda was all smiles as she said, "Thanks for your support."

129

"I was in the neighborhood," Harry was smiling. He had a feeling of satisfaction, but the booze and the dope were confusing him. He felt ungrounded.

Velda swung her legs around and sat up. She straightened her blouse and skirt. She found her shoe and put it on.

"Safe sex," Velda said. "It's better than a dick. I've tried vibrators, dildos, men, women, and a dolphin in Key Largo too." Velda stood and leaned across Harry who was naked to the waist. She got the bottle of champagne and sat in his lap. She arranged her rear end on Harry's erection.

"I always get mine," Velda said. She swigged from the bottle and gave it to Harry. Her other arm was around his neck.

"You're one hell of a woman, Velda," Harry toasted her.

"You know, the Don has this literature for his Sperm-care products," Velda talked to him. "There's an article about these two Frenchmen who both lived to be one hundred and fifty years old. It's documented. They said they owed their longevity to each day drinking their sperm. They don't say who drank whose. But I figured out that it wasn't the sperm, or some hookers I know would live forever. It was the orgasms. I've had one a day one way or another ever since I came out of rehab. Look at me. I look great. I'm in better shape than ever in my life. Thanks in part to Billy for getting me out on that bike. Here, feel my ass. Like two bowling balls. Billy used to say that I

130

could crack nuts with my ass."

Harry felt the round firmness resting on his legs. He knew Velda was right. Billy was right too.

"I know you'll stop when I say so," Velda said and rubbed the knot on the back of his head where she had hit him the day before.

"I can see why Billy liked you," Harry said and kept his hand on her hips. "You're a rascal too. Always busting somebody's balls."

"You, me, and Billy, we're from the old school," Velda ran her hand through his hair.

"You're right," Harry said. "But I think we broke most of the rules."

Velda's cheek was in front of Harry and he kissed her. She giggled like a girl. She kissed him fully on the mouth, hungrily, but she kept her legs together.

"Remember," Velda said. "You're on the six month plan. I don't want to put you in a position to have to make a critical decision in your present condition. That's why I did it myself."

"I could have done it for you," Harry said.

"When I was a young girl," Velda said, "I read a girlie magazine advice column. The question was whether masturbation was bad for you. The answer was that you could wind up liking it more than other forms of sex. There's certainly less guilt and less fear."

"Modern times," Harry said and shook his head in agreement.

"Screwing Billy was like masturbating," Velda said.

131

She was drinking heavily from the bottle while her other hand was feeling Harry's legs. "Nice legs. Don't get me wrong. He satisfied me and we did things that will always be a secret between him and me. But there was a piece of the arc missing to complete the circle."

"His legs," Harry said.

"No," Velda said. "That was never a problem. We loved each other. He just couldn't feel it."

"He couldn't feel love!" Harry was fading.

"No," Velda said. "He couldn't feel anything from the waist down. No orgasm, no climax, no intercourse the way you know it. With Billy, it was an internal orgasm. Maybe the body goes into shock when it releases sperm. His balls used to pulsate. It was incredible. Poor Billy couldn't feel a damn thing down there."

Velda was at the bottle again. She was determined to crawl inside tonight. Harry took it from her and set it aside. She looked at him hard then smiled and kissed his cheek. She knew that he was only trying to help. And for the moment she wasn't telling him to mind his own damn business.

"Billy said he got the same feeling as sex when he raced his wheel chair against my bike on the beach at Daytona," Velda was reminiscing. "Increased heart rate and respiration, change in blood pressure. And then it would stop. We did a lot of long distance rolling. We had some good times together before Candy showed up."

"Who was Candy?" Harry asked. He was comfortable with Velda in his lap. Since he knew he didn't have to

132

decide if he would have intercourse with her, he could relax; and that's what his body longed for. Sleep. But he wanted to stay awake.

"She was the perfect blonde," Velda said with admiration. "She had the white teeth, the California tan, and a cute little ass with the open space between her thighs even when her knees were together. Billy said that Candy was a virgin."

"How did they meet?" Harry asked. His eyes were closed but he was listening.

"Frisky brought her over one day," Velda was solemn. "And Billy took her in. It was love at first sight."

Velda was blending with Harry, her head was tucked under his chin, she was breathing on his chest. One hand played with his breast. The champagne had put everything into soft focus. She wanted to keep talking as if she hadn't talked to anyone in a long time and she had a lot of tales to tell.

"Did it make you jealous?" Harry asked.

"No," Velda said. "How the hell could you be jealous of someone who looked that perfect and was blind."

"What do you mean, blind?" Harry said

"Blind," Velda said with emphasis. "She couldn't see anything. You're the one who's had too much to drink. Some retina disease. She told Billy that she was a runaway, but never said what it was she was running from. She wasn't on any hot sheet or missing persons list that I could get. She had a lot of problems. He used to go with her to her therapist in Miami. Billy wouldn't tell me anything.

133

So, I had her up to my place one night to check her out. She was familiar with the bottle. Maybe we drank to much. She could have been a virgin. She was horny enough. I mean we got wrecked on krypto and wine coolers. She was a good kid. What a body! We did everything, assholes to elbows and she gave as good as she got. She was almost as good as the twins. The difference was, Candy made me feel like a slut and the twins made me feel like a goddess."

Harry was listening, though the fatigue of the day was smothering the curiosity of the night. Velda felt good in his lap but his legs were asleep before the rest of him. She felt his discomfort and moved so that Harry could stretch out on the couch. She found the bottle and finished it. It seemed to give her new energy.

"I know I'm no spring chicken," Velda said. "You can't stay twenty-one forever."

"I don't know the twins," Harry said. The recirculation of his blood giving him a moment of clarity.

"They're in the book," Velda said sitting on the floor at Harry's side. "Pleasure Therapists. They have ads in all of the new age magazines. Massage, body work, Tantra and colonics. The Chinese have a saying: `You're only as young as your asshole.'"

Velda started to giggle and then laughed out loud. He could feel her organizing her thoughts as she rubbed his full belly. The robe he wore had come completely open and it was flesh against flesh. He enjoyed it but couldn't move.

"You can't tell a soul about this," Velda tried to

whisper though her lips were thick with drunkenness.
"Billy and Candy wanted to consummate their relationship,
but like I said she was fucked up. The therapist in Miami
referred them to the twins who had a mating ritual guaran-
teed to heal traumatized women. But, they wanted a lot of
money. Billy told me about it. So I decided to check them
out. Billy split the cost with me since it was work as a P.I.
Strictly business. It was fun. They certainly give you your
money's worth. I can't say I never had to pay for it. Hell,
what are my choices? Half the men in this town are gay.
The other half want to be Ernest Hemingway. What
woman likes a man with a beard? A woman with chapped
thighs."

Velda laughed at her joke and a flood of memories
took her away. Harry ran his hand through her soft hair. It
brought her back to the present.

"Nobody wants to hear my tale of woe," Velda
straightened up. "I was telling you about Billy's sperm.
And the twins. The Don hired me to get a condom full of
Billy's sperm. Ten grand. A lot of scratch but then the
Don must have had a big itch. Billy and I weren't having
much to do together once he went from cookies to Candy."

"Billy always had a sweet tooth," Harry said.

"So, I was a little bit jealous even though she was
blind," Velda admitted. "She had such a cute young ass.
They kept to themselves most of the time, so the sperm
wasn't going to be that easy to get."

"Why didn't you split it with Billy? Five grand."
Harry could still do simple math.

135

"Billy give his sperm to that pervert!" Velda pretended to spit. "You know Billy better than that. The damn fool was in love. So, maybe I was more than a little jealous even at my age and with my experience, but business is business, I needed ten grand to close on a strip mall on Stock Island. I told Billy that the twins were legit but that he should be sure to wear a rubber for Candy's sake. Her being a virgin and all that. Safe sex. Billy hadn't ever been tested and neither had I. There wasn't time. It didn't make any difference to Billy. He couldn't feel the difference. Candy would do anything for Billy. True love. It sucks."

"Only when its done right." Harry cracked himself up but still couldn't function. The fog was getting thicker and all systems were down. He listened.

"You and Billy have the same sense of humor," Velda laughed. "Quiet down, I'm talking. So, I take an offer to the twins. I'll lay a grand on them if they give me Billy's condom after the ceremony which is supposed to end in intercourse. They call it a uniting of the mind, spirit and body. Candy liked that kind of talk. She wanted to be a Buddhist. Frisky took out one of Billy's kayaks for his part of the mission. He was supposed to pick up secrets for our side at the twins boat. He didn't charge me a thing. He did it for the rush. Me and Bogart, the skinny black kid that worked for Billy. We were waiting at the dock. He was telling me the best way to snatch a purse on a bike and I was showing him what I would do to him if he ever tried it with me."

"Where's Billy?" Harry asked suddenly, opening his

136

eyes to the firelit room, then relaxed.

"Billy's on the boat with Candy and the twins," Velda slapped his thigh. "And Frisky comes back empty handed. I smacked him across the collar bone with the .45 to make sure he wasn't scamming me. I was convinced so I let him crawl back in his hole. I take Bogart in the back of my car and have him jerk off into a rubber. That cost me fifty cause he was wise to what the Don was paying runaways for the same score. He rides off thinking I'm some kinky old white woman."

"The sperm," Harry said remembering the cooler the Don had given him that was now back on the boat.

"The sperm," Velda smiled. "I gave it to the Don. I swore that it was the real Billy. I get to keep the full ten grand. Frisky thinks it's a drug deal gone bad. Bogart knows from nothing, and the twins leave a message on my machine saying `Sorry.'"

"No witnesses," Harry sighed. "You're the only one that knew."

"Me and Billy," Velda laughed. "I had to tell Billy. We both nearly busted a gut when the Don came around and asked us what we thought of the new lotion he was using on his face. He had that smug look when he asked Billy. Billy said he thought it made him look darker. When the Don left, we rolled on the floor for a solid half hour. We both wet our pants."

"A couple of rascals on the howl," Harry couldn't suppress a yawn.

Velda got up from the floor and took out her blouse

137

and unzipped her skirt. She lay down at the other end of
the couch with her head at his feet, her arms around his
calves. She kicked off her shoes and tucked her feet and
legs between Harry and the back of the couch.

"Billy and Candy," Velda said. "Who'd a thought it?
But they were happy. She would jog alongside his wheel
chair and he was her eyes. I used to see them go by here
late at night after all of the traffic was gone. I'd drop by
there once in a while to smoke a doobie and watch Candy
dance. That girl loved to dance and look as sexy as hell. I
loved her and hated her in the same breath. Then Billy had
an accident about nine months ago and she left him."

"What accident?" Harry asked. It was a struggle.
The feel of the woman next to him so smooth and warm,
like a blanket. Her voice was like a lullaby.

"I don't think you ever knew about Billy," Velda
yawned. "He wanted it that way. You see, the most important thing in Billy's life was his bowel movement. We take
it for granted. Nature calls and we answer. Well, Billy
couldn't hear the call and never heard the answer. But he
could smell it. So he ate almost the same thing at the same
time every day, a lot of rice and beans; so when he got up
in the early morning, he could swing himself up on the
toilet, smoke a joint, drink his coffee, that was it for a
complete gastric cycle. A regular fellow. You could set a
clock by him if you got up that early. He didn't want you to
know about his problem. He wanted you to think that he
was the same as always, only shorter. He used to put one of
my kotex pads in his shorts at night in case he leaked."

138

Harry didn't want to hear it. There was a leak. The deck was rolling under him. He was bailing buckets when a rogue wave drowned him in sleep.

CHAPTER SEVEN

When Harry woke up he smelled the coffee. He noticed that he had been covered with a summer blanket. There was a brown leather skirt and a pair of brown pumps under his shoulder. He could see Velda in her granny outfit at the counter that separated the kitchen. He pulled the blanket around him. The white silk robe had disappeared. He took a seat next to Velda on a stool at the counter. The coffee was already poured. He stirred in some sugar.

"I guess I really took a tumble off the wagon last night," Velda said. "I hope I didn't do anything to embarrass myself."

"I enjoyed every second of it," Harry said. "You're quite a fascinating woman. Any guy who dumped you should be shot."

"He was," Velda said. "A couple of times but they couldn't kill the son of a bitch. Not like Billy."

"Tell me about Billy's accident," Harry said and sipped the coffee, added more sugar.

"Another guy with a sweet tooth," Velda frowned. "I must have really run my mouth. What else did I say? Jesus, what else did I do?"

"You got yours," Harry smiled at her and looked at those big dark eyes. She laughed and kicked at his leg.

"The accident," Velda said and her mood went sour. "To make a long story short, Billy shit all over the bed and Candy vomited all over Billy. They had been smoking krypto, eating oysters and drinking beer the night before. Billy called me. When I got there, Candy was out in the yard crying like a baby and stinking to high heaven. Billy was inside crawling around trying to clean up the mess. It was an accident. But Billy said it was the worst day of his life. I helped him get rid of the sheets. I cleaned her up and comforted her trying not to tell her what she couldn't see but could smell. I went out and bought some sage, an old indian purification, to cleanse the place. It covered up most of the smell but nothing could cover up the memory. Billy was more careful after that; bladder bags, diapers and his old regimen rice and beans. Candy never got over it. She kept throwing up and one day she went out and never came back."

"How did Billy take it?" Harry asked.

"Like a champ," Velda said. "Like a real champion. He was back to his old self again. Always a smile, always a good word, always a game going on. We spent more time together. Me on my bike, Billy in his chair. Daytona, Cape

141

Kennedy, the Gulf Coast. We even went skiing up in North Carolina. They had a special chair on a ski. Billy was terrific. After one lesson, Billy was King of the Hill. What a guy! That was his life for a while. I was part of it. I loved it. I loved Billy. Everybody loved Billy. So why would somebody want to blow his brains out?"

"Maybe a jealous lover," Harry said.

"Maybe a greedy brother," Velda said.

They were both silent and drank their coffee. They caught glances of each other but no one talked. A buzzer in the background stirred her. Velda went into the corner of the kitchen and took Harry's clothes out of the dryer. They were hot when she handed them to him.

Harry dropped the blanket and put on the shorts and shirt. Velda watched him as he dressed. Being on a boat, he was used to nudity but he still held his stomach in when he knew she was looking. He checked the pockets and they were all empty.

Velda slid a small wicker basket along the counter top in front of him. It contained his belongings: a wallet with one credit card, a drivers license, another picture I.D. from the NYPD (retired), a swiss army knife and a package of condoms.

"Were these meant for me?" Velda smiled. "Doesn't matter. I always liked boy scouts. Be prepared."

"The jealous lover crack was a cheap shot," Harry said. "Sorry."

"Me too," Velda said. "I knew the money in that account was yours. Billy told me about it. He told me

142

about when you were cops and kids. But what have you been doing for the last five years?"

"Me?" Harry said. "I've been around. When I got my retirement I was seeing this model from California. She took me out to Tahoe. We lived in a cabin. But the second time we made love, we knew it was only physical. So, two years later we went our separate ways. I'd been waiting for this boat to come up for auction after a big drug trial, so when the doper made a deal, I came back East and got Peaceful Coexistence. A great name for Catamaran. I didn't have to change it. That would have been bad luck. After two years in a police dock, she was a mess. For a long list of reasons in every port from New York to Florida, it took me three years to get her together and bring her down to see Billy."

"And what happened to the California model?" Velda asked.

"She moved to Hawaii and joined a tantra group," Harry said. "She visited me on the boat about six months ago. It was still only physical. This time it only took one night and a rough storm to bring her to her senses."

"I saw a card you sent to Billy with an eagle on it that said only `Free as a bird,'" Velda said.

"The post office is the biggest bargain we have," Harry said.

"And Miss Six Month Plan?" Velda said.

"We met in Miami three months ago," Harry said. He filled the pockets of his pants and shirt with his belongings. Velda had the condom package in her hand and slapped it

143

into his palm.

"Come on down to the office," Velda said. "I've got something to show you from Billy."

In the office, Velda unlocked the file cabinet and took out a folder. It contained a black and white photo and bank deposit slip. There was a newspaper clipping about an accidental drowning victim. It was very brief. It probably had been buried on page ten so as not to scare the tourists. Harry looked more carefully.

The bank receipt was for ten grand. The victim of the diving accident was Adam Wise, Ph.D. of Miami. The photo was blurred as if the camera was hand held and not too steady. It didn't change the subject matter.

There was a blonde bent over the hood of a *Jaguar* sedan. A bald paunchy guy wearing only a Lone Ranger mask was humping her from the rear. A circle of young boys stood around with their dicks in their hands. Even in black and white it was easy to see the girl's even tan, her perfect white teeth as she smiled and her wide open eyes that saw nothing.

"When was this taken?" Harry asked.

"I don't know," Velda said. "Maybe Candy was only half a virgin."

"And you got this from Billy?" Harry said.

"I got it from his place," Velda said, putting the items back in the file. "The police missed it, but I knew where he hid things. Billy operated at a different level, if you know what I mean. It was the only thing under the carpet. The last couple of months Billy kept mostly to himself. He was

144

preoccupied with something that he didn't tell me. I think this was it."

Harry watched Velda return the file to the cabinet.

"I recognize the car," Harry said.

"So did I," Velda sat in her executive chair very business like. "I think you're a stand up guy Harry. Billy said you were coming. It made him happy to know that you would finally show up. If it was the old days, I'd be on this case with you. But I'm in the cookie business now; and as far as investigations go, I stay away from any case where I could get hurt. At my age, it takes too darn long to heal. If I can do anything for you, or with you after Miss Six Months dumps you for a younger guy, you know where to find me. I'm also a notary, if you need one."

"You said you have a car," Harry said.

"I'll give you the keys," Velda picked up her bag from the floor.

"It's not for me," Harry said. "It's for Billy."

When Harry and Velda got to the dinghy dock, Billy was in the backseat of her brown Mercedes with the tan leather interior. He was wrapped in white cloth as if he was starring in *The Curse of the Mummy*. The tinted windows of the car kept him hidden from any early morning gawkers.

Eve was waiting with the dinghy when they pulled up. After Velda, Eve looked kind of boyish with her close cropped hair and flat chest covered only by a tank top. But, her short shorts showed those legs that could only belong to a woman.

Nobody wasted any words as they quickly took Billy and placed him in the dinghy. There was an old ball cap and a pair of sunglasses with a lens missing under the seat. Harry put them on what was the Mummy's head. The two women took a moment to check each other out as Harry untied the boat and set the oars in the water. Eve sat next to Billy on the stern seat with an arm around him so that he wouldn't topple over. The boat and the brown car both pulled away from the dock at the same time in opposite directions.

"Thanks," Harry said to Eve and gave her an approving look. "I thought I might have to swim out and get you."

"I figured when you didn't make it back last night, you'd be coming home this morning," Eve said. "Or, I'd be visiting you in the county jail. I see you found a safer port in the storm."

"How was the boat after the cops got through with it?" Harry asked and kept a steady stroke. It was early and there wasn't much activity. The fishing boats had gone out earlier and the dive boats hadn't yet started. It was a clear path to the catamaran. His timing was good. He was still lucky.

"The coroner guys took the big pieces and left me the slop," Eve said flatly. "I did a good job. It looks better than before except where they dug the slug out of the aft frame."

"Did they take anything else," Harry said looking back over his shoulder to check his course. He pulled harder. The added weight made a difference.

"They took the cooler with Billy's sperm in it," Eve said.

Harry started to laugh as he got closer to the boat. Eve paid no attention and didn't see the humor as she looked around cautiously. There was no one on deck of any of the nearby boats.

The sound of metal pounding metal was ringing from the belly of some boat, but on the water it was hard to tell exactly where.

Harry wasn't concerned. He had come to know boat people and knew that they were all islands unto themselves, and respected your right to be the same. They were the first to come if you called for help and the last to interfere. Anything Harry put on his boat was his business, even if there had just been a murder there. And by now the two-way radios had spread the news up and down the coast. Boat people didn't look for trouble. There was enough of it out there on the water for everybody. The mummy in the ball cap and sunglass was private. There were no witnesses at the anchorage. At least none that would ever show up in court.

Eve lifted Billy up while Harry lifted from the deck after they tied up. She held the dinghy steady with those beautiful strong legs. She sprang aboard after Billy was secured.

Billy sat at the back of the cockpit, tied upright by a line over the boom and around a winch. Eve came up from below with a pot or coffee. They relaxed in the cockpit after the exertion of their efforts.

"Safe at home," Harry said and let out a breath as if
he were a spouting whale. "Sometimes I think I will never
go ashore."

"Did she whack you again?" Eve asked and took the
remainder of the joint they had shared in the tree out of her
hip pocket. It was bent and burned but big enough to light
with a lighter they kept near the compass binnacle.

"No," Harry said and took a hit when she passed the
roach to him. "She talked me into a coma, but I learned a
lot about Billy."

They both looked back at the restrained Mummy with
the hat. The sunglasses had been lost and his face was
blank. He was at peace with the world.

"Anything about who killed Billy or who is trying to
frame you?" Eve asked.

"Just a lot of pieces to a puzzle," Harry said, "And
some of the pieces, a girl named Candy and a couple
known as the twins, are still in the box."

Harry took another toke on the roach , burned his
fingers and tossed it overboard. He motioned Eve to come
next to him. He covered her mouth with his and exhaled
into her breath. She held her mouth against his in a big wet
kiss before she sat down and let out a little wisp of smoke.

"That was very nice," Eve said. "You learn something new every day."

They sipped the coffee and drank some good water
from the jug that they always kept filled in the cockpit.
They sat quietly enjoying the buzz, knowing that they

would have to move into action soon, taking Billy out to sea. Harry began to giggle.

"What?" Eve said. "What?"

"I was just thinking about a story Velda told me last night about that sperm," Harry grinned. "It's Bogart's."

"Billy's sperm that the cops took?" Eve was puzzled.

Harry told Eve the story about the sperm switch and Velda collecting the ten grand.

"Bogart's sperm!" Eve laughed. "What makes you think the Don would give you the real stuff? How would you know?"

"DNA?" Harry said. "But what the hell's the difference. I didn't know what to do with it anyway. I was going to feed it to the fishes with my progeny."

"Will we be back in time to go to the health clinic?" Eve said in a way that gave Harry an erection.

"We better get ready to go," Harry said.

"What exactly are we going to do with Billy?" Eve started to stretch. "We don't have to unwrap him, do we?"

"We'll take him out to the Gulfstream," Harry said. "I've got a fifty pound storm anchor and one hundred feet of rusted chain. We'll wrap him up and send him over the side into the big blue. It's the last tribute to a rascal. No harm meant. No harm done. This is the last collaboration of the Knight brothers. It's what we talked about once, being buried at sea or cremated. Billy said buried at sea because it would be more trouble. We also considered being burned on a barge like the Vikings. But we knew that even if we agreed when the time came, neither one of us would ever

149

spend that kind of money on a dead guy."

"I understand and I love you," Eve said. "Whatever you say, my captain."

Eve leaned on his shoulders and pressed her face close to Harry's. She rubbed against its smoothness. There was a smell of cinnamon in his hair.

"Velda took good care of you," Eve said kissing him all around his eyes and ears and neck until he became tickled. She rubbed her hands against his chest and felt his breast pocket where she found the package of condoms.

"Safe sex," Harry said.

Eve opened the small paper box with the pretty girl on it. She took out five individually wrapped prophylactics. She kissed Harry.

"They're all here," Eve said. "That Velda may be able to fool those Yankees on the dock with that granny act, but I saw her legs and butt when she was getting Billy out of the car. She has a killer body."

The word "killer" hung in the air between the three of them. "Do you think she could have?" Eve asked hesitantly.

"Did Velda kill you, Billy?" Harry asked the mummy tied up in the back of the cockpit. It wasn't Billy in the sperm cooler. Maybe it wasn't Billy in the wraps. Sometimes you just had to trust somebody. This time it was Mr. Charles Abbott, first in the book. Harry would never think of looking inside the Mummy outfit to see if it was his brother. He would always see Billy smiling, joking, telling a good story and dancing up a storm with a beautiful girl.

150

After today, Harry would see Billy in every wave.

Nothing more was said and they moved as one to ready the boat for sailing. Harry started the engine, while Eve went forward to weigh anchor. He watched her as she squatted,then stood lifting with her long lean legs. It was a sight for sore eyes. As they moved forward, she lifted the anchor out of the water, dipped it once to clean off the bottom mud and then secured it on the net between the hulls. She came back to the cockpit as they motored out of the anchorage. There was no wind.

"What if the police come looking for us?" Eve asked.

"It's easier to find forgiveness than it is permission," Harry said as they headed for open water.

It was flat calm, the air hot and humid, disturbed only by the hum of the motor and occasional sea birds that came looking for food. Eve relaxed under the shade of the bimini top and left Harry to his thoughts. As he steered the boat through the slick water, he smiled as he thought about his brother. His love for his brother did not end with death. He was thankful that he had been blessed with a one man family. Billy was a rascal. Harry knew that there was more to his death than just murder.

When they reached the dark blue waters of the Gulfstream, Harry cut the engine and they drifted. There was no ceremony. Harry wrapped the mummy in chains and shackled the fifty pound anchor to a couple of rusted links that kept the package secure. Eve carried the anchor while Harry carried Billy back to the afterdeck where they set it all down on the edge and unhooked the lifeline to the stern pulpit.

They both stood over Billy in silent prayer for a moment. From the top of Billy's head, Harry found the end of the wrap wound around his brother and unwound it a couple of turns. Harry got down on his knees and moved the anchor to the edge of the deck. The water was crystal-line. The sky was never bluer.

Eve was right next to him with her hands on Billy's back. Harry gave a nod and heaved the anchor overboard as Eve shoved Billy in unison. Harry caught the end of the wrap as Billy splashed into the water. He held it and they watched it unravel until Billy's hair started to show. Then he let it go. They watched as it snaked wildly into the depths following the white sinker, becoming a distant lure.

Harry put his arm around Eve's waist and she hugged him. Down deep they saw a large fish strike at the trailing bandage. It surprised them and they laughed. The air became light and they hugged each other for a long time. Then they got back to the cockpit and started the motor for the return to port. Mission accomplished.

On the way back to Key West, Harry told Eve about his night with Velda. He told about the old time office with the bottle of booze in the bottom drawer. He described Velda's apartment, what she wore and how she looked. He explained her relationship with Billy and his accident. He told her what he could about Candy and the twins; and how Velda had checked them out.

"Lipstick lesbian," Eve surmised.

152

"Switch hitter," Harry said.

"I think she's looking for a triple header," Eve said. "I could tell from the way she looked me over at the dock, she was more interested in checking out the merchandise rather than checking out the competition."

"A trio," Harry laughed. He hadn't thought about that before. That would be an interesting decision to have to make.

"I've always liked chocolate," Eve poked him in the ribs. "But I'd have to go one on one with her first."

"I'd like a picture of that," Harry said.

"Better than that, you can watch," Eve said.

She stood up behind him as he steered a compass course. Her arms went around him and her hands were at his crotch. She kissed the back of his neck. They stood quietly for a time feeling the sea and their unity.

"I think the secret lies with the twins," Eve said. She then went forward to the net where she enjoyed the sun. She took off her clothes and bundled then into a pillow. Naked and spread eagled on the bow, she was as fine a figure head as ever graced a ship.

They anchored in their old spot and took the dinghy ashore. They pulled into a marina where they gave a guy five dollars and tied up. They also filled the jugs of drinking water from a hose at the slip.

As they walked out to the street, Bogart skidded to a stop on his bicycle.

"Police are looking for you," Bogart said. "Did you really bury Billy at sea? That's cool!"

153

"Who told you?" Eve asked.

"Mrs. Brown told me," Bogart said. "She knows I keep it quiet."

"Is that what the cops want?" Eve asked.

Bogart broke into a wide grin and started to laugh so hard he dropped his bike.

"What did they say?" Harry asked.

"Bomb scare!" Bogart bent over double before he got control of himself. "They saw your boat was gone. I was nearby and heard them say to go ahead and radio for the bomb squad from Miami. And this other cop in a suit says, `No, we can do it ourselves.' I followed them on my bike back to the police station but they had all the streets blocked so I had to go through some backyards. From a roof across the street I could see two guys with a fishing pole behind some riot shields that they use during Spring Break. They have a beer cooler on the line and they take it out in the parking lot. One guy gets close and when he goes to open it, smoke comes out and they all run and hide behind cars."

"A beer cooler," Eve said.

"Yeah," Bogart said, "Like the one you had yesterday."

Harry and Eve looked at each other and then at Bogart who was in a hurry to get on with the story.

"It took a while for the Miami cops to get here with a robot and this big metal mother looking barrel on wheels pulled behind an armored car. It was fantastic. The robot picks up the cooler and lowers it into the extraterrestrial

154

barrel. It takes a long time. Then they all drive out to the airfield with the armored car way out in front. I hopped a couple of fences and layed up in the grass off the runway. After the car gets the barrel to the middle of nothin', it pulls away. After it stops, a siren goes off and the barrel goes boom, shakes a little and smoke comes out of different places. There were helicopters, mobile units, satellite dishes from TV stations buzzing all over the place. One good looking chick from Miami reported that the police had to blow up a bottle of nitro glycerine with a stick of dynamite to prevent possible harm to the public. They said it was part of a drug war. Man, what a day! Then a half hour later, everything is back island style. You missed it."

"Smoke from the dry ice," Eve said to Harry and shook her head.

"I better go by and talk to Captain Art Adkins before somebody shoots me on sight," Harry said.

"I'll go back to the boat in case they want to come aboard again," Eve said. "I'll meet you back here in a couple of hours." She looked up at the position of the sun.

"I'll have time to go by the clinic," Harry said. He kissed her. He and Bogart went into town. They parted company at the Post Office.

Harry had the key to Billy's box. There was nothing but junk mail. He went to General Delivery to see if there was anything forwarded to him from his box in New York. They didn't forward junk mail. He had no outstanding bills, but it was a habit he had at every port when he was getting cards from Billy. Harry heard a whisper from

155

beyond the grave when the clerk handed him a letter that he recognized as written in Billy's hand. He shoved it into his pocket and went out into the street. He wanted to be on the boat when he read it.

It wasn't far to the police station and the streets were in an afternoon shade. There were big flowering mimosas, frangi pangi, a few oak and mango trees in fenced yards. It was a quiet part of town away from the attractions.

He walked in the front door of the police station and a couple of uniformed cops nodded and said hello. At the desk, he asked for Captain Art Adkins. When he gave the woman desk sergeant his name, she stepped back and drew her gun. She called the cops from outside who came in fast, put Harry against the wall and patted him down and cuffed him. The woman cop was on the phone.

"We got the mad bomber," she said.

Harry recalled a mantra he had used some time after Billy got hit and transcendental meditation seemed like a good chance for peace of mind. He let it run through his mind and his muscles. He remained calm. This too would pass.

CHAPTER EIGHT

When Captain Art Adkins came out of the back room, he looked at Harry in his meditative calm and laughed. He had the officers unhook Harry and walked him back to his office. He was friendly and apologetic.

"There's been an All Points Bulletin out for you all the way up and down the coast," Art Adkins said, offering Harry a small paper cup of Cuban coffee from a larger styrofoam cup.

"What for? I didn't leave the jurisdiction."

"Your boat was gone." Art Adkins downed his Café Cubano like a shot of rum. "We had a bomb threat involving a parcel taken from your boat. What's a cop to think?"

"That was no bomb," Harry said and sipped the dark sweet liquid. He could feel the caffeine hit his nervous system. He wanted to get on with it.

"The bomb guys from Miami said it was nitro set to

blow on a thermal fuse," Art Adkins followed the café with a glass of water. "When they blew it up, it didn't ignite. What the hell was it?"

"Sperm," Harry said.

"Sperm!" Art Adkins poured some more coffee. "It must have been some pretty hot stuff. It was smoking."

"Packed in dry ice," Harry said. "I got it from the Don."

"Smoke from dry ice," Art Adkins smiled. "That explains it. Tell you the truth, I think everybody wanted to try out that new bomb bucket. The Don donated a bundle to upgrade our department."

"What a guy," Harry said.

"He bought us flack jackets for the war on drugs," Adkins said. "He wants to protect the kids."

"Especially little boys," Harry said.

"You seem to know about one of our leading citizens," Art Adkins unwrapped a cigar and bit off the end.

"Sperm-care products," Harry said. "What a joke! What else is he protecting? Kiddy porn. Child prostitution. Pedophilia. I know the citizen from way back."

Captain Art Adkins sat back in his seat. He seemed surprised that Harry was so well versed. He lit the cigar and looked around to be sure there wasn't anyone who would complain and make him go outside.

"Are you reading from a Grand Jury indictment?" Art Adkins talked around the smoke.

"Yeah," Harry said. "He'll get indicted when pigs get wings."

"Don't be so sure," Captain Art Adkins leaned forward through the smoke in a confidential tone. "For the last six months Billy was working with me to nail the son of a bitch. Didn't you know about it?"

"No," Harry said. He leaned away from the Captain. There didn't seem any reason for this confidence at this time especially after Frisky's death. It was possible Adkins was pumping him for information.

"Billy had contact with the runaways" Art Adkins leaned back. "It was like a battle between good and evil. Billy trying to set them straight. Frisky and the Don trying to get them into his hell. Frisky got a commission on the sperm, and a premium for pictures he took of selected clients who were the guest of the Don at his circle jerks."

"What about Candy?" Harry asked.

"Billy started working with me after she left," Art Adkins looked at his cigar.

"Do you know where she went?" Harry asked.

"I could get an address," Adkins had something to trade. "Give me a little time."

Captain Art Adkins got on the phone and ordered Harry's APB lifted. Harry told him about Velda and the sperm swap. Adkins choked on his cigar.

"I recommended that the State's Attorney not file charges in the Frisky death." Adkin's smiled. "We blew up Bogart's sperm!"

"You're a real good cop," Harry said.

"Frisky was a piece of shit," Adkins said. "He worked for the Don and any other creep who wanted

159

something illegal. Billy knew who he was; what he was."

"Billy must have known about the Don's other businesses for some time," Harry said. "Living right there on the estate, he had to see something."

"You know your brother," Adkins puffed. "He was a live and let live kind of guy. But he was still a cop at heart. He was on to something that would stick. Maybe it was Candy or that therapist they went to see in Miami. Something made him change."

The Captain took an envelope from his desk. There was a page torn from a slick magazine. It was a display ad. Two people. Eve and Adam Wise, therapists at the Eden Clinic specializing in sexual disorders. There were snapshots of the two doctors. He was bespeckled and smiling. His hair slicked back, his white jacket pristine. She was thin with long brown hair also wearing glasses and a white coat. The picture didn't show her legs.

Harry looked at the picture for a long time.

"Maybe she has a twin," Captain Art Adkins sat up and looked into Harry's eyes. "Adam Wise died in a diving accident off of the jetty where Billy was killed about four months ago. There was no evidence of foul play. His wife closed the clinic and as you can guess, being a doctor and a business, there was quite a bit of insurance. But they had the coverage for ten years, so there were no red flags at the payoff. Just another rich widow in Florida. It happens. I want to talk to her."

"About what?" Harry said. "An official accident. Lying isn't a crime unless it's done under oath."

160

"Impeding an investigation," Captain Art Adkins said.

"It wouldn't take a lawyer to beat that wrap," Harry said. "And if she is a therapist, what went on between Billy, Candy or her is privileged."

"I'll have to take another look at her statement," Adkins wasn't quite so friendly anymore.

"Don't waste your time," Harry said. "That gal is too smart to make dumb mistakes. Her reasons for lying are her own. She was with me when Billy was killed."

"And she was with you when you killed Frisky," Adkins added.

"I can see the wheels turning," Harry smiled. "Your cop's mind is working overtime."

"You're kind of sweet on her," Adkins relaxed.

"We get along pretty well," Harry said. "It seems to me the Don was the one with a reason to have Billy killed."

"Possible," Captain Art Adkins knocked the ash from his cigar into a desk drawer. "It was a typical mob assassin's gun, but not the style. They like to shoot somebody from behind in the back of the head, not face to face with the guy's eyes open. But who knows? We'll never match the slug other than calibre. You know what that's worth. A shell casing maybe, but a rim fire at that. No, we can only match the calibre. There was one round missing from the gun we retrieved from your boat. Her gun."

"An empty chamber under the hammer," Harry said. "That's good gun safety."

"You have all the answers," Art Adkins said.

161

"It wasn't her gun," Harry said. "Somebody planted it."

"She said it was in her underwear drawer," Adkins pressed him. "That's where we found it."

"Maybe you should have shut the drawer," Harry said.

"She's your alibi for Frisky," Adkins was making a point with the cigar as an indicator, "And you're her alibi for Billy. Maybe the two of you are in this together."

"Fuck you," Harry momentarily lost his center but a deep breath and the resounding mantra kept him under control. "You know the rules, Art Adkins, Captain. Get the evidence. Give it to the State's Attorney. If he finds it to be more than conjecture, you might have a case and a collar. Right now, all you've got is dead people and no witnesses."

"Listen, you old whore," Adkins warned Harry, "My dick is getting bigger and it's pointing in your direction. I read the report from New York. You fucked up your brother's life once. Maybe you'd do it again. You're the reason he had no legs. Don't say a word. We're not so backward down here. We have computers, faxes, telephones and informers. We solve most of our cases and we get convictions. You're either guilty or holding back on me. You know more than funny stories about sperm and I'll find out what it is. You may be all there, but you're not half the man your brother Billy was."

Harry got up and left without saying anything. He asked the desk sergeant for directions to the health clinic. Without looking back, he went outside to freedom. The

162

clinic was only a few blocks away. Harry had to hurry because it was close to closing time.

When he got there, an obviously gay nurse looked at him through a locked door and with a wink let him in. Wearing purple eye shadow and earrings. In any other town, it might appear strange except for Provincetown or the Village. In Key West, a waiter in heels and a skirt was not unusual. Freedom of expression was alive and well in America.

"Hey, good looking," Harry said. "I want to pick up my HIV test results."

"I understand," the nurse said. "You're not the first nervous nelly to show up late. I know. I've been there before."

Harry gave his name and the nurse went behind a reception desk and played with the keys on a computer.

"There's another name attached slash, West, Eve," the nurse looked at the screen and then looked up and smiled. "Oh, are you getting married?"

"Yea," Harry said. It was easier than an explanation. He gave the right answer. "You might want to sit down there," the nurse pointed to a couple of chairs in a waiting area. "I have to go in the back to get the results."

Harry took the nurses advice and sat down to wait. He waited. He watched a clock on the wall tick off the longest two minutes of his life. Tragedy usually happened fast in the police business, but this was a slow death. The red second hand on the clock moved ever so slightly in its circumnavigation of the numbers that measured time. Why did he have to wait? Was there something on the screen that warned of an outcome that he wouldn't be able to stand? Was he HIV positive? That last time with his Tahoe tootsie? When he had his teeth cleaned? Every open wound that he suffered as the normal part of boat life became a potential danger that he let pass through him. He was sure that he was clean. But what about Eve West/ Wise? The thought that she might be infected slapped him across the face and he winced at its sting. Could it be possible to find a woman you truly love only to have her fade from life at the moment of discovery? No, Harry thought. I've always been lucky. It can't happen to me.

The sound of the nurse's footsteps were in time with the pulse beating in his temples. As the nurse's face came into view, Harry tried to detect the results, but nurses had done this many times before and he was sure she had developed a deceptive technique. She had papers in her hand as she came up to him. She looked from the papers down at Harry in the chair and her mouth fell open and her eyes opened wide.

Harry's heart skipped a beat. He could feel tears welling up in his eye. His hand shook noticably as he reached for the results.

"You're Billy's brother," the nurse gasped.

"Yeah," Harry tried to clear his throat. He wiped at his eyes that were moist. "I forgot my glasses. Could you please read those for me?"

"They're both negative," the nurse said off-handedly. "From this angle, you look so much like Billy."

164

Harry exhaled a long slow breath. Eve's smiling face waited for him in the future.

"I usually saw the back of his head," the nurse said and sat down in the chair next to Harry putting a comforting hand on his forearm. Harry recoiled. "Oh, not that, silly. Billy was straight as an arrow. I meant the kayak races. He was better than any man in that kayak of his. He had a special seatbelt that bonded him to the boat. It became his legs on the water. And oh, deary, those big arms and shoulders turning like a windmill as he pulled out in front. He blew us all away. Oh, it was such a shock when I found out about Billy."

"Do you have any idea who killed him?" Harry tried a longshot.

"The murder! Maybe it was a blessing," she wiped at her nose and sniffled. "I was talking about the blood test."

The silence gave the answer.

"You didn't know?" The nurse put a hand to her lips. "He could have had counseling and treatment, but Billy didn't want any of that. He took it like a man. It didn't stop him or change him. He caught his breath and wheeled on down his path in life. He wasn't the type that would fall apart and kill himself over it. We knew he had gone through so much shit in his life up to then that one more turd wasn't going to matter. He was such a great guy. We all loved Billy. He was the champ."

A moment ago, time had been a slug dragging itself across the sidewalk of life. Suddenly it had become a

165

hummingbird darting past Harry faster than the mind could follow and he only got glimpses of its hovering existence. He had to get back to the boat.

Harry folded the test results and put them in his back pocket. Billy's letter was there. The nurse hugged him when they got up and he returned the gesture.

Outside, there was still daylight, but clouds appeared from time to time casting shadows. He walked at a brisk pace. He could feel his muscles working. He let his mind open to the nature of his path, its light and shadows. Harry absorbed the pleasure of being able to love freely without the fear of AIDS with Eve. He let Billy's life and death pass through him. He hung on to the expectation of Eve.

Eve was smiling when Harry saw her sitting in the dinghy tied up to the end of the dock. He saw that look of happiness and knew he could never destroy it by questioning. This was the moment for celebration, not investigation. Harry didn't give a damn about Eve Wise. Eve West was waiting for him at the end of the dock and six months of restraint would be released before he ever doubted her sincerity.

"We passed the test," Eve Said.

"How could you tell?" Harry asked as he got into the boat.

"By the fact that you were walking," Eve laughed. "If the news had been bad, they would have had to bring you back in a cab."

"Am I that predictable?" Harry untied them.
Eve was sitting on the rowing seat and had the oars in hand.

166

He relaxed in the stern.

"I've got a surprise for you," Eve said, dipping the oars to get them in motion.

Harry was in his favorite position; between Eve's legs resting with his back against the transom. He watched the woman he loved living a vibrant life. It gave him great pleasure to be a part of that life.

When they got aboard, it was not unusual that they didn't speak. They had quietly established routines that they enjoyed. This one had become known as the cleansing of the land.

Eve went to the foredeck and brought back a two gallon plastic bag, clear on one side and black on the other. She had put it out in the sun earlier in the day. Water had been heated through the clear side and heat absorbed by the black. She hung the bag from the boom over the cockpit where she had opened the bimini top.

They both undressed and tossed their dirty clothes into a common pile near the steering station. Harry had already emptied his pockets and set the contents near the compass binnacle. The letter from Billy was still unopened on top.

They took turns kneeling under the bag which had a small hose with a shower head at the end. The one standing sprayed the one kneeling with just enough water to wet the hair and body. The water was very hot. Then they filled their hair with shampoo working up a lather that they spread over the rest of their bodies, helping each other with places that were hard to reach, their backs and buttocks and feet. Then they went to the back of the boat and jumped into the water. They submerged and rose several times shedding the soap bubbles and the dirt of the land. They came back aboard by way of the steps molded into the back of each hull.

When they were back in the cockpit, they again accompanied each other beneath the hot water of the sun shower rinsing away the salt of the sea. It all ran down through the scuppers back to the ocean completing another cycle. There was a serenity of living in harmony with the natural world that calmed the fiercest heart.

They toweled off in their separate cabins. Harry shaved at the small stainless basin in his bathroom. There was no hot water. It didn't bother Harry. He found salt water and shampoo was as good a shaving cream as any on land, and he cut himself less often. There was an old bottle of body lotion scented with myrrh that he had bought from a street peddler in New York which he used as an aftershave. He ran his hands through his hair. He liked the bad light of the head because it showed less grey, fewer lines and less age in general. He saw more of himself in soft focus, not distracted by details. Harry liked what he saw. He was lucky.

There was a clean black and white caftan on the back of the door to his cabin and he threw it on as he went up top. Eve was waiting with a bottle of tequila, a lime and a shaker of salt. She wore a simple loose short dress in a Bali print. She had already fired up a joint and handed it to him as he sat near her.

"Bogart," Eve held her breath and gave him a thumbs

up sign.

Harry smoked a little and passed it back. There was a shot glass behind the tequila bottle which Harry filled. After he exhaled, he did the shot.

"Another celebration," Harry said. "Just like the night we arrived."

"I figured you'd need it one way or the other," Eve said and squeezed the lime into her mouth, took a shot and then licked salt from the back of her hand. "Is that the proper procedure?"

"It doesn't matter," Harry took another hit and another shot, squeezed the lime and licked the salt. She laughed at him when he was finished. He enjoyed her laughter.

Eve came close and kissed his eyes shut. She ran her hands and her face against his face and her touch removed the tension in his head. She kissed lime juice onto his lips and touched the tip of her tongue in the salt and then touched it to the tip of his tongue. She then took tequila in her mouth and transferred it to his mouth with a kiss.

"Yesterday, the human bong," Eve laughed, "Today the human shooter."

"Is that the surprise? I like it. I like it a lot."

"No," Eve said. "I got us an appointment with the twins."

"The twins!" Harry tried to sit up but it seemed easier to just recline and do another shot. He had enough surprises for one day. They were becoming so common as to be mundane. He took another hit and layed down on a cockpit cushion while Eve sat in the Captain's chair.

"They're in the Dry Tortugas," Eve was excited. "We can either take a seaplane or if we sail all night we can get there tomorrow before sunset. Harry, this is important to me."

"How did you find them?" Harry asked. The liquor was already in his brain. The relief from the HIV test and being with Eve put him in a peaceful receptive mood. He wanted her, but if he had to wait another night and another day, it was okay. The possibility now existed. That in itself was a victory. He'd do whatever she wanted. He was in no position to resist. He sucked the lime.

"They're in the yellow pages," Eve said. "I looked them up after you went off, I called them on their cellular phone."

"Modern times," Harry yawned. He knew he was drinking too much lately. He finished the joint.

"Something happened on their boat that night with Billy and Candy," Eve pleaded her case to Harry. "It's the missing piece. I think that once we know what happened, we'll know who killed Billy, or maybe why."

"And you think it has something to do with Candy," Harry said.

"I know it does," Eve said. "Maybe they know where we can find her."

"Captain Art Adkins said he might get me her forwarding address," Harry said. There was something he had to do before he passed out. He reached over by the compass binnacle and got the envelope on top.

170

"What's that?" Eve was at his side.

"I got a letter from Billy," Harry said and sat back down. He held it in his hand unopened. Eve took another shot and knelt on the deck.

It was a serious moment as Harry used his thumb nail to lift up the flap. Harry unfolded a letter size sheet. At the bottom was Billy's signature. There was nothing else on the page. Harry started to laugh.

"I don't get it," Eve said.

"It's just like Billy," Harry stopped laughing and nodded affirmatively. "I can fill it in whenever I want. Say whatever I want and he'll sign it. Velda will notarize it if I need it."

"It's like a blank check," Eve smiled.

"Or best evidence," Harry said.

"Then he knew," Eve said the obvious. "Billy knew he was going to die and wouldn't be here to testify, but about what?"

"I guessed a while back," Harry said. "Velda told me how concerned he was that I not find out his limitations and problems. That's why he cleaned out his place, the bladder bags and diapers, before he left for the last time."

"So Billy knew he was going to die and he got ready for you," Eve said. "Or someone who knew how he felt, got ready for you."

"Velda!" Harry said, but his voice was clearer than his mind.

"She knew what he wanted. You said she killed before," Eve was convincing.

171

"Billy was also working undercover with Captain Art Adkins to pin something on the Don," Harry wanted her to know. "Sometimes something goes wrong."

"There's no such thing as an ex-cop," Eve mused.

"It was only for the last six months since Candy left him," Harry said. Somehow he felt defensive.

"Maybe Candy knew what he wanted you to find?" Eve was thinking out loud.

"A blind girl couldn't have gotten out on those rocks to do the killing," Harry said. "She would have needed help in cleaning out his place."

"And Billy knew it was coming," Eve pointed to the blank sheet of paper with the signature. "When was it mailed?"

Eve took the envelope from Harry and looked at the front. "The day he died." Harry said.

"Maybe the Don had a contract on him," Eve was figuring all the angles. "Billy knew he couldn't get away. He couldn't even hide."

"Billy wouldn't hide," Harry said. "He faced life in the open. He was the same way with death. Maybe he wanted to die."

"What in the world would make you think that?" Eve looked sideways at him.

"Billy was HIV positive," Harry said.

Eve looked at him and silence descended. Her mouth started to speak but she thought better and continued a quiet consideration. She fell into Harry's arms and he held her. He was drifting with her when she pulled away.

"I'll take the first watch," Eve said. "You're in no condition to drive. We need to get there by tomorrow night. The twins have created a special ceremony for us. I told them that you wanted only the best."

"Ceremony?" Harry was confused. "The twins have us booked? What's this going to cost me?"

"A couple of grand," Eve smiled. "Remember, you're a rich man. They're giving you a discount provided they get to keep the catch."

"What does that mean?" Harry said. "You didn't charter a fishing boat."

"They want your sperm," Eve said.

The tequila had paralyzed Harry. The joint confused his thoughts. It had all become surreal. His eyes were really tired. He forced them open as he watched Eve ready the boat for sailing. She was a marvel. It was like watching himself in her body. She did everything the way he had taught her. She could handle the boat herself. There was a southeast wind and they were headed west. They sailed out of anchor with only the mainsail hoisted. When they had cleared the harbor, she unfurled the jib. They were on their way to the Dry Tortugas.

"If we can make it to the Tortugas and back, we can go anywhere in the world." Harry recited common belief.

Eve looked back at Harry, smiled, and gave a thumbs up as the wind took them away.

When Harry opened his eyes again, it was dark and he saw Eve's face lit by the red light of the compass binnacle.

She leaned back in the captain's chair with both bare feet up on the wheel. She steered her course. She picked up a cup and sipped something. She took a flashlight from the cabin top and read a chart across her lap.

The passage to the Dry Tortugas was marked with beacons and red and green lights that flashed a certain sequence to identify themselves. They were numbered. It was necessary to read one in the front and one behind to properly pilot the channel. A heading was always taken from the compass and periodically corrected to account for any crabbing movement of the boat. Also on the chart with the depth readings were little pictures of half sunken masts indicating a sunken ship. "P.A." Position Approximate.

Ahead, Harry saw red, green and white lights pulsing different heartbeats. As he looked upward through the ambient glow of the running lights, he could see the map of the stars washed out by the glow of a nearly full moon. He figured he had slept about six hours. His mouth was foul and he ached in a lot of places. Eve looked back to take a fix on a marker and saw him looking at her.

"I knew you were awake," Eve said.

"How come?" Harry muttered and sat up.

"You stopped snoring. And whistling too."

"You don't say," Harry said and stumbled down to his cabin.

He took a cold shower to wash the salt from his eyes. He remembered shaving earlier but not much more. He pulled on some shorts and a tee shirt, brushed his teeth and stood for a while thinking about what he would need to

174

take over to the helm, for the next four hours watch.

Eve had a Cuban coffee pot ready to be perked, when he got to the galley. There were some biscuits and a squeeze jar of honey. He got two clean cups out of the cabinet and waited against the bulkhead for the café to perk.

He set the perked coffee and food on a tray on the cabin top. Eve stood up. He hugged her and he could feel each of her vertebrae pop as she let the tension of the watch transfer to Harry as he replaced her in the Captain's chair. She leaned over slowly stretching her spine as she pointed with a pencil to a spot on a line drawn on the chart. It was their position and heading.

While Eve exercised her body on the outer deck always holding on to a line or a cable, Harry rechecked her calculation and found them to correspond with his own. He sat back, put his feet on the wheel, and checked the sails. It was all trim, doing about ten knots. He chose the catamaran for its speed as well as its comfort. Eve stood behind him, handing him his coffee.

The moonlight on the water gave it a priceless value that could never be matched by man. The fact that it would disappear soon. The fact that it was ephemeral enhanced the moment. They both gazed into the land of lights.

"Remember all of those big mansions we saw when we were walking around Key West?" Eve said.

"The Victorian palaces," Harry said.

"They were all built by salvers," Eve said. "They would move the lights in the Florida passage causing ships

175

to run aground. Then they would reap the rewards of salvage rights. They were in it for the money."

"Please, take the wheel a second," Harry remembered what he had forgotten while waiting for the coffee. He went back to the stern and urinated, watching it splatter into the phosphorescence of their wake.

"We're in the Quicksands," Eve said as Harry retook the helm. "The depthsounder has been reading between eight and nine feet for the last hour. The winds have been steady ten out of the southeast."

Eve looked ahead and then behind. She looked again at the chart with the flashlight. She slapped Harry on the back.

"I'm going below," Eve said. "Drive careful."

She kissed the back of his neck and mussed his hair. She held his shoulders for a moment. Then she was gone.

Harry was alone. For four hours she would be gone and he would be at the wheel. He knew that the skippers of all those half masts on the charts were probably better sailors than he. But as the French said, "There are no good sailors, only old sailors."

He checked the red and green running lights, the white stern and the mast light. There was a jack for the radio or a microphone cord from down below that he could use, but Harry had no desire to be in touch with anyone in the world. He finished his coffee and started on Eve's. He smiled just thinking about the look on her face when he got the test results.

There was the rush of the water as the two hulls

plowed on toward the lights. A rogue wave came at them from the side and the sail flapped, the rigging talked, the boat gave a slight pitch and plowed on. This was their path.

Harry knew he wasn't going to confront her with the Eve West/Wise issue. There was no reason to detour from the meeting with the twins. If he was to find out who killed Billy, they would be on the path to the solution. Flying fish sailed along beside him in the moonlight. They were good omens. He thought of Billy.

Harry was going to find out who killed him. It was more than intuition, it was experience. If you kept finding out more and more about a crime, eventually you solved it. If the trail ran cold, it didn't happen. Billy knew that. And Harry was finding out more and more all the time. He was sure that Eve's explanation would satisfy him. She was that kind of woman. Harry knew that she was smarter than he was.

He also knew Billy saw it coming. He prepared for it. He didn't try to fight. He had never given up before. HIV positive wasn't the death sentence as it used to be. That wouldn't have scared Billy. That wouldn't have beaten him down. He figured, as long as no one else got hurt, whatever he got he deserved. That was the way it was except that one time with that pimp who had a gun.

It had to be something else. Harry moved on. Did Billy have something solid on the Don, besides a picture of Candy and the ten grand receipt Velda got for Billy's sperm. Billy would have kicked the...knocked the shit out

177

of that two bit fancy hood. The Don didn't scare Billy. Maybe Billy found out something between the Don and the cops. That would hurt. Nobody liked a bad cop. Harry figured the time line. A year ago, Billy met Candy. Nine months ago, Candy left Billy. Six months ago, Harry got laid. Four months ago Adam Wise died. Three months ago Billy called him. A little later, Harry picked up Eve West/ Wise. A few days ago just after Harry and Eve arrived, Billy was killed. And now Harry and Eve were on their way to experience the twins. The same path Billy and Candy had followed.

Harry didn't try to delve into it. It would come. He knew it as well as he knew the lights on the chart marked the channel. Unless one of them was moved.

Harry could hear the buzz of the small travel alarm that Eve bought to wake her for her watch at the helm. Harry could usually wake up in four hours without any help. He guessed the tequila and pot had upset his internal clock. He could hear Eve humming in the galley and soon smelled coffee. He was glad she hadn't stayed up with him. He would have talked and one thing would lead to another. Questions with answers he didn't know and didn't want to hear at the moment.

It was still night when Eve came up with the coffee. In a pair of ragged tights and a sweatshirt to protect her from the early morning dampness. Harry showed her their position on the chart and waited while she rechecked his calculations. Without a word he kissed her and she smiled

with that thrill of childish expectation that chilled him.
Harry quickly went below with his secret thoughts. He
took a valium from the medicine cabinet where he had put
Billy's prescriptions. As he lay down he could hear the
sound of the water coursing between the hulls singing over
the through hull fittings with a song of speed. The wind
had picked up. He could feel the bow drop as the boat
began to surf and heard an exultant cheer from Eve up top.
The next rush dropped Harry down the wave of sleep that
came so quickly.

        Harry didn't wake up until Eve called him from
topside.
        "We're here," she yelled. "We're here. All hands on
deck. All hands on deck."
        Harry saw the bright sunlight through the porthole and
could tell it was midday. They had made great time. And
he had overslept again.   Harry was alert in an instant. He
was moving up the companionway with all his senses
kicked in when the full light of day hit him in the face and
he stopped in his tracks. His sunglasses hung on a cord by
the cabin door and he reached for them without looking.
She had dropped the sails and was motoring.
        "I'm sorry to wake you," Eve said kissing Harry as he
moved next to her. "But I need you to drop the anchor and
fend off if needed. From the chart, it looked like a tricky
place to stop."
        "You made great time," Harry said, "and you stood
my watch."

"You needed the rest," Eve said and grabbed him by the hair. "You need to take better care of yourself. I took an upper and was wired. Come give me a hug before we have to go to work."

Harry held Eve from behind as she stood and steered. His arms embraced her chest and he covered her breasts with the palms of his hands. He could feel the nipples come erect.

He looked over her shoulder at the chart. He had reviewed the harbor on the map but had never been there before, knowing that new places could always be tricky, the chart was years old, the sea ever changing. He reluctantly released Eve from his arms.

"I'll take it," Harry said and she gave up the helm to him.

Eve went forward on the deck and stretched in the sunlight on the shrouds that held the mast.

"What a glorious day," Eve shouted and then went to the bow pulpit where she looked down into the clear green water. She went to the net and readied the anchor, and signaled Harry that they were set.

Harry turned the wheel as they came around a small island with a stand of trees and not much else. It was probably formed when the Army Corps of Engineers dredged the harbor. It acted as a barrier against foul weather. As he passed the channel marker, Fort Jefferson in all its red brick glory rose up on the right. It was as large and imposing as it was meant to be. Cannon could be seen along the ramparts. A large flock of gulls screamed past.

Around the tip of the barrier island, the channel opened into a wide harbor within a triangle of islands with the Fort set on its longest side, protecting the rest of North America from the dangers that lay beyond its most southern exposure.

Harry motored past the large dock in front of the fort where a Coast Guard cutter had tied up. There was a strong current that ran through the channel and he pulled back on the throttle. There was one fishing boat tied up to a large mooring can and two cruising sailboats anchored across from the Fort. The weather was good, especially with a full moon, so tonight all the lobster and shrimp boats would be out. In bad weather, fifty or more boats could find shelter in the lee of the Fort.

Harry decided to anchor at the far end away from everybody. He took a quick look at the chart. The boat didn't draw much water and it was a sand bottom so he could go places other boats couldn't go.

At the far end of the harbor, he turned the wheel hard to port and came up into the current. He idled the engine and drifted back. Eve had the anchor in hand.

"Now," Harry yelled.

She let the anchor drop and the chain rattled into the water. The anchor rode ran out through a chalk and she looped it over a cleat. The line became taut as the anchor grabbed.

"Tie her off," Harry said and idled the engine waiting to see how they would hang. Eve waved an okay, and the boat rested on its hook. Harry cut the engine.

"I never notice how loud that engine is until it's turned off," Eve said stepping over the rail into the water with a splash.

Harry checked the anchor rope and slipped a piece of leather around it where it ran through the chalk to prevent chaffing. He then watched Eve undress in the water. She tossed her pants and shirt into the net.

"You should do this too," Eve called. "You've been wearing those clothes for two days."

It was well into the afternoon. A seaplane on pontoons landed in the channel and taxied over to the dock behind the cutter. Harry looked around the boat and saw that everything was in order. Then he dived in after Eve.

The water was warm. The salt tasted good. It stung his eyes as he followed the anchor chain under water where he buried the anchor in the sand. Eve swam down next to him. She pushed on the flukes deepening the bite of the danforth. Her body slid next to Harry as they worked. Then they rose together in a swirl of bubbles and he hugged her until they sank with their mouths sealed by a kiss. She undressed him and their bodies were lubricated by the sea as they entwined in an underwater embrace. They were breathless when they surfaced.

The boat hung so that the Fort and dock were in full view off the port bow. They maintained a sweeping view of the harbor while at the same time they had privacy astern. They swam around the boat, Harry looked closely for any flaws in the hulls. There were none.

When they came aboard, they sprayed each other

182

down with a mist bottle, then toweled off the salt. Harry shaved at the stern pulpit with salt water and shampoo. When he was finished, Eve had a bottle of red wine breathing in the cockpit with some canned potato sticks and hot peppers. She was opening a tin of crackers when he sat down. She had covered the cockpit cushions with a sheet so they wouldn't stick to the vinyl.

"We should have poked up a couple of lobsters," Harry said and poured two plastic cups full of wine.

"I'm really not hungry," Eve said. "I'm a bit anxious about tonight."

"The ritual with the twins. They aren't going to kill a chicken are they?"

"No," Eve laughed. "I just hope you get your money's worth."

The sunset was hidden by thick clouds to the northwest. The wind had clocked around and the tide changed so that they were now hanging with the Fort to starboard. It was breezier and they put on caftans. Eve wore socks.

"The weather service said that a mild front was going to pass through quickly," Harry said. "Then it will be clear and fair."

They were talking about the weather. It was small talk to Harry when there was so much more on his mind. What were they doing here at the end of the earth. This was where they imprisoned Dr. Mudd.

"Do you know about Dr. Mudd?" Eve asked and poured more wine.

"I was just thinking about him," Harry said. "Aiding

183

and abetting Lincoln's assassin."

"I'm not familiar with the charge," Eve said. "He was later freed after he saved many lives during a cholera epidemic."

"He did his time. But this place isn't exactly Sing Sing."

"They thought it was the end of the earth back then," Eve said as if she read his mind.

She wore a plain white gown, clean and flawless. The day of sailing had touched her skin with a rosy glow. Freckles stood out across her nose. Her green grey eyes were a bit glassy from the salt water. She smiled a perfect white smile. She never wore makeup. She never needed it. Harry guessed that she never would. She would always be beautiful. He was staring at her. She was enjoying it when a dark form passed behind her.

The "Gemini" was a boat with a well shaped transom and its name in gold, above a home port of EARTH. She was an old converted fishing smack. The ports in the transom were like those of an old pirate ship. Even the wheelhouse set far aft gave it a poop deck atop the cabin. Forward was a wide open deck with a large main hatch. Forward of the hatch was the thick round wooden mast that held a long boom that was covered by a furled sail. The bow was high so that the deck sloped back to the hold. High gunwales ringed the deck with plenty of openings to spill back any water and to clean away the trash. The deck had been redone in teak and her bright work was polished. The black hull was trimmed in white and she flew a party flag from the stern light pole.

The wheelhouse was well protected from the weather. Harry couldn't see who was steering. A white anchor was released automatically and splashed into the water on a heavy chain that rumbled around a winch. The big boat swung back its shapely stern and Captain Blood ports looked at them.

"There are the twins," Eve said. Her nails dug into Harry's arm as she grabbed him. He could feel a current of excitement in her touch.

A small grey outboard with a Park Ranger at the wheel pulled up next to the Gemini. While the Ranger in his brown uniform held the boats steady against each other, two women came out of the cabin and down a ladder into the smaller boat. They both wore long shorts and jersey tops, carried handbags and a travel bag. Even from a distance, the radiation from their sunburns showed on their naked arms and legs. They were laughing and waving as they pulled away.

The women were forced to be seated as the Ranger opened the throttle and tossed them back. He sped over to the dock where the seaplane was tied. The women boarded and were airborne before Harry finished his second glass of wine.

Eve let out a sigh of relief.

"For a second I thought they were the twins," Eve said. "I was very disappointed."

"What do you know about them?" Harry asked.

"Not much," Eve said. "Just what I've heard and it's

all been good. The one I talked to was very nice. We had an instant rapport. She said they are the very best at what they do."

"Pleasure therapy," Harry said. "The mind boggles with possibilities. Did they ever work Vegas?"

"We'll ask," Eve said. She was standing, taking off her socks. "We're next. Let's go. And bring your VISA card. I don't know if they take American Express."

That got a good laugh out of Harry. The sun had dropped down below the line of clouds. And the moon would be rising very soon. Harry pulled on a light blue cotton sweater and a pair of white shorts. He didn't need shoes. They weren't going ashore.

The dinghy had been stowed on the port deck when they were under sail. Eve had it in the water when Harry came back up top and grabbed the bottle of wine. There was a good slug left and he finished it. He smiled back at Eve who had the white gown tucked between her legs, and was ready with the oars. Harry felt the hard flat form of his credit card zipped into the pocket of his shorts. He had to admit that the wine hadn't taken the edge off of his senses. That caused him to be a bit anxious stepping off into the unknown. Eve seemed ready, willing and able.

"Cast off," Harry said taking his place in the stern.

Eve sat with those lovely legs braced to each side of Harry as she rowed to the Gemini. Harry put one hand on each foot and felt her arch flex as she leaned into the stroke. She was grinning at Harry. She knew something he didn't know and she wasn't telling. From her expression it

186

would be a pleasant surprise. Not telling seemed to be the story of her life, what little he knew about it, if any of it were true. It seemed to Harry that every time he had ever become interested in her history, Eve always diverted him with sex. And right now, he wasn't complaining.

"THIS IS A CLOTHING OPTIONAL VESSEL"
The sign hung next to the boarding ladder. From the wheelhouse came a woman's voice. It was warm and light.

"Tie up, and welcome aboard, Doctor Wise."

The cat was out of the bag and clawing at the air. Eve winked at Harry and the cat hid in a corner for later.

Eve stood in the dinghy and slipped the bow line over a cleat at the top of the ladder. With two steps she was aboard and her white gown unfurled. Harry followed with less grace but equal enthusiasm. This is where his path led. He had no choice but to enjoy it while it lasted.

"I love your hair," a different huskier female voice called down from the bridge. "That picture in the yellow pages did nothing for you. I'm so glad we have finally had a chance to meet. I've been an admirer for so long."

"You're very kind," Eve said.

"We'll be down in a minute," the lighter one said. "Just straightening up after those last two. Walk the deck. Feel the energy of the men who worked this boat."

Harry and Eve walked the deck past the hatch to the bow.

"Doctor Wise," Harry said.

"I'll explain later," Eve kissed him on the cheek. She took his hand and led him to the mast where she embraced the large round pole and laughed at Harry who was still checking out the boat.

The mast was stepped through the deck. The boom swung over the hatchcover and was rigged to lift and swing it aside. There was a block and tackle with an additional pulley that would make the job easier. It could be handled by one woman instead of two men.

Harry looked at Eve who had continued her phallic fascination with the mast. On her it looked good. He was at the end of the earth, so Harry felt very little pressure. There wasn't much farther he could go. After this adventure with the twins, there would come a time when he and Eve would be alone on deck. Then she would tell all. For the moment, there was no need for inquisition. His path had led to a session with "the world's foremost pleasure therapists." It was printed on a brochure that lay near the mast. Harry picked it up. "Tantra. Tao. Kama Sutra, Founders of the Maui Goddess Retreat. Yin Yang Specialists."

On the back was an endorsement:

"Highly recommended..." Doctor Eve Wise, Eden Clinic, Miami Florida."

Harry showed the folded paper to Eve.

"This is not the time or place," she told him. "If this was the last day of your life, how would you want to spend it, being a cop or making love to me?"

"I was wondering about the truth," Harry said.

Eve looked directly into his eyes and touched his arm.

"Is truth so important if two people love each other?"

188

Eve's lips stayed parted when she finished.

Harry was caught in a whirlpool that pulled him into her mouth. She soul kissed him and held him with her mouth. She certainly had a way with words.

"The power of the eyelash at the edge of the veil is more cutting than the cleaving scimitar."

The words came from the husky voice along with the scent of musk. Eve released him and he turned to see the twins. Harry smiled. It was easy to see why they were called the twins.

They looked nothing alike. As different as night and day. Hot and cold. Yin and Yang. A cat and a mouse. They were so opposite, they had to be different sides of the same coin.

"Welcome," the naked blonde said to them. She was glorious, with frosted tosseled shoulder length locks, she had an even tan, muscular definition so fine she could have been carved marble. Her mouth was painted bright red. Her fingernails and toenails were flame red. Her pubic area had been shaved clean.

"Welcome," said the small wavy brown haired woman in the faded shirt and pants. Her hair was tied to one side and she looked away as meek as a mouse. At first glance she was as plain as her twin was brilliant.

Harry immediately registered them as the Cat and the Mouse. The graceful feline came forward and embraced Eve. She was muscular. Her breasts were firm and her abdominal muscles put to shame any washboard Harry had ever seen. She then hugged Harry and he rubbed her back,

feeling it ripple down to the hard curve of her hips. She
then turned her attention back to Eve.

The Mouse on the other hand stayed at Harry's side. She
was looking up at him. When he caught her, she quickly
looked away. Then, she looked slowly back at him.

Her eyes were a beautiful dark blue, the color of the
Gulfstream. Harry was lost in her sea colored look. Her
fingertips touched his hand. He was helpless. From the
dark crystalline depths of her eyes there was a passion. He
knew she wanted him. And he wanted her. Perhaps, it was
the setting, the scent, taste, feel or sound. Whatever trig-
gered the chemistry, the totality of his senses craved this
small meek woman.

"What's your pleasure?" The Mouse asked holding his
hand like a teenage date, her shyness drawing him in.

Harry saw the fin of a dolphin out in the channel and
he thought of Billy. He opened himself to Billy's spirit. He
let his brother dwell within him. He knew Billy wouldn't
want to miss this.

"Look," the Cat pointed a perfect arm out to the
channel where the sun was slipping into the sea, sliding
down until it was a spot of fire at the edge of the world.
The Green Flash. It came in an instant, an emerald explosion that disappeared as soon as it was perceived, a mass
hallucination.

"Did you see it?" Eve asked, holding onto his
free arm.

"You couldn't miss it," Harry said.

"This truly marks a blessed event," the Cat said and the

Mouse nodded their agreement.

"We usually like to start with a colonic irrigation," the Cat said. "We don't want any accidents or interruptions during the service. It will also purify your bodies. We use a special solution that makes it all very comfortable. We can start any time after it gets dark. We use soothing healing herbs. Do either of you have a preference as to your attendant?"

"You and Doctor Wise have so much to discuss," the Mouse peeped up.

"You don't mind?" Eve asked him. She already had her arm around the Cat's perfect waist.

"No," Harry said. "It's fine with me."

He watched Eve brighten even more as her eyes met the Cat's eyes. She took Eve by the hand and led her to the aft part of the boat. Eve had taken off her gown. Watching the two women walk, Harry knew that perfection came in more than one form. They disappeared behind the wheelhouse.

As soon as the two blondes disappeared, the little brown haired girl next to Harry kissed him passionately with her lips, her tongue and her teeth. She stopped to breathe and catch a glance aft as if she was afraid of being watched. Harry looked into her eyes and saw volcanoes erupting blue fire.

While Harry stood accepting his fate, the Mouse took off her shirt and pants. As big and beautiful as the Cat exhibited herself, the Mouse was small and beautiful. Naked, she was lean and strong, perfectly formed with the

191

legs of a ballerina. Her skin had an olive cast and her hair which she unpinned fell in a cascade of curls past her shoulders in a thousand shades of brown.

She didn't look up at his eyes when she unbuttoned his shirt and untied the drawstring to his shorts. He could feel her hair brush his chest as she removed his shirt. As she pulled down his shorts she got on her knees. With those blue eyes and a thin firm hand she examined his penis. It was fully erect. She kissed it to show it had passed inspection. She looked up in his eyes and smiled. Harry was enjoying the moment.

She stood up and looked at his face as though she were examining a map.

"You look much better than before," she smiled.

"Before what?" Harry said. She was standing next to him with their bare bodies touching. One of her hands held his hand, the other held his penis. With his free hand, Harry touched her hip and felt her shiver.

"Isn't it exciting to see each other again in a new life," she said and squeezed with both hands. "I know you recognized me. I could tell the first time you looked in my eyes."

"It was something," Harry said. He looked at her and had to admit that her presence was familiar though specific features were all new. There was a large winch at the foremost part of the bow. There were coils of rope and a cushion where she led him.

Harry sat on the ropes with the cushion between his back and the winch. He was looking out over the bowsprit at the day vanishing into night. She sat in his lap and looked back at the rest of the boat. When she was sure that they were alone, she hugged and kissed him again curling her body into his, feeling as much of him as she could with her skin. She took a deep breath and relaxed with him, her mouth against his as she sighed.

"Make it last," she said. "It's been so long. Let's make it last for a while this time."

Harry held her and rubbed his hands over her body and closed his eyes. She was different from anyone he had ever known, but somehow the same as someone he remembered.

"Do you understand reincarnation?" The Mouse asked softly in his ear. Her breath was warm and her tongue flicked at his lobe. Harry laughed.

"I understand it a lot better now," Harry said and kissed her electric blue eyes each time she blinked.

"We've known each other for over five thousand years," she whispered to him. "In so many lives. Sometimes I was the man and you were the woman. Sometimes we were both women. Sometimes both of us were men. But we were always lovers. We will always be lovers for eternity, in different shapes and forms. We will share blessed moments when we can."

Harry held on to her quivering body as she cried tears that rolled down his chest. It was dark now. The stars had appeared as the only light. Harry sat with the small woman in his lap, while she played with his nipples. The tears were gone and her breath was smooth and even. She sprang up and was gone.

Harry turned but could only see her shadow in the light from the wheelhouse where he could see Eve and the Cat sharing a joint on the bridge. The Mouse came up between them, took a hit and then kissed Eve on the mouth and then did the same to the Cat who held her a little longer. In a moment the Mouse was back on deck coming toward him with a bucket and a straw mat rolled up under her arm. Without a word, she spread the mat on the deck. From the bucket she took a large enema bag with a hose clamped at the end near the nozzle.

There was a yin yang symbol on the bag, the two halves of the circle each within the other completing the circle, as a man and a woman, forming a unity without relinquishing their selves. She tossed the bucket over the side and held it with a line attached to the handle. When she brought it back aboard it was half full. She set it near the mat. She draped a small white washrag over the side of the bucket.

She came to Harry and took him by the hand. He was impressed by her strength as she helped him up, leading him to the mat. She hugged him and kissed him, directed him to lay on his side on the mat looking out to sea. There was a strong scent of strawberries that seemed to envelope him. He could feel her moving behind him, stroking his side and his arm with the tips of her fingers, teasing up goose bumps all over his body. She began to chant in her lovely light voice as a songbird calls to a mate.

Harry was caught up in the rhythm of her song when

194

he felt her hand massage something slick between his buttocks. Then the nozzle of the enema hose entered him and his sphincter muscle grabbed it. She rubbed his back and his neck following her tracks with little kisses and he relaxed and let the nozzle move into him. The liquid was warm and he felt it flood his lower bowel as she lifted the bag and undid the clamp. Harry heard her giggle at the sounds coming from him as he filled up. Harry was afraid to laugh. He was full and squeezing like crazy.

"You're only as young as your asshole," the Mouse said.

Harry was seated on the bucket as the Mouse took away the enema bag. He felt a bit woozy as he evacuated his bowels to the point that he could feel his sinuses drain. There was a tremendous rush as he stood to empty the bucket over the side. He refilled and rinsed it and refilled it again to be used as a douche. He cleansed himself with seawater and the washrag. He emptied the bucket and from habit refilled it halfway to be used later. That was boatlife.

It seemed such a long way back to the mat where he lay on his stomach feeling the warm evening breeze dry him. He was levitating. There had been something in that enema besides strawberries.

As an Army medic, Harry had tried every legal drug in the pharmacy. It was one of the benefits of taking specimens and giving shots which was his main function, no war being fought near him at the time. Serious accidents happened occasionally but the doctors liked to handle them for the experience. As a cop, Harry had tried every illegal drug so he would know what he was up against when he faced a jumper on coke, or a thief on crack. He hadn't picked up any habits but he certainly had his preferences. He still did an occasional joint especially since Eve liked it. He still drank booze. And he never turned down good hash. He considered himself somewhat of an expert, but whatever it was that they put in that enema bag was better than anything he had ever done. He was happy, relaxed, mildly euphoric, sexually up and looking forward with wild imaginations to the rest of the ceremony. He landed gently back on the mat as the Mouse came with another bag.

"Another one?" Harry said. "I already gave at the office."

"This one you give to me," she smiled and her blue eyes flashed thunderbolts as she handed him the bag. She saw the half full bucket and placed a clean washrag on the handle. She rolled him onto his side and he rose to his knees without the use of any muscles that he could feel.

She knelt on the mat, sitting back on her feet with her head bowed and her hands together. Harry hummed along as she repeated the enema chant. When she leaned forward to kiss the deck with her ass in the air, Harry figured that it was his cue. Her smooth round buttocks parted and her anus shined with lubricant. As Harry touched the nozzle of the hose to the radiant hole, she accepted it easily with a sigh. He was on his knees behind her now. He unclipped the hose and she drained the bag as he raised it. There was a different fragrance in the fluid this time. It was stronger,

196

less sweet but just as stimulating. He lowered the bag and slid the nozzle out.

Harry turned away as she went to the bucket. He heard an endless river that lasted so long, he began to laugh and she laughed too. She emptied the bucket and he watched her douche in the mariner's bidet. She carefully wiped herself with the washrag, set the bucket aside half full and took the bag from him as he sat on the mat crossed legged.

When she finished her chores, she shivered a bit. She came to him and tried to hide her body in the warmth of his arms and legs. She was completely giving and they blended together to form their own yin yang.

"We just released all the kundalini energy from our lower chakras," the Mouse purred. "Can you feel the current?"

Harry could feel the current. He could feel her very blood sustaining her life. He could feel her arms and legs around him. He could feel his breath against his own cheek. He had become the Mouse. He was drugged and was enjoying it. Some herb had awakened his senses but slowed down his mind, making time creep by with the girl within and without and he was loving it.

When his fire had consumed her chill, she brightened and blossomed out of his hold and his soul. She took him by the hand and tiptoed naked back to the wheelhouse. They heard a bucket of water tossed from the poop deck. Eve was laughing. She hauled up half a bucket on a long line. It would now be the Cat's turn.

197

Harry stood with his arms around the Mouse holding her breasts, warming her back, their legs enmeshed. They heard the chanting, the sighs and the moans. It reminded Harry of the song of the hump back whales. He stood with the small girl in a timeless embrace that could only be shared by eternal lovers.

Eve and the Cat eventually came down from the poop deck with a half bucket of water that was placed in the stern. The Cat came over to the Mouse who stood with Harry and she kissed her fully on the mouth at the same time feeling Harry's penis which was a hazard to navigation as the two women parted and moved to the wheelhouse. Eve smiled at Harry in passing doing the same as the Cat and giving him a wink.

Through the mahogany paneled wheelhouse was a companionway down into the hold. But it was dark down there and he could see nothing but the shiny wooden entrance. There was a large old wooden wheel at the helm. It had been worked bright with varnish and polished where it was held together by brass. A raised Captain's chair commanded the wheel and a panel of lights and switches were mounted within easy reach. Through the large glass ports he caught a glimpse of the moon large and yellow rising above the horizon. A switch was thrown and the cabin was bathed in ultraviolet.

The Cat poured an aromatic tea into four cups and distributed them to each person with a blessing. Harry tasted it. It was sweet and sour. He drank it in silence as did the others. He took a few deep breaths and felt the boat

fall away beneath him. She had slipped him a "mickey".
He was becoming unconscious.

Harry could feel the Mouses' nails dig into his arm
when he dropped the cup. She knew that the motion, the
swirling was not the boat moving. He was on his knees
with the Mouse easing him down, her mouth to his ear.

"Your life is in danger," she whispered.

Harry caught one last look at her before he fell into
the dark blue Gulfstream of her eyes. He was sinking fast.
The trailing shroud that was wrapped around Billy's body
had unraveled and he was caught in it. Harry tried to climb
hand over hand up the trailing white twisting linen strip.
He tried to kick to the surface but his legs were gone. He
climbed faster but he was going deeper. He tried relaxing,
comforted by his resignation to his fate.

When Harry resurfaced, his head ached and he
couldn't see through the fog. He tried to rub his eyes but
he couldn't reach them. His wrists were shackled to beams
to the side of each shoulder. He was on his knees resting
forward. As he raised his head, the Mouse was in front of
him, but he couldn't touch her. There was a scent of musk
coming from a small amphora set between them. He tried
to say something to get her attention as she chanted with
bowed head before him. He flexed his back and thrust out
his stomach to reach her. She looked up, raised her face to
his and kissed him on the lips. Her eyes were wide open
reflecting the moonlight flooding through the open hatch
above them. Its white light created a fog in the darkness of
the hold. Then she vanished.

199

Harry could feel a mat beneath him and he was not uncomfortable. His shoulders relaxed and his elbows rested at his sides. His bindings were made of cloth and were not too tight. He doubted he could slip them. He was still naked.

The Mouse ran naked through a shaft of moonlight that glistened on her flawless form. A shiny black shadow followed her causing the smoke to swirl behind it as it passed him. The smell of sage cleansed the air as it drifted up through the open hatchway. As the smoke lifted, he could see at a distance in front of him, the large black mast stepped in the keel of the boat. A white drape hung from the mast near the top where it passed through the deck. The cloth began to flutter. It took form. Harry recognized the legs. Eve had her hands tied to the mast above her. Her feet just touched the floor. Her legs were apart and she was looking around until she saw him in the moonlight.

Harry and Eve's eyes met for the first time since they had boarded the Gemini. There was a look of quiet desperation as she pulled at her bonds. There was no sign of fear. It was more a look of longing for him to satisfy her desires. Harry was helpless, but her struggle excited him, watching the muscles of her legs strain. It was a sight that was quite familiar to him but never ever boring.

The Mouse came up behind Harry and pressed her body against his back. She put her mouth to his ear. Her breath was hot.

"I'll help you to escape," she whispered.

A new incense of fragrant blossoms filled the hold of

the ship. His eyes had now adjusted to the moonlight and he could see where he was. The interior of the ship was painted black with a map of the sky in the southern hemisphere painted in iridescent stars. If you looked up through the hatch and could see the stars of the northern hemisphere, you would be the center of the universe.

There was music. Sounds he didn't recognize mixed with the song of the whales, crashing waves, bells and gongs, then periods of silence. For a moment a cloud passed and the moonlight vanished but not the stars. They glowed in the darkness.

When the moonlight returned, it seemed more brilliant. It lit the bottom of the boat between Harry and Eve where the yin yang symbol lay sculpted on the floor. The black and white glistened in the circle. Eve thrust herself toward Harry, he wanted her, uniting as the yin yang in an embrace of total love. He hoped that he wasn't just feeling the drugs.

The smoke from the fragrance danced with the wind. As it thinned, the sculpture unfolded as the Cat in black patent leather and the Mouse in bare skinned satin fluorescence withdrew their heads from each others' lap. It was like the cracking of an egg and the birth of two spirits.

The Cat stood in front of Eve. She wore black patent boots that covered her knees, tight black shorts and a black vest that was custom made to her form, showing her abdominals through the leather. It accentuated the trimness of her waist and the swell of her hips. She wore long black gloves. As she turned, Harry could see that her bare breasts were cupped within openings in the vest. The shine of the patina was complimented by the glow in her eyes and the smile on her lips.

The Cat stepped in front of Eve and Harry watched as the black gloves traced the contours of her body. The Cat stepped to the side so that Harry could see the gloves as they circled the areola of Eve's nipples. He watched the black hand as it moved down over Eve's stomach stopping at the union of her legs where it stayed while the Cat kissed Eve's face with little fluttering kisses until their mouths met and Harry could only see the Cat's back as she ground her hips against the helpless woman who didn't put up any resistance. The motion of the Cat's hips had caused her shorts to ride up in the crease of her buttocks. Framed in the black patina, her smooth round ass and firm thighs looked like antique gold in the moonlight. Harry wanted her as much as he had wanted Eve only seconds ago. He knew it was the drugs but he wasn't complaining.

Harry had lost track of the Mouse while he was assessing Eve's situation. He noticed her again as she went to where the Cat stood with Eve and placed a seashell at their feet. Even at a distance, Harry could tell by the gloss that it contained lilac scented oil. He watched as the Mouse touched oil to places on Eve's body: her shoulders, ribs, and thighs. The Cat spread the oil with her black leather clad hands massaging gently then more deeply. When Eve was completely covered, the Cat and Mouse began to play.

They started with Eve's feet. Kneeling to kiss them, their rear ends were both pointed at Harry. He was sure that this was intentional. It was a show for his benefit as they expressed love for each other and Eve as they stroked her body. Embracing it with their own at the same time pleasuring each other with sexual contact. Eve too was an observer to their ardor as it increased in intensity before her, against her and with her.

The music was now sitars, birdsongs and the sound of rain so real Harry looked up through the hatch. The moon was full directing all of its light at them. He pulled at his shackles but did not feel like struggling. But he did want to join the twins in their devotion to Eve who was laughing as the Cat and Mouse sucked her nipples and rubbed both sides of her pubic mound. The laughter turned to erratic breathing and then the long guttural sigh that Harry recognized as her orgasm. Eve hung limply from her bonds as the Cat lowered her with her hands still bound. There were a number of black cushions with the painted stars that were moved near her to make her comfortable. They untied her hands. She looked at Harry and smiled. Harry laughed.

The Cat and the Mouse turned their attention to Harry. With the shell of oil in hand they came to where he was kneeling in his pillory. The Mouse put a finger into the shell then touched it to his nose and the fragrance expanded his mind. The Cat was standing behind her, perspiration on her skin outshined the patina of her costume. She was looking at Harry and her mouth was open as if she could eat him alive. But the Mouse touched his face and her eyes trapped his and he looked down the front of her small sweet body and his stomach growled at the thought of

203

devouring her.

As the Cat stood in front of him with his face against the black leather of her bodice, Harry could smell the sweat beneath it mix with the scent of leather to create a new intoxicant. The Mouse had gone behind him and he could feel the hot oil as she anointed his head and it ran down his cheeks and neck over his chest and down his back to his buttocks. He closed his eyes to keep out the oil. The Cat pulled his face up between her naked breasts and spread the oil with them brushing her nipples across his lips and against his closed eyes. From behind the Mouse's small strong hands spread the oil to his loins down between his legs all the way back to his tailbone. Then she lifted his testicles and the Cat slid her boot under them until she lifted him to his knees and the Mouse grabbed his erection with both hands and rubbed it against the slick black leather.

The Cat lowered him back to his haunches. The Mouse stood up and the two women made love with him between their bodies. One high black boot was over his shoulder and his face was next to the small hand that rubbed the crease where the leather shorts had ridden up. The Mouse was sitting on his other shoulder fucking the black leather glove on the Cat's gentle hand.

It was a terrible strain on Harry's back but he was feeling no pain. The Mouse slid down his back and the Cat crouched in front of him teasing his penis with the tip of her tongue. The Mouse was massaging his chest from behind concentrating on his nipples until they were as hard

204

as his cock. She wrapped her legs around his waist so that
her feet could rub oil into his thighs and onto his penis.
The Cat nipped at her toes and pawed at her legs catching
her by the ankle and biting her heel. She then kissed the
foot, rose to her knees to grab Harry by the neck and kissed
him as completely as two mouths could. She then turned
and crawled on all fours back to Eve where she curled up
next to her. Eve's eyes were open and she was enjoying the
show.

The Mouse eased Harry down so that his arms were
stretched back and up in the shackles and his face thrust
toward the pair of women reclining with each other. She
put all of her weight on his back and though she was small,
Harry had to strain to prevent dislocating his shoulders.
His chest swelled with the exertion and the Mouse's fingers
dug into his pectoral muscles. Slowly she slid from him
removing her weight and allowing his muscles to relax so
she could make her fingers dig deep massaging to the bone.

The release was incredible. Aches from injuries
acquired in a lifetime ceased to exist. The pressures of
society and civilization never existed. The love that he had
for these women dominated his soul. He leaned back to
stretch and felt the Mouse behind him. Her hands were
under his arms and he squeezed them to let her know that
he wanted her their forever. They were blending again with
her head on his shoulder and her hair against his face as
they both watched the Cat rise.

Eve was prone on the floor with her head propped
against a starry pillow. The Cat stepped across Eve's

outstretched legs so that she was astride facing Harry. The Cat looked directly in his eyes as she knelt down with her knees at Eve's waist and her face above her thighs. Without taking her gaze from Harry, the Cat rubbed what looked like vaseline over Eve's thighs and belly down to and including her vagina. The music had turned to a jazz saxophone. The mood, with a scent of mint, was cool. The Cat's simmering black outfitted torso and high boots blocked the view of all but Eve's legs, twisting feet and curling toes.

Occasionally Harry could see Eve's short cropped hair above the Cat's black buttocks. He couldn't see what Eve was doing back there but from the way the Cat was gyrating, he could imagine. From the way Eve's thighs held the Cat's frosted head, it was obvious that no one was attempting to escape.

The dark blue eyes were in front of his eyes, sparkling even in the shadows. The moonlight behind created a silver aura. When her mouth covered his, he truly understood soul kissing for her tongue reached beyond his mouth to the very center of his being. He wanted to grab her, hold her, move her, feel her body in his arms but he was restrained by the bindings.

With a twist of his hips and lift from his arms, Harry was able to swing his legs out in front of him. Leaning back stretching his calves and thighs enabled the Mouse to sit on his chest. The oil made all movement so easy, no friction, no accidents. He was able to lay on his back with his arms up as she placed her feet over his shoulders and

206

rubbed his ears with her arches. Her knees were wide apart. She looked back over her shoulder, waited for a moment then turned and grabbed him by his hair and pulled his face up into her, sliding slowly so that he received everything from clitoris to coccyx.

She shuddered and quaked without a sound and released his head which fell back against the mat with a thud. Even the thud felt good. Harry licked his lips and took a deep breath. He exhaled against her thigh which he could feel with his cheek. He looked up at the small sweet beautiful woman who had him at her mercy.

Harry rested on his back with his hands suspended above him. With a flash of her eyes, the Mouse spun around on his chest so that she faced his legs. She stretched out on top of him so that her feet were under his chin and her hands were at his feet. Harry couldn't raise his head to see, so he let himself fall through space sniffing lilacs as she began with the tips of his toes.

As he felt the small strong hands massage every cell in his body, Harry reminded himself to add on a thirty percent tip when he paid the bill. She used accupressure at all the reflexology points on the soles of his feet. She dug deep to break up any blockage. He could feel his internal organs. She breathed her breath into his pores. As she worked her way up his body, she used her arms and legs, feet, face, chest, pelvis, knees and her elbows to massage him. It was a total transfer of energy from one being to another.

The temperature of their bodies had equalized. They became one slippery being dissolved in solution. She slid past his face and their mouths met tongue tasting tongue. Harry drank her last atom as the tip of her tongue left the tip of his tongue. When she stood the last of his strength went with her.

She had massaged away the history of his body. Every pain, from a scrape on his knee as a child to Velda's bump on his head, felt like pure liquid without structure or form. His skeleton no longer existed. His skin would soon dissolve and his body would flow into the scuppers and be mixed with the seas. Harry knew that Billy's spirit was really enjoying this.

Harry didn't even consider trying to move. The music had stopped and he could tell from the angle of the moonlight that some time had passed. A sharp crack and a moan alerted him. He hadn't lost all of his adrenaline. He was able to lift his head and realizing that he was now on his stomach with his arms raised above his head. He pulled himself up easily because he had no spine. His head was swimming, his eyes were blurred and his mouth was dry.

The Mouse came to him and slid his legs around so that he could rest back against her. He sipped a spicy tea from a seashell and she fed him slices of mango and papaya. The sweetness stimulated him.

Harry was able to see that Eve had once again been strung up to the mast by her hands and the Cat stood next to her with a black strap. She whipped Eve across her naked rump. It was a loud sharp smack. Eve hung from the mast as a flag on a windless day. She moaned not from pain but with pleasure. She fluttered a bit with the next stroke and

208

leather slap.

The Mouse helped Harry into a sitting position with his legs crossed in front of him. She wiped the juice from around his mouth and neck. She looked over her shoulder and gave him a quick kiss on the lips as the strap struck again.

"You and I can escape together," the Mouse whispered as she cleaned him. "When Eve is brought to you for consummation, I'll be behind you. She'll have to be carried over here. I'll release your hands so you can push her away. It will surprise both of them. Then you and I will escape. Just follow me."

She captured him with her dark blue eyes. She held him. He didn't have to answer. The chemistry between them was more than drugs. The elements had become volatile. She stroked his erection with the tips of her fingernails. With all of his strength he tried to hold her. He wanted her now. The shackles held.

The Mouse joined the Cat as they took Eve down from the mast. They laid her out in front of him on her back in the full moonlight. Her eyes were closed and she didn't move but for the slight rise and fall of her chest as she breathed. She was strikingly gorgeous by any standard. Her long body glistened with the fragrant oils. She began to stir turning on her side and pulling those long legs up to a fetal curl. Harry could see the red welts across her rear end.

The Mouse sat at Eve's head lifting it onto her thigh so that she could give her a potion from a slender phial.

209

Eve's eyes opened. She reached behind her and ran a hand across her wounds. She looked up at Harry and smiled.

The Cat was now dropping flower petals on Eve. They fluttered down and touched her skin. Each one giving her strength as she became more animated and she was able to stand.

Eve was unsteady and leaned against the Cat with her cheek resting on her naked breast that protruded from her shiny black patina. Now the Cat had one bare hand. She rubbed a lubricant between Eve's legs deep into the hair that decorated her pubis. This gave Eve a second wind. The three women embraced and the Cat and Mouse began to chant. Without effort, the Cat lifted Eve with an arm around her waist and one under her legs and brought her to Harry. Eve looked down at Harry and sighed.

The Mouse had moved behind him and he could feel her breath on his neck and her hands at his wrists.

The Cat stood Eve over Harry so that she could lower her on to him. Eve's legs were around his chest. The Cat had her by the ass and was letting her slip away closer and closer to the head of Harry's penis, which was reaching new heights.

"Now is your chance to escape," the Mouse said.

Eve had her arms around Harry's neck and the Cat had his penis in her hand and was guiding it into Eve's vagina when his hands came free.

"Follow me," the Mouse said.

Harry grabbed Eve and held her as he penetrated deep inside of her. Her legs grabbed him and he erupted like a geyser, Old Faithful, in spurts and bursts and one last draining blast of sperm that exploded forth like none he had ever felt before. He would have considered it premature ejaculation but he had been hard for hours.

Then Harry held Eve in his lap with her head resting on his shoulder. From behind him the Mouse kissed her on the forehead. From behind Eve the Cat kissed Harry on both cheeks. Then they all wrapped together in a unified embrace while the Cat and Mouse chanted and offered up a prayer for eternal love and happiness. The Mouse ran her hand down Harry's belly to his crotch where his erection once stood.

"Congratulations," the Cat said.

"Shit," the Mouse yelled. "Damn it. I'm going to kick your ass."

"What's wrong?" the Cat cowered.

"You did it again," the Mouse was irate. "You and your damned vaseline. The condom broke."

Eve tossed back her head and laughed.

"It's all inside me," Eve told Harry. "I have your sperm."

"That will be extra," the Mouse said.

CHAPTER NINE

They were all up on deck naked in the moonlight that now cast long shadows. They were drinking tea and a joint was circulating among them. Eve was next to Harry. The Mouse was bathing the Cat with a sponge as she removed her black costume.

"I bet it gets hot in there," Harry said and passed the spliff to the Cat who was on her stomach as the Mouse did her back.

"Some like it hot," the Cat said in her best Marilyn imitation. Harry and Eve laughed. The Mouse put up her hand.

"Don't encourage her. She'll start singing Happy Birthday, Mr. President."

The Mouse wouldn't look directly at Harry. Her attitude was cool but friendly. She was business like. She pulled off the tall black patent leather boots and tossed them aside.

"You're not still pissed about the sperm," the Cat said to her.

"You and your damn patent leather," the Mouse said.

"But you said you liked it," the Cat protested.

"It's all my fault," Eve said. "I should have read the label on the package."

"The one with the picture of the foxy lady," the Mouse said. "I told you on the phone not to get the kind that require a water soluble lubricant."

"But Harry already had them," Eve said. "And we were in a hurry."

"I didn't even feel it go on," Harry said.

"You're not supposed to," the Cat smiled.

"Just like his brother," the Mouse shook her head.

"You made the right choice," Eve kissed Harry on the cheek. The Mouse looked at him disappointed. The Cat purred.

"You chose me instead of freedom," Eve added.

Harry didn't comment. It had not been so much a choice as fate. It was so much easier to stay with someone he knew rather than to run off into the unknown with a stranger and probably have to wait another six months.

"Damn vaseline," the Mouse said.

"It's great for patent leather," the Cat defended herself. "That other stuff leaves a film. Vaseline makes my boots shine and you know how you like the feel of that. And besides, I like the taste."

"But it doesn't go with some condoms," the Mouse

was pedantic in her authority with the Cat. It was easy to see who wore the pants in this relationship.

"We'll pay the difference," Eve nudged Harry who nodded agreement.

"I told you what happened to Billy," the Mouse told Eve.

"The Don is going to be mad as hell," the Cat said. "The sperm was supposed to be on the first plane out this morning. What will we say?"

"He couldn't get it up," the Mouse smiled. "That's always believable."

"Do you think you could have another orgasm?" the Cat asked Harry.

"Are you kidding!" Harry said. "My balls would collapse. Like Billy used to say, `Once a Knight, always a Knight and if you do it right, once a night is enough'."

"Speak for yourself," the Mouse said still not looking at him.

"I have your sperm," Eve whispered hotly in his ear.

"What exactly happened with Billy?" Harry was coming down from the drugs.

"The same as you," the Mouse stopped washing. "They both enjoyed the ceremony. Then at the end when she slid down on his cock, and screamed, Billy couldn't stop. He broke her cherry, the rubber broke, and he came inside her. You guys are just alike. There was sperm everywhere."

"And blood too," the Cat added. "Billy said she was a virgin."

"The only difference," the Mouse looked at Harry,

214

"Was that when Billy came, he had one hand up my ass."

"And my tit in his mouth," the Cat said.

"Billy wanted it all," the Mouse said. "And the girl couldn't see what he was doing anyway."

"Billy was a rascal," Harry smiled at the Mouse.

"We told Velda he never got off and she seemed to accept that as normal," the Mouse said. "Who knows?"

"Who would have thought that it would be worth so much?" the Cat said.

"It's the beginning of life," Eve said.

"Sperm," the Mouse frowned, wiping the Cat's boots. "It's a pain in the ass."

"That's the way you like it." the Cat purred.

"Sometimes," the Mouse locked those blue eyes on Harry's as he sat holding a dozing Eve in his arms. She turned and bent over to pick up the Cat's boots so that her cute round ass and those ballerina straight legs were in his face. She turned and flashed her dark blue eyes at him. Harry wanted her. He could have another orgasm. Maybe.

"And what if I had chosen you," Harry said to the Mouse.

"You'll never know," the Cat said.

"Maybe you'd like to come back and try it again," the Mouse teased him.

"And the danger to my life," Harry said. "For a while, I believed you until I remembered that I hadn't signed the credit card slip."

"It's all theater," the Cat said. "Doctor Wise wrote a very good paper on the subject. She's quite well respected in her field of therapy. She says all sex is theater."

The Cat stretched out while the Mouse tidied up her discarded outfit. Harry looked at her body and then at the Mouse. They were twins only in different sizes. Perfection came in different colors, shapes and sizes.

"I could have chosen you," Harry said to the Cat.

"Then Eve would have been very disappointed," the Mouse interrupted. "This was a true wedding service where you chose the one you loved."

"I love you too," Harry whispered to the Mouse so that he didn't disturb Eve who was now asleep.

"The titillation of promiscuity," the Cat laughed, "Does wonders for the testosterone level. You're just like your brother."

The Cat helped Harry place Eve in a comfortable position on a mat. Her body was still hot and they decided not to cover her. Then she led Harry back to the wheelhouse where the Mouse was waiting with his shorts and credit card.

"We have a lot of repeat business," the Mouse said and prepared the slip.

"I'm going to get a sheet and lie down next to Eve and watch the sunrise," the Cat said. She hugged Harry and kissed him on the mouth before she left him alone with the Mouse.

Harry added a thirty percent gratuity and signed. Money. He could have bought a new inflatable dinghy and an outboard but the boat would someday leak and the engine would quit. He'd been through it before. But this

216

was an experience of a lifetime. Besides, he was a rich man.

"Thank you," the Mouse said and concluded business.

They stood facing each other for a long silent moment.

"Come on," the Mouse said and led him to an aft cabin. It was small and sweet. There was no doubt who lived there. In the dark, they found her bunk. She got in then pulled Harry in around her like a blanket. That's how they fell asleep.

In the morning they had pear nectar and melon on the poop deck. The Mouse spent a lot of time on the cell-phone making arrangements for the next party. The Cat and Eve discussed therapy.

As Harry was leaving after having helped Eve into their dinghy, the Mouse got him alone and gave him a wet kiss.

"I'm still going to have you to myself one day," she whispered and he could feel himself getting hard.

Harry and Eve set sail as soon as they got back to the boat. The front that had come through brought the wind out of the northwest. It was favorable, having following seas rather than a constant pounding into the wind. Harry took the first watch after Eve had weighed the anchor. She sat silently near him for the first two hours. Then she stretched out in the shade of the sail and slept while Harry was alone with his thoughts.

It was not unusual to have these silent periods while under way or even holed up in an isolated cove. Harry reran the ceremony with the twins in his mind over and

217

over again and at the conclusion, he always chose Eve. He would rather die than hurt her.

Harry had chosen her in a fit of passion and an instant of enlightenment. He had followed his heart instead of his hard on.

It was a tough choice for a man. He knew he had made the right decision. He realized that the dark blue eyed Mouse was part of the show and she played it right to the last goodbye. He was sure they had repeat business. But still there was that spark at the back of his mind, that instinctive knowledge that through time they had met before and they would meet again and they would always be lovers.

It was past noon when the shade had vanished on deck and Eve returned to the cockpit where she hugged and kissed Harry in a revelation of delight.

"You've made me the happiest woman in the world," she said.

"You sound like we just got married," Harry said.

"It was better than a marriage," Eve held on to him. "It was a unification of lovers. The completion of the circle."

"I still feel like I'm on a honeymoon," Harry kissed her and gave up the wheel. There was plenty of light and the channel was well marked. She took over without reading the chart. The markers were all numbered and they had been this way before.

Harry did some stretches and watched her. He loved the way she felt the wind on her face and relayed that information to the boat. She turned the wheel slightly, pulled in on the jib sheet and sat back as the boat surged forward. She was a natural.

They were kindred spirits, constant lovers, alone in a floating universe. They were the last two people on earth. They were Adam and Eve in the garden.

Eve and Adam Wise. The Eden Clinic.

Harry forced all of the questions out of his mind and centered on his love for this woman. There was no past. There was no future. All that existed was their present unity. He was never going to be the one who would break the spell cast by the ceremony with the twins. He would not be the one to make her cry. He would not force apart what fate had joined. He liked being with her.

She gave him the companionship that he hadn't known since he and Billy were kids.

Harry didn't sleep. He read the charts, made a couple of tuna fish sandwiches which he shared with Eve. He brewed coffee and enjoyed the domestic life.

Harry had the sunset watch and Eve got the moonrise. They exchanged places during the night; one piloting while the other slept under a blanket nearby in the cockpit. The only talking they did were words of love; very private intimacies shared between mates.

The honeymoon was over with the first sight of the Key West jetty early in the morning. It was where Billy had died. Harry saw a yellow flash of a cane pole and saw an old black woman fishing. If it hadn't been for the cane pole, she would have gone unnoticed, just another round dark object amid the round dark rocks of the jetty. It brought Harry down to earth.

After they dropped anchor and furled the sails, Eve made coffee and brought it up on deck. Harry was trying to remember where he wanted to start. She read his face.

"Evelyn West was a patient of mine," Eve said to his surprise. "She wanted to get out of a dead end life as a lawyer at the same time I wanted out of a deadend life as a therapist."

"So you're not really a lawyer," Harry said, "And not really a paralegal."

"I didn't want to intimidate you," Eve said. "One of her problems was she couldn't find a man who could deal with her success. I had to pull that card on the cop, and I hadn't told you, so I covered a lie with a lie. We were getting on so well. I'm just a foolish woman."

"And a legitimate therapist well respected in your field," Harry reminded her.

"Correct," Eve smiled. "It's crazy. Evelyn wanted a new life and so did I. We both had good credit histories. We had birth certificates, passports. We are similar in stature anyway and nearly the same age. She had baggage she wanted to lose and so did I. Since we wouldn't be practicing each other's profession, what difference did it make. I became Eve West, retired lawyer and adventurer. She became Eve Wise, widowed sex therapist who joined an ashram in Brazil."

"So, there's another one like you out there," Harry

said. "Which one got the insurance money?"

"I have more money than you do," Eve said. "It was declared a diving accident, quite common in Florida. He came up too fast, hit his head on the bottom of the boat and drowned. I've seen the report. I needed it for the Insurance Company."

"There were no witnesses," Harry said.

"No," Eve said. "He was a stupid man. He liked to dive alone."

"You don't sound like you miss him." Harry said.

"I'm happy he's dead," Eve said.

Harry was resting on a cockpit cushion with his coffee cup on his stomach. It was empty. He looked inside for no reason, just killing time until he asked the big question. Eve waited patiently. She found a jug of water, drank and offered some to Harry. He took it and wet his mouth.

"Did Billy have anything to do..." Harry stopped and came at it again. "It happened right out here in the channel off the jetty."

"Yes," Eve said.

"Did Billy kill him?" Harry asked.

"No!" Eve was emphatic and stood up. "That's not possible. Billy wouldn't do something like that for all the money in the world."

"You knew Billy," Harry said and she sat back down.

"Harry," Eve said. "My life is a work of fiction. Any resemblance to persons living or dead is purely coincidental. The names have been changed to protect the guilty."

She was calm. She looked directly at him and sat up

221

straight. She was on the witness stand but she wasn't under oath. Harry knew that it wouldn't have made any difference.

"I loved Billy," Eve stated. She smiled. "Everybody loved Billy, especially his brother. He sent me to make sure that you'd show up sooner or later. He said it had been years but you always had a good excuse. This time it was special. There was an urgency in his request at the same time my own personal crisis was resolved. I owed Billy a lot."

She looked up at the sky. The sun was well risen. The heat was coming into the day. Harry drank some water. He knew when to shut up. She was a smart girl. She could figure out the questions ahead of time. He would have to figure out the answers.

"He promised me the world," Eve said. "The switch with the lawyer was Billy's idea. He said it would free me from my old self. He gave me confidence, taught me about my strength and my beauty. He taught me to have fun. He taught me to be a rascal."

Eve came over to Harry and kissed him on the forehead and played with his hair. There was still that closeness between them. Nothing she said disturbed him. He knew that it was true. Billy was that kind of guy. He could change people's lives. He could show them how to have fun even if you were dead from the waist down. Harry remembered the burial at sea and restrained a laugh so as not to appear to be laughing at Eve. Billy had even shown them how to have fun even when you were dead from the head down. The streamer unraveling in the depths.

"He was right about me having the world," Eve said and leaned in next to Harry. "He gave you to me. He told me where to find you. Dress like a Dallas Cowgirl. He even told me what to say, because he knew you pretty well. He was right on."

"And you were right for the part," Harry said. He looked at her legs folded next him her feet tucked under his hip. She was leaning on his shoulder. He felt his strength in supporting her.

"Billy was someone I could talk to about my problems, after I listened to those of other people. I loved my job as much as you loved yours. I helped people too. I heard thoughts more depraved than any crime scene you ever saw. I helped people who were fucked up."

"Like Candy," Harry said.

"Like Candy," she sat up and testified. "Billy was so in love with her. She brought out his strengths, his need to be protective. She was the definition of beauty, but very troubled."

"She was your patient," Harry said.

"That's how I met Billy," Eve said. "He started bringing her to my office after she moved to Key West. Frisky would drive them up. I never met him. He always waited in the car. Billy waited in the garden usually smoking a joint if no one was around to talk to. He made people laugh. He made me laugh. He was so positive. A breath of fresh air, a sight for sore eyes. I should have never sent them to the twins."

"You arranged it," Harry kept learning something

223

new.

"I had heard such good things about them," Eve said.

"I had written to them after they said they were using some of my methods at their Goddess Retreat in Maui. We became pen pals. They flattered my ego and appealed to my vanity. Billy and Candy wanted a ceremony to celebrate the fact that they loved each other."

"But she was `fucked up'" Harry said.

"That never stood in the way of love," Eve answered. "She was a virgin. Yes. A virgin. Her hymen had never been broken. Everything was in confidence. I couldn't tell Billy. That girl depended on me."

There was a silence as Harry watched Eve wrestle with a career of ethical honesty in a time of total freedom. She was immune from any punishment. When she took his fingers to her lips and kissed them, he knew that he was now her world.

"She could never have vaginal sex," Eve continued. "It was very painful. She had a small vagina that minor surgery could have corrected. She was extremely hormonal, masturbating three and four times a day. She became a lap dancer. This was before she became blind. She had so much sexual energy. Then she had anal sex. She loved it. Then she went blind."

"She was blind when she met Billy?" Harry said.

"A little over a year ago," Eve knew the answers. "It was love at first sight. Billy never asked any questions. He had found a rose in the garden. It was a blessing. Candy told him she was a runaway and in a way she was. She was a fugitive from her sinful life that she blamed for her blindness. There was no clinical collaboration. She was `fucked up'. Billy loved her. I loved Billy so I sent them to the twins who had muscle relaxers, lubricants and potions guaranteed to loosen her up. If it failed, maybe Billy would come to me. It was a fantasy. As Velda told you, Billy couldn't feel a thing down there. He got excited just looking at her."

"So you and Billy never..." Harry started but was interrupted.

"It was not a consummated love," Eve said.

"But you're so good at what you do," Harry was honest.

"I know the cues," Eve put her foot between his legs and wriggled her toes. "I know behavior patterns, fetishes, partialisms, instinctive response. Staging and execution."

"Sex is theater," Harry quoted her. "This could all be an act."

"I never planned on falling in love with you," Eve said. "You're so much like Billy."

"Only taller," Harry said. She had all the answers. She put it so well rubbing his chest and his nipples.

"You think it's an act?"

"I'm not complaining."

"You never would. You're my kind of guy."

"Just like my brother," Harry added.

"There is so much more between you and me than there ever was with Billy." As Eve said this, she realized that it could be taken the wrong way. "I don't mean from

225

the waist down."

"And what about Adam Wise?" Harry wanted to clear the air.

"The filthy son of a bitch fucked me when he knew he had AIDS," Eve showed her bitterness. "I'm glad he's dead. His specialty was sexually disturbed children. I thought that he was helping them. He would take them camping in the Keys. I was busy with my own patients. I know that is no excuse. We discussed our serious cases like Candy. He was the one who brought her to my attention, a difficult referral from a colleague. Bullshit! She told me he was a regular at the bar where she danced before she went blind. That didn't bother me. It was safe sex and I was busy. I was glad to get him off of my back. The shoemaker's daughter goes barefoot."

"The lawyer wears Chanel pumps and Versace dresses," Harry remembered her valuables.

"I was fucked up too. You changed all that."

"Not Billy?"

"Six months ago," Eve told her story. "A few months after Candy left him and disappeared, Billy told me about a picture of Candy bent over the hood of a car with someone fucking her in the ass. He never told me where he got it, but he was sure it was after she left him. He didn't say how he knew. There were little boys masturbating in the background. Billy said he knew who owned the car."

"The Don," Harry said.

"The Don," Eve said. "Billy swore he would nail him if it was the last thing he ever did."

"Maybe the Don got there first," Harry said.

"From what Billy and Candy both told me," Eve said. "Billy would meditate on the jetty every morning at sunrise. Everybody knew him. If somebody wanted to get him, they knew where he could be found."

Harry was trying to tie the new information into the time line he had conceived. Six months ago Billy had started working with the cops. Four months ago Adam Wise died. Three months ago he met Eve.

"He saw it coming," Harry said. "He wanted to see it coming."

"He did," Eve said pointing to the rocks. "Right there."

"And where was it your husband died?" Harry asked. She pointed to the middle of the channel.

"Why do you keep tying the two together?" Eve said.

"This was Billy's beat. Nothing happened on Billy's beat that he didn't know about."

"Adam was diving for old bottles and artifacts. It was early in the morning."

"So if Billy was there, he would have seen something," Harry said.

"He told me that he didn't see a thing," Eve said.

"Maybe he lied." The conversation ended.

Eve prepared the dinghy for going ashore. She put it in the water. She loaded the empty water jugs. Harry sat watching. The rollercoaster was picking up speed. He was heading to a resolution of the problem. He was on a collision course with the Don. It was like old times. Good guys

227

and bad guys. Cops and robbers. Only this time he wasn't bound by any code of conduct.

As they were getting into the dinghy, Eve stayed away from him. She sat in the stern and let him row. He looked at her. Whatever she said didn't matter. Lies. The truth. Harry didn't care about the truth. He cared about Eve. He smiled at her and winked. She smiled back and rubbed his leg where he had braced himself with his foot next to her hip.

"Somebody who knew Billy and his habits," Harry said to her. "Somebody who was connected to the Don. Someone who would kill him and he wouldn't fight back."

"Let's finish what Billy started," Eve leaned forward. "Let's nail the Don."

"Revenge is sweet?"

"No. It's a bitter pill. But sometimes we have to take the bitter with the sweet."

"Sweet like sugar," Harry said. "Sweet like candy."

"Sweet like cookies," Eve said. "Billy never talked to me about Velda. He had his secrets."

"Did he ever tell you how he got hurt?" Harry asked.

"No," Eve said. "I talked. Billy listened. Do you want to tell me?"

"No," Harry said and pulled harder on the oars and watched the sky for weather.

CHAPTER TEN

They tied up the dinghy at the Marina across from the Coast Guard base. They paid their money, then Eve began filling the two five gallon collapsible jugs. Harry blew her a kiss and pointed to the jetty. He began to walk. He walked through the Marina out to a large leveled waterfront lot that was soon to be the sight of another Marina. The lot bordered the wall where the jetty began. Large grey and black boulders of granite were piled up for fifty yards to act as a breakwater for the channel into the Coast Guard base. The tide was high and splashed foam against the seaward wall; the leeward side was calm as a pond.

Harry walked out as far as it was easy to go; as far as a man in a wheelchair could go, about half way. Then he went a little farther because he knew Billy would. It was still some twenty yards to the end. There were beer cans down between the rocks, potato chip bags, cigarette packs, butts, broken glass and snarled fishing lines.

Harry walked to the end of the jetty and turned around in a circle. The panorama included the anchorage where his catamaran waited with the open sea beyond. As he turned around, he could see the entire island and the sky above.

Harry sat down and looked out to sea. He meditated for Billy. He felt for him. He thought for him. He became Billy.

"Billy!" the woman yelled. "I thought you was dead."

Harry turned and looked down to his right where he saw the black woman with the yellow cane pole whom he had seen as they were coming in to port. In the bright sunlight with her in the shade, he could barely see anything but the pole.

"Hey," Harry greeted her and stood up. He could see her mouth drop open and her eyes grow big. She looked up to heaven, put her hands together and prayed.

Harry walked down to where she knelt. She put one hand over her heart. The other hand held a bucket with a few small pan fish in it. She was going to hang on to it. It was her catch.

"I'm Billy's brother," Harry said.

"Praise the lord," the woman wailed. "He said you would come."

"You knew Billy?" Harry kept his distance. She was nervous, holding a handkerchief that she dipped in the water. She wiped her face and arms, leaving the dark skin wet. As it evaporated, it would cool her.

"Everybody down here knew Billy," she said as if he was kidding her. "But me and Billy. This was our spot. He would sit up there praying, or meditating, he liked to call it. I would be down here fishing. This is the holy spot where we both met with the Lord."

"Did he always come out this far to pray?" Harry questioned her.

"I don't know 'bout most times," she looked Harry over real good while shading her eyes from the sun with her hand. "I only comes out here the hour after the slack high tide 'cause when all the nutrition comes rushing out, the fishes comes in to feed and I gets them."

"It looks like you have dinner there," Harry nodded at the bucket.

"Oh, those are not for me," she smiled and he came closer. "These are for people who have less than me. I takes care of them that can't do for themselves."

"And who takes care of you?" Harry looked at the woman in her late years, big and black in a dress that was probably never new. Her sandals were the kind men wore with big straps that she had opened to ease her swollen feet.

"The Lord provides," she said and looked up to heaven. "I am a witness to his bounty and his generosity. Praise the Lord."

"So you only come down here once in a while," Harry changed the subject.

"And most times," she remembered, "Billy is sitting back farther."

231

She pointed to where Harry had stopped the first time. He smiled to himself. He knew Billy.

"Just over the side," she said. "Close to the water. But you could still smell what he was smokin'. That last day, Billy came all the way up here to the end. You know how he used to use his arms to swing himself forward in that way that he did. When he saw me he said he was going to meet his girlfriend and I know that meant he wanted privacy. So I went back a ways so we could both be alone with the Lord."

"Did you hear the shot?" Harry asked.

"I did but I didn't know it was a shot," she said. "I was back there on the quiet side. Just a pop. The next day after I read the paper about Billy being killed. I thought that pop just as the sun was coming up must be the shot. The tide had just turned. When I left an hour later, I didn't see Billy but maybe I didn't look. I caught me some fish. Praise the Lord."

"You didn't see anybody?" Harry asked.

"I wasn't looking," she said as if she were talking to a cop. "I was fishing. Noise is noise. I went on my way. I didn't see nothing."

"Did the police talk to you?" Harry asked.

"The police!" she laughed. "Me tell those white police I was where a white man got shot. The Lord didn't make no dummies in my family. I never talked to no one but the Lord and he will be my final judge."

"Amen," Harry said.

"The only one I ever told 'bout what I saw was Billy."

232

She had moved around to avoid the sun in her eyes and looked him over. "Billy told me not to worry, that soon his brother would be here and the two of you would take care of that evil man."

"What man?" Harry was on to something.

"The one with the green Jaggywire," she spit out the words. "The devil's disciple with the white hair who got my son Bogart hooked on crack until Billy straightened him out. Praise the Lord."

"He is the devil," Harry agreed.

"Bad with young boys. Something so evil I can't speak it," she looked at the sea. "You know what I means. That morning I saw him waiting down there by the car, his white hair marking his head like Cane. Then that other man, the big one, came out of the water like in the movies, all in black. He must have seen me 'cause he come this way with a knife. So I move to where I know Billy was. The man comes up behind Billy and when Billy sees me point, he turns and this devil all in black with the knife turns and he has this tank on his back. One look from Billy, and he picks up his fins and goes to the green Jaggywire and he and the other devil leave. That was what happened that day that doctor from Miami drowned while diving for bottles. What a fool! Lord knows you can't feed nobody with old bottles."

"You and Billy were witnesses," Harry said.

"I only witness for the Lord," she said. "For anybody else, I didn't see anything."

"I got here too late," Harry said.

233

"Too bad," she shook her head. "Maybe you could have saved Billy, but I think he had plans that day."

"What plans?" Harry eased his tone.

"Plans to die," she said. "I think he knew."

"Why do you say that?" Harry asked.

They were both sitting on the rocks now. He hadn't rousted her or put her under pressure. She was a grown woman. He figured she knew right from wrong as well as anyone.

"He throwed away his wheelchair," she said. "Like he wasn't going to need it anymore. I thought maybe he was going to be picked up by a boat. Billy was back there where I saw that big man that other fateful morning. Billy was up on the rocks and he picked up that chair, and heave ho it goes flying out there most to the middle of the channel. He starts coming out to where we see each other. I gave him respect for his privacy. Lord, bless his soul. Amen."

There was a tug on the line that she had in the water and she pulled in another little fish. Most people would have thrown it back. She put it in the bucket. It was worth more than an old bottle.

"Praise the Lord," she sang. "Hallelujah!"

Harry dropped a twenty dollar bill in the bucket when she turned to cast the line again.

"For those that got less than me," Harry said.

Harry walked back along the jetty to the vacant lot where Eve was waiting next to a police car. Captain Art Adkins was on the passenger side with a cop driving. As

234

Harry looked inside, he saw a box of doughnuts and coffee on the console. Eve turned around to greet him and was holding a gun. It looked like a .22 Magnum.

"Good morning, Captain," Harry said, then nodded to the driver.

"Good morning," Captain Art Adkins said. "You returning to the scene of the crime?"

"Everybody has to be someplace," Harry said. "This island isn't very big, not too many places a person can be."

"We're just a small town," Captain Art Adkins defended his turf. "We don't have a big city force, but we've got a new computer. And you know what that computer found out, that this gun was bought last year in Miami by Doctor Adam Wise. So, I'm returning it to it's rightful owner, the widow Mrs. Wise."

"West is my maiden name," Eve informed him.

"And you're a therapist and a lawyer?" Captain Art Adkins investigated.

"Is it a crime to want to be a lawyer?" Eve said.

"No, it's a sin," Captain Art Adkins laughed. The cop next to him almost spilled his coffee. Eve smiled.

"If you're giving back the gun," Harry said, "Then you must have another suspect."

"How were the Dry Tortugas?" Art Adkins asked. He offered them doughnuts. They both refused.

"It's inside the county," Eve said. "We weren't trying to hide. We went for a day sail. Have you got someone following us?"

"Oh, no, no, no," Art Adkins put up his hand and

235

looked at Harry. "We don't have the manpower for that. We have other crimes. Some even more important than who shot Billy. The Ranger down there didn't get the cancellation on the APB and he reported you. How are the twins? That little one is in love with me. Did you have a good time?"

"It was a pleasure," Eve said in a way so sensual that Captain Art Adkins dropped his doughnut in his lap.

"While you were gone," Adkins said, brushing the sugar from his pants. "We had a little action of our own."

"Another bomb scare?" Eve smiled.

"Something other than our normal drug smugglers and domestic miscreants," Art Adkins ignored her. "Related perhaps to Billy."

"So the Ranger is our alibi," Harry said.

"Guess so," Art Adkins threw half the doughnut away. "It would be pretty hard to run someone off the road and pop a couple of caps into them while you were with the twins getting `therapy'."

"And the gun used was a .22 mag like the one that killed Billy," Harry said pointing to Eve's hand. "And this .22 had an alibi."

Eve put the gun inside the bag she carried. She leaned on the car roof and looked down at the Captain Art Adkins. He couldn't handle her gaze and went for another doughnut.

"You'll have to find another suspect," Eve said. "Do you have any leads?"

"Maybe I owe you an apology," Adkins said to Harry.

He didn't want to talk to Eve. She backed off.

"Maybe," Harry said.

"Maybe," Art Adkins repeated and took a slip of paper from his breast pocket and put it in Harry's hand.

Art Adkins said, "It's the address you wanted. Candy."

The name burst in the air. It went back and forth between Harry and Eve's eyes. A radio call broke the silence as the driver picked up the mike to respond.

"We gotta go, Captain," the cop said. "Trouble in Little Africa."

"The last time we went in there," Captain Art Adkins said. "They spit on me and threw a brick through my window. Let me finish my doughnut."

The two cops sat in the car with the motor running. They sipped slowly and chewed with deliberation. Harry looked at Eve with an expression that let her know that this was the way cops acted when they had to go into a place where they knew they weren't wanted.

"They called me a pig," Adkins bemoaned.

"They'll call you officer again," Harry said. "When they start calling you officer again you'll feel better."

"Officer," Captain Art Adkins drawled. "Officer, help me. Someone got hurt. Someone got shot. Officer, please help me."

"Who was it that we didn't shoot while we were away?" Harry asked. "Anybody we know?"

"Velda," Captain Art Adkins said. "She pistol whipped a sailor at Captain Tony's and was riding her bicycle home when she got run into a canal and got shot

237

twice. She's a tough old bird. She'll live, but she didn't see who did it. They got her from behind."

"The sailor?" Eve said.

"He has an alibi," Art Adkins said. "Out cold with his buddies. Claims he was jumped by a bunch of bikers. Never mentioned a woman on a bike."

The radio squawked again. The windows went up and the air conditioning came on. They drove off slowly without saying goodbye. It wasn't until they were out in traffic that they put on the siren and the lights. Emergency.

"Velda" Eve said. "There goes my number one suspect. Maybe she was shot in retaliation for Billy."

"I don't think so," Harry said. "Not with the same gun."

"It's a common enough gun," Eve said anticipating him. "I have one here."

"Bought by your late husband," Harry said.

"I don't know what to say," Eve said. "It's more of a surprise to me than it is to you. Honestly, Harry, I never knew he owned a gun. I'm not lying."

"Let's go see Velda," Harry said and started across the vacant lot. She caught up to him, taking his hand as they walked. Just another couple of honeymooners in Key West.

There was only one hospital. According to their records, Brown, Velda, Hit and Run, had checked herself out. As they walked to Velda's office, Harry told Eve about his conversation on the jetty with Bogart's mother. He told her about the wheelchair being tossed.

"He knew he wouldn't be needing it," Eve said.

238

"Suicide."

"No," Harry protested. "Not Billy. Not suicide. Billy could handle whatever cards he was dealt. He would never fold. What did he do, shoot himself in the head, throw away the gun? No, Billy would never kill himself. He knew I was coming."

Harry could feel Eve's eyes on him. He knew she could see the hurt in his face. He tried to hide it.

"So, Adam's death wasn't a happy accident," Eve knew when to change the subject.

"Maybe he bought the gun to protect himself?" Harry said. He breathed easier. Adam Wise's demise was a simpler matter. "He couldn't take it in the water. He thought he would be safe. Somebody had it in for him."

"It could be a long list," Eve said. "Your witness says that the Don was driving the getaway car. With Adam's penchant for young boys, there could be a connection to the Don's sperm products."

"Or his other enterprises," Harry said.

"Adam had done sperm research," Eve said. "Scientific stuff. Protein content. Zygote count. Preservation. All those camping trips to the Keys. I never knew him. In all the years we were together, I never really knew him. He was going to publish his findings. He talked of a Nobel Prize."

"Maybe the Don didn't want any publicity," Harry said. "It might breed competition and he had a corner on the market that he didn't want to lose."

"I think someone killed Adam to rid the world of

239

assholes," Eve said. "As a public service."

"I'm sure you had an alibi," Harry said.

"Yeah, copper," Eve was sarcastic. "I always have an alibi. I was in Miami at the clinic with a patient. The police have her statement as well as the staff."

"Billy was meditating on the jetty," Harry said.

"And they knew Billy saw them," Eve said. "But he never went to the police. Was he scared?"

"Not Billy," Harry said. "He only saw a diver. There was no witness to the act. Maybe it was a contract killing?"

"It was ruled an accident," Eve said. "They found evidence on the boat propellers. Hair plugs. Adam was very vain. There were no witnesses."

"Billy knew and he didn't tell anybody, not you, not me not the cops," Harry said as they walked.

"Blackmail?" Eve said.

They had reached the storefront with the Mrs. Brown's Cookies sign on the window. There was a light on and the door was unlocked. Harry pushed the door open and held Eve back to one side as he surveyed the room. He didn't see anyone but the back door was open. Eve followed him and quietly closed the front door behind them. Harry stopped at the back door and peeked around the corner into the stairwell. He could see light coming from the top of the stairs. The light was just enough to show the gloss on the drops of blood that led up the steps.

"Velda," Harry yelled and pushed Eve back against the wall behind him. He noticed the .22 gun in her hand. She held it pointed up to the ceiling. She knew what she was doing.

"I took lessons," Eve said. "From the Police Protective League. Combat violence against women."

"Friend or foe?" Velda's voice came out hoarse and rasping. There was a slight slur. Harry knew what her breath would smell like.

"Friend," Harry yelled. "Billy's brother."

"Come ahead with your hands up."

Harry and Eve went up the steps in unison making a single sound. He entered the apartment while Eve stayed outside. She held the gun with both hands.

There was no missing the size of the hole in the barrel of the blue steel automatic pointed at him over the back of the brown couch. There was a mess of black and grey hair in the background. Harry smiled and moved slowly forward with his hands up. The silver and black inched up and a pair of dark brown eyes dilated to the size of the gun barrel looked at him.

"Hey, handsome," Velda said. "Come over here and give Velda a big hug and a kiss."

"I came for the cookies," Harry grinned.

"Oh, fudge," Velda said and they both laughed. The gun dropped heavily to the floor and Velda fell back behind the couch. Harry picked up the gun and went around in front of the fire place.

When he looked at Velda, he froze. She was face down on the couch, naked but for the bloody bandage on her back and another falling off of her left hip. Most of her back and right leg were discolored by purple and brown

241

bruises. Part of the back of her head had been shaved and a line of purple stitches laced up the pure white skin.

"They came at me from behind," Velda's voice came from under her arm where her face was tucked. "Sometimes I like that kind of thing, but this time they were too rough. Find a place that isn't damaged and kiss me."

It wasn't easy but Harry found a smooth tan spot on her right buttock and bent over and kissed her ass. Eve had come quietly into the room when he stood up. She had the gun pointed at him and said "Bang."

"Who's there," Velda tried to turn on her side but Harry comforted her with a hand on her unbruised shoulder.

"You've met Eve," Harry said to Velda, "When we took Billy to the dock."

"The dame with the great legs," Velda said and rested.

Eve came around the couch next to Harry. When she saw Velda, her mouth fell open and her eyes teared. She knelt down by Velda's head. She touched Velda with that stroke that women save to comfort women. Like a secret handshake or a password, it was a bond born of gender. No men allowed.

"What did they do to you!" Eve felt her pain.

"I lived through worse," Velda said and moved her arm so she could make eye contact with Eve. Both of Velda's eyes were blackened and her nose swollen and scratched. "The commies back in the early sixties were a lot rougher than this bunch of pencil dicks. We showed

242

them a thing or two about the American spirit. We left their bodies pinned to the Iron Curtain with an icepick through their balls. We were pretty rough ourselves."

"You're tough," Eve smiled. "I like that."

"Damn pain killers," Velda choked back some tears. "Make you lose control. I need to be ready when they come. Where's my gun? Any man who ever hurt me, wound up dead. What I didn't do myself, my ex did and he was the best. He was a killer and he looked after me. Now I'm on my own. I'll have to do it alone. Do you know what it's like to be a woman alone?"

"I know," Eve said.

"It hurts," Velda said and started to cry.

"You'll be okay," Harry said. "You're a tough cookie. You'll heal. You're a tough cookie, Mrs. Brown."

"Fuck you," Velda said. "It's not the wounds of the flesh. It's life. Life hurts."

"I understand," Eve said and put her face close to Velda and they both cried like babies.

Harry went back downstairs to lock the front door and see if there was still a bottle in the desk drawer. He was still carrying Velda's .45. It made his arm ache and he put it on the desk where a folder was out. It was Billy's file. He went to pick it up and there was a white fluid spilled on it. There was an overturned phial.

"Sperm," Harry said and wiped his hand on the blotter.

Harry turned on the desk lamp, found a dry corner to the folder and opened it. There was a medical report

243

showing William Knight to be HIV positive. Velda had been investigating. The photo of Candy being violated with consent was still there, but the receipt for Velda's ten grand was gone.

Harry found the booze in the bottom drawer. It was a new one, unopened. He found some paper towels in the bathroom and cleaned up the mess on the desk, then washed his hands. He took the file and the bottle upstairs.

Eve was changing the dressing on Velda's two nasty red holes, one in her back, the other in her butt. Eve squeezed on an ointment and covered them with clean gauze that she had gotten in the medicine cabinet. There was a jar of brown salve that she rubbed on the back of Velda's legs and feet. She was careful not to rub too hard. Velda was dozing. Eve covered her with a fresh sheet.

"Smells good," Harry whispered. He put the gun and file on the mantel and opened the seal on the bottle of brandy with his thumbnail.

"Cocoa butter and eucalyptus," Eve said.

"Cognac," Harry said and pulled the cork. Velda's head popped up. She saw Harry next to the mantel.

"Sperm," Velda said. "Bogart dropped it off yesterday with the medical report. Are you going to hold that all day or offer a lady a drink?"

Harry looked around for a glass to pour a drink and Velda glared at him. Eve changed places with Harry. He held the bottle for Velda and Eve looked at the file.

"The son of a bitch," Eve muttered but they heard her. She saw them staring and brought the photo over. She handed it to Harry after Velda took the bottle and maneuvered onto her good side.

"The picture Billy told you about," Harry said.

"Meet Doctor Adam Wise," Eve said. "I guess Billy didn't want me to know. He wanted to keep me from being hurt as much as he was. He must have sat on this for over a year."

"I don't know," Velda took a quick sip and gave Eve the bottle. She did the same.

"Wait," Harry said. "You said Billy told you this was taken after Candy left him nine months ago."

"It couldn't be," Eve showed him on the photo. "Look at the bastard's hair."

"What hair?" Velda asked and went for the bottle but Harry got it first.

"Adam started getting transplants over a year ago." Eve said. "This is an old photo."

"Then why would Billy say it was more recent?" Velda asked. She waited for Harry to pass the bottle and come up with the answer.

"Someone he trusted," Harry said and gave Velda the brandy. "Someone he believed in told him."

"Frisky did this kind of shit for the Don," Velda said. "You better replace this if you drink it. That liquor store across the street won't deliver."

Harry capped the bottle.

"He wouldn't trust a scumbag like Frisky," Eve said. "Billy was smarter than that."

"Did you know about the health report?" Harry asked.

245

"I was the only one Billy told," Velda said. "He had wanted me to get tested after Candy left and we got back together in an intimate way. But I hadn't been with anybody but Billy for years."

"What about now?" Eve asked.

"So far so good," Velda said. "Another five months and I'll get tested again. Until then, I'll have to make do."

Velda looked at Eve for a reaction but got none. Harry hadn't told her everything that had happened at Velda's the last time. Harry smiled at Velda.

"When you're well enough to get up and around," Harry said. "I'll buy you a new pair of shoes."

"I'd like that," Velda said to her friend. "You're thoughtful and kind."

"Just like Billy," Harry said.

"What happened to Candy?" Eve asked.

"She disappeared," Velda said and rested back on her stomach. Eve rubbed her neck and shoulders being careful of her wounds. Harry took a piece of paper from his pocket.

"Captain Art Adkins gave me her forwarding address," Harry said. "Some place up on Elliot Key."

"And where did he get it?" Velda asked.

"He didn't say," Harry said.

"Where's my gun?" Velda started to get up suddenly. She saw Harry take it from the mantel. "Just put it here next to my bottle. That gun saved my life. My pal. Fortyfive forever, not getting older like Velda. It was in the bag around my neck when I went into that drainage canal

246

when that car hit me from behind. The weight took me straight to the bottom. When they tried to shoot me, the water slowed down the bullets so they only nicked my skull and stuck in the muscles of my back and butt."

"You're in great shape," Eve said. "You're a real tough cookie, Mrs. Brown."

"I love you too," Velda said and winked at Eve.

"You know who did it?" Harry said.

"What am I, stupid?" Velda said. Her eyes were closed. "That white haired cocksucker and his big buddy with the little dick."

"Do they know you're here and alive?" Eve asked.

"I snuck out of the hospital, got a ride from a cabbie who knows how to be quiet for a twenty," Velda droned on. "I made it as far as this couch. The only way to get to me is through that door and I got it covered."

Without opening her eyes, Velda found the gun and cuddled up with it next to her chest.

"Will you be okay for a couple of hours?"
Eve asked her.

"Alone," Velda said. She yawned. "That's the way you come into this life. That's the way you go out. Alone."

"Can we borrow your car?" Harry asked.

"The keys are on my dresser," Velda pointed somewhere.

Eve followed Harry into a room with a bed and a dresser. The bedspread was brown and white. Harry wasn't surprised. The dresser was an antique with a pol-

247

ished mahogany finish. The keys were on top.

"Maybe we should call the police and get someone over here to watch her," Eve said.

"The police," Harry bit his lip. "I only told two people about that sperm switch with Bogart. You and Captain Art Adkins. You're going to be with me. I don't know where he's going to be. It's pretty bad when you can't even trust the cops."

"Don't trust anybody," Velda called from the other room and they went to her. She was asleep. Eve touched her silver and black hair ever so gently.

"Tough cookie," Eve said.

"The original," Harry agreed.

CHAPTER ELEVEN

Harry and Eve were in the brown *Mercedes* heading north on U.S. 1 when they heard the news.

"...another senseless drug related death in Key West. Humphrey Edgar Wallace was shot to death in an alley. Another drug deal gone bad according to police sources who say Wallace had two bags of crack cocaine on him at the time. Known to locals as Bogart, Mr. Wallace..."

Eve turned off the radio and they rode in silence. Traffic was slow due to construction. Harry stayed between the lines and stopped at all the lights. Eve was staring at him.

"Candy," Harry said. "The missing link. She was what Billy and Adam Wise had in common."

"They also had me," Eve said.

"How did you find out that Adam had AIDS?" Harry asked.

"He told me," Eve said. "One night he put some designer drug in my wine. We had impassioned sex. In the morning he told me that he had AIDS, then went to his room. I was dumbstruck. The first thing I thought was, what had I done to make this man hate me this much?"

"Did you come up with an answer?" Harry asked.

"Billy," Eve said. "For the six months prior to that night, we hadn't been intimate. That was the six months when Billy was coming in with Candy. I raved about him to Adam to everyone. I was in love and I didn't care. I never loved Adam but it was the right thing to do, for our careers. It was a partnership more than a marriage. That's what I thought."

"But not what Adam thought," Harry said.

"Adam thought that what I felt for Billy was pity," Eve smiled. "He never knew Billy. Candy had already left Billy and we kept in touch. We became very close."

She stopped talking and Harry knew she was leaving out personal details that he didn't care about. She seemed content with the memories of Billy. Then again, that was all that was left.

"Tell me about Candy," Harry said. The memories vanished and she looked at the traffic.

"I told you she was my patient. She was drop dead gorgeous. I understood why Billy fell for her. She was a lap dancer, a professional prick teaser. Until she went blind."

"Was that psychological?" Harry asked.

"Hysterical blindness? No. Adam could site the

250

statistics of how many young people go blind from the eye disease Candy had."

"No cure?"

"None yet," Eve frowned. "But she never told Billy about her job. She told him she had run away from a rich family that had abused her. That's why she had money. He believed her. Billy didn't care. Candy was no rocket scientist, but she made more money than they did."

"Until she went blind." Harry said.

"And met Billy," Eve said. "She thought her blindness was due to having anal sex. She was brought up Baptist and masturbation was sin enough. It was a sin to dance. Her life has been a rebellion against her values. She was being punished for her sins."

"Billy changed all that," Harry said.

"He lit up her darkened life," Eve said. "He made her laugh. He made her feel secure in those big arms of his. She was safe. The Don wouldn't touch her. The month Candy and Billy had their session with the Twins was the happiest I have ever seen two people until I met you."

Harry kept his eyes on the road. He remembered the trip back from the Tortugas and the elation he felt with Eve beside him in the cockpit. She was with him now in the car. He hoped he could feel it again. There were questions he had to ask.

"And Billy thought the photo with Adam was taken after Candy left," Harry was digging.

"That's what Billy said," Eve answered. "He cursed the world for what it had done to her."

"How often did you see Billy?" Harry continued. "I mean, after Candy left."

"He came up to Miami once," Eve said. "He told me about the photo. I told him about Adam trying to kill me."

"Death by sex," Harry said. "The praying mantis hasn't got anything on mankind. You say Billy only came up to Miami once?"

"Once," Eve repeated. "I saw him in Key West when I claimed Adam's body. I saw him again in Islamorada when he suggested the change to Eve West and sent me to bring his brother to him."

"Did he mention the Don?" Harry asked.

"He wanted to be sure you'd show up," Eve said. "That was my assignment. It was a chance to get my mind off of my own problems. Do you know what the last six months have been like for me?"

"HIV positive," Harry said. "That was another thing Adam and Billy had in common."

"And you and I don't," Eve forced a smile.

Harry reached over and put his hand on her head and tossled her short hair. She loosened her seatbelt so that she could kiss him on the cheek. Then she reclined her seat and let him drive.

Harry thought about Billy, Adam, Frisky, Bogart and Velda. The dead and the near dead. What did they have in common? Sperm. It's production and distribution. The Don didn't hide the fact that that was why they tried to hit Velda. And Bogart was an obvious second choice. Vain men didn't like to be embarrassed. Frisky was in the wrong place at the wrong time. Adam Wise was killed by the Don's hired assassin and made to look like an accident. That would cost extra. Maybe ten grand. It was hard to know the price of life when you were out of that business. Billy knew and they knew he knew. Billy was a rascal, but that didn't include blackmailing hoods. Not even hoods who ruined the woman you loved. That wasn't a reason for blackmail. That was a reason for murder.

The address that Captain Art Adkins had given Harry turned out to be a small hospital set back off a side road on a well manicured site hidden in the tall Florida pine and scrub oak. Everything was very clean inside. When they asked the desk nurse for Candy Love, they said they were family. They walked down a hallway toward a room at the end with a door half open. As they passed each room, they caught a glimpse of the ravages of disease and dying. At the last room, they heard a baby crying.

If Harry hadn't seen the photo nor had he heard the description of Candy, perhaps the shock would have been less dramatic. As it was, he had to grab onto Eve's arm to remain standing. The only thing that remained of the perfect blonde were those skyblue eyes that could not see. Harry thought of the holocaust, the skeletons stacked in barracks their muscles drained to threads strung on bone covered by mottled skin. There were dark blotches on Candy's face. A small thin baby cried its breath against her cheek.

"I think we should come back later," Harry said. "I don't think this is a good time."

"Wait," Eve said. "I want to look at them."

Suddenly the devil's madonna lifted her head away from her wailing child.

"Eve," Candy said, "Is that you?"

"Yes, dear," Eve said and approached the bed on the side away from the baby. She kissed Candy's forehead and stroked the once golden blonde hair that had turned white. Harry stayed by the door.

"There's someone else here," Candy held her baby.

"It's Billy's brother," Eve said.

"Oh, wow," Candy said. "You hooked up with Billy's brother. Billy would have liked that."

"You know what happened to Billy?" Eve asked.

"I know," Candy said. She turned back to where she could feel the breath of her baby who now slept. She touched a finger to its lips. There was an IV in the back of her hand that came from a bottle hung at the back of her bed. There was a multi display monitor on the back wall that pulsed weakly with her heart.

"He looks just like Billy," Candy said.

"He's beautiful," Eve said looking at the little body with the plastic bracelet falling from its thin wrist as he felt his mother.

"Billy never got to see him," Candy said. "He could never make it. Guilt, I guess."

"Guilt?" Harry said.

"He thought he was the cause of our problems," Candy sniffled a little. "He thought he gave me and Billy Jr. AIDS. I tried to tell him that wasn't true. But he said he

254

knew that I was a virgin until we met the twins. He didn't understand about the contact I had before I met him. I just couldn't tell him the truth about my past. I didn't want him to think that our love was based on a lie. I'm glad he never came here. I never wanted him to see me like this. I wanted him to remember me the way I was when we were with the twins. I was so beautiful once. We were so happy. How are the Twins?"

"They're fine," Eve said. "They send their love."

"What a night!" Candy said and a tear ran down her cheek. "Billy was my first real lover. That was the night I got pregnant."

"So, that's why you were throwing up at Billy's," Harry said. "Morning sickness."

"Yes," Candy said. "But I didn't know then. I guess I wondered out into the street and the police picked me up. The next thing I knew, I was in a State hospital. I think that's where I am now. They don't tell me anything. I don't tell them anything either. Only that cop and I talk. He and Billy were out to bust the Don."

"Captain Art Adkins," Harry said.

"He's so nice," Candy said. "He told Billy where I was, but Billy didn't want to see me. Finally after Billy Jr. was born, Captain Adkins called Billy from here. That was such a short time ago. Now, Billy is gone."

"Did you tell him you had AIDS?" Harry asked.

"No," Candy said. "But he knew. Maybe the Captain told him. When they asked me who the father was, I said I didn't know, but maybe they found out and contacted Billy

255

and told him. I don't know. Everyone here has been so good to me. They're giving us the latest drugs. I am going to get better."

"Hang in there, kid," Harry said.

"I'm no kid," Candy protested. "I'm a full grown woman. That's what I told the Don when he brought me to his house where he had all those little boys. Frisky and a man I didn't know were there. They said I was going to get my eyes fixed, but the next thing I know I was bent over a car and somebody was poking me in the ass. He tried to split me open and I passed out while they laughed. And the one laugh that was loudest was the Don. I'd recognize that bastard's laugh anywhere. He was a partner in the club where I danced. When my eyes got bad, I fell off of a table and injured a John. The Don laughed then too. Later we got sued. Eve remembers when I came to her."

"I thought you were a teenager," Eve said.

"I always looked young," Candy said. "Men like that."

"And you never told Billy about the night at the Don's" Harry said.

"I told the cop," Candy said. "He told me about Billy. It's too late for him. But me and my baby are going to beat this thing. Billy told me how to do it. One breath at a time. Breath in the wonders, the scents, the sounds, the touch of my baby."

Candy smiled and you could see the beauty that was once so apparent. Harry couldn't talk. Eve had tears on her cheeks but was silent.

256

"Me and Billy Jr., we're survivors," Candy said. "I talked to Billy the day before he died. He said his brother was going to get the Don and stop him from ruining people's lives. Billy told me how to visualize us together. He was so upbeat. He was so positive. He was Billy."

Candy had sunken back into her pillow and her eyes closed. A nurse came to take the baby. She didn't resist. She didn't like it but didn't have the strength to fight.

Harry cleared his throat to speak but Eve nudged him. Candy's eyes were closed. She was within herself at that place that was not diseased, at that place inside her that was pure.

"For my few precious moments with Billy," Candy spoke softly, "With our baby Billy Jr., I feel that I have been blessed with the greatest joy possible in this life."

She rested. Harry and Eve quietly backed out of the room. They quickly walked back down the hallway without looking to either side. They hurried to the car. Harry nervously searched his pocket but came up empty.

"I have the keys," Eve said and unlocked the driver's door.

"Thank heaven," Harry exhaled. "For a second I thought I had left them inside. I don't think I could have gone back in there to get them."

Eve drove, cruising south with the sun setting over the thousand islands of Florida Bay. They hadn't spoken at all except to order something to drink at a fast food drive in on the way out of town. It was dark by the time Eve spoke.

"I know why Billy died," Eve said.

257

"Tell me," Harry said.

"He wanted to," Eve looked at the road. "He couldn't stand the pain of having caused such misery for Candy and their baby. He thought he gave them AIDS. It was more than even Billy could bear."

"But didn't you tell him about Adam in the picture?" Harry was looking for another answer.

"I never saw the picture until now. I don't think Billy ever met Adam. Billy told me that he himself was the cause of Candy and the baby's pain."

"So he waited on that jetty for an assassin to come and blow his brains out," Harry disagreed with his words.

"Who gave him that picture?" Eve asked.

"Captain Art Adkins," Harry said. "Billy would believe a cop. And if the cop told Billy that this is what had become of his love at the hands of the Don, Billy would be glad to help bust the son of a bitch."

"And the Don must have found out" Eve added, "And wanted Billy dead because he could tie him to Adam's death even if he couldn't prove it in court. He was on the case."

They were both feeling wired from the caffeine in the cokes they drank.

"The stupid bastards," Harry said. "They always overdo it. They didn't have to kill Velda for ripping them off for a lousy ten grand. She knows the way the world works. A simple beating would have been enough."

"Not with Velda," Eve said. "She is a tough cookie. They knew she would come back at them and come back hard."

"And Bogart," Harry said.

"That was more personal," Eve figured. "The Don didn't want anybody to know who he was using on his face."

"And Frisky," Harry said.

There was a silence as Eve put her thoughts in order. This was going to be a tough one. Harry waited for an answer. An honest answer.

"I thought it might be Frisky," Eve looked at him and then back at the road. "It all ran through my mind. And then considering that night with the cop being shot at and what happened to Billy, I thought it might not be Frisky. I had to make a decision. The gun was next to me. I erred on the side of safety. I had no choice."

"I know what you mean," Harry said to his own surprise. He looked at the oncoming lights. They shined into the depths of his mind.

"So we know someone with a .22 magnum like Adam's shot Billy, Velda and I'll bet Bogart," Eve told him.

"The big guy with the Don," Harry said. "The one who killed your husband."

"And the Don was behind it," Eve said. "But we don't have enough evidence to convict anybody. Just speculation."

"Bogart's mother said Billy threw away his chair," Harry remembered. "I just can't imagine Billy sitting there waiting for some goon to kill him. Somebody he hated. It's not like Billy."

"So, tell me, Harry, what is like Billy?" Eve probed now. "Stories from ten years ago? Billy dancing up a storm with some pretty girl. Billy, the cop? Billy, the rascal?"

"Billy wanted to see it coming," Harry told her.
Eve said nothing.

"Billy with a wife and kid," Harry had to smile. "That would have been something."

"Some people don't deserve to die."

"Some people don't deserve to live."

"What do you think will happen when you tell Captain Art Adkins what we know," Eve asked.

"He'll tell the Don," Harry said. "Art Adkins knows there is no evidence to convict him. So, he'll sleep with the enemy. The Don will give him a ton of cocaine with no owner. It will play big in the press and they'll solve all the crimes that are still open on the books."

"And call it justice."

"Just us, against them."

"So what are we going to do?" Eve asked.

"I'm going to think about what Billy would do," Harry said.

"Lure them into an alley and whack them on the head," Eve recalled.

"That's what he would have done," Harry said. "But that was before White Rage died."

"You would have done it when you were the Law," Eve said.

"I'm not the law any more," Harry said.

"The law is the way politicians control the wealth,"

Eve mused. "You two were just soldiers for the King."

"Billy said we were peace officers for the people," Harry was serious.

"Billy's dead," Eve reminded him. "They killed him one way or another. They beat him down until he didn't want to live."

"That was his path," Harry said. "He was an adult. And he should have been able to know what was good for him by that time. He didn't need lawmakers to tell him how to live or die."

"Well my path leads by a couple of tombstones," Eve took the gun out of her bag.

"Do you think a cop would hand you a loaded gun?" Harry took the gun from her so she could keep both hands on the wheel. He flipped out the cylinder and showed her the empty chambers in the oncoming headlights.

"Did you know that back at Velda's?" Eve asked.

"Don't go off halfcocked," Harry lectured. "Let's think this out. What would get the Don into a dark alley?"

"Sperm," Eve said.

It was late when they got back to Velda's. They parked out front. It was quiet. The tourists were farther downtown. They let themselves in the front door with a key on the chain with the car key. Nothing had changed in the office and they went to the back door and called up to Velda.

"Oh, fudge," Velda laughed. She pushed a buzzer that opened the door. They went up. Velda wasn't on the couch.

The brandy bottle stood empty on the mantle. Velda was naked crawling out of the kitchen with her gun in one hand. She had the file in her teeth. Harry and Eve watched as she looked under the couch with her ass in the air. Eve checked the dressings on her wounds. She took the gun and the file and helped Velda to the couch.

"What are you looking for?" Harry asked.

"Money," Velda said. "It has wings but leaves tracks."

"What the hell are you talking about?" Harry said.

He looked at the empty bottle. Eve was covering Velda with a sheet.

"The broker's receipt for the ten grand," Velda took the file from Eve and the photo fell to the floor. She emptied the folder and the other paper fell out. "It was in here. Ten grand."

"The money you got for Billy's sperm," Harry said.

"What the hell are you talking about?" Velda said. "That's cash. Do you think I want a record of that cash so the IRS can get on my ass? Kiss my ass. Kiss it and make it better."

Velda let out a laugh and stuck her butt in the air. Harry could smell the liquor on her breath. Eve patted Velda's rump ever so gently.

"You can kiss it too, honey," Velda winked at Eve. Eve kissed her fingers and then placed them on Velda's behind as it slumped to the couch. Harry picked up the folder and the papers. He put the photo back without looking at it.

"That receipt was missing when we found the file on your desk with the sperm on it," Harry said. "I thought it was the ten grand you ripped off the Don."

"You didn't look at the date on it," Velda said. "Some cop you are. It was dated four months ago just before Dr. Adam Wise had his accident. That was no accident. It was a contract hit. That was the money for the hit according to Billy."

"Did he say who paid the contract?" Eve asked. She still had Velda's heavy .45 in one hand. Harry took it from her and put it on the mantel.

"Billy never said," Velda closed her eyes. "He never had the chance to find out."

"We know who filled the contract," Eve said. "The Don's assassin."

"That white haired cocksucker," Velda said and jerked up. "Where's my gun? Nobody tries to kill Velda and gets away with it. I'll kill the both of the guilty bastards."

"Calm down!" Harry said. "What are you, the jury?"

"I, the jury," Velda said, "find the two guilty as charged. I sentence them to death because no court in the land ever will. There's a law more basic than anything on the books. Survival of the fittest. And those two aren't fit to live."

Harry didn't have an answer for her, but then there wasn't any question. It was a statement of fact. The receipt that connected them to the crime was gone. The receipt that Billy had uncovered. They killed Billy? You

263

didn't have to be a Perry Mason to figure out this one.
They tried to kill Velda. They killed Bogart. The Law
couldn't stop them. Who would be next? Would they
come after him when they knew what he knew? Would
they come after Eve, the widow? There was no telling
when their bloodlust would be satisfied. They had to be
stopped and everybody in that room was thinking the same
thing.

"If you can't trust the cops, who can you trust?" Harry
said. Eve looked at him and agreed. Velda was silent.

"I've got a plan," Eve said.

"Count me in," Velda told Eve.

"These guys aren't going to put up their hands and do
what you tell them to do," Harry told Eve. "If they see a
gun and no badge, they'll take a chance of you missing.
When they pull a gun it will be to kill. Kill you. You have
to hit them hard and fast by surprise. Don't give them a
chance."

"I shot Frisky, didn't I?" Eve said. "Did you ever
have to shoot someone?"

"In twenty years," Harry thought, "No. The first ten
years were my education. Graduate School of Life with
Billy. The last ten I spent saving lives and collecting the
remains where we were too late."

Harry sat down in front of the fireplace that had no
flames. He stared into it. Eve came and sat next to him.
Velda was breathing on the couch behind them. It sounded
as if she were asleep.

"What an education!" Harry said. "Billy and I were

264

riding in a car together. There were a series of bank robberies where we'd always get there late. We could be a block
away and get the alarm call and still get there late. So, Billy
went to the Captain and told him what we were up against.
The Captain told Billy not to worry. It wasn't our fault.
The banks had a fifteen minute delay on the alarm. They
didn't want us to get there while the crooks were there.
Somebody might get hurt. It would be bad for business.
The one guy we did catch stopped to talk to the reception-
ist. He wanted a date. He had a toy gun. Billy wanted to
let him go because he would be too stupid to survive in
prison."

Eve held his arm and kissed him on his ear. When he
turned his head, she kissed him full on the mouth and
lingered long enough to let him know that she wanted it to
last forever. Harry was the one to pull away.

"We want to get them alone somewhere," Harry said.

"The boat," Eve said. She was anxious. It showed in
her voice. But she wasn't afraid.

"Are you sure you want to commit murder?" Harry
asked.

"If that's what it's come to. Why should they live and
Billy and the others die? Are they some higher life form
that can prey on a lower species? Should we surrender or
run from their lawlessness? If the Law can't stop them, we
can."

"Something could go wrong," Harry couldn't look at
her.

"I'll take my chances," Eve said. "I would rather die

265

than bring our child up in a world with them in it."

"Our child!" Harry swallowed hard.

"Our night with the twins coincided with my most fertile time," Eve spoke softly. "The full moon. The ritual. Your sperm inside me. It could be true. It happened with Billy."

"You want to have my baby." Harry said. It was a statement of understanding, not a question. He suddenly felt very warm. It was a dimension he hadn't thought about.

"If I couldn't have Billy's baby," Eve told the truth. "I want yours."

"It's great just to be nominated," Harry said.

"After we get them to the boat," Eve changed the subject. "We can't do it in the anchorage. Too many boats."

"Garrison Bite," Harry said. "It's a shallow anchorage on the other side of the island. Most boats can't get in there, but we can with the catamaran."

"I'll tell the Don that the Twins said that he would pay a premium for your sperm if you could ever get it up." Eve was calculating. "I'll tell him he can get it at the boat at Garrison Bite where we anchored for privacy."

"He'll just send the big guy to fetch it," Harry said. "The Don won't come himself."

"He will when I tell him how I'm going to get it," Eve said. "You know what he likes. Candy told you."

"He'll suspect a trap," Harry said. He didn't want to hear her details. He wanted to focus on what had to be

266

done.

"Then he won't come," Eve said. "But I'll bet his salaciousness overwhelms his caution. He'll have his bodyguard with him. It will be safe."

"Human nature," Harry said. "Ask for a lot of money. Everyone understands greed. It's a gamble we can take, since we're the ones setting the trap. If they don't show, we can try again. We'll need another gun or some ammunition for the .22 mag."

"There's a sporting goods store on Stock Island," Eve said. "We passed it on the way to see Candy."

"Make the call," Harry said.

CHAPTER TWELVE

Harry and Eve went down to Velda's office. He sat at the desk and she sat in a wooden chair at the side near the phone. There was a rolodex next to the desk lamp and Harry found the Don's number and gave it to Eve. She began to dial.

Harry had brought Velda's .45 down with them. He dropped the clip on the desk pad and ejected the round in the chamber. It was wet. He took a handkerchief from his pocket and began to clean the weapon. He didn't want a misfire.

"Hello," Eve said into the phone. She was composed. "This is Mrs. Adam Wise. I would like to speak to the Don."

Eve took a deep breath and smiled at Harry while she waited. He made a fist to show support. Eve sat up straight.

"Hello," Eve said. " Yes...Yes the same. No, this has nothing to do with my husband. It has to do with money. Yes...The Tortugas were wonderful. It is a shame."

Harry looked around for an extension. There was none. Eve looked at him with her confident air and it settled his nerves a bit. It was great to have a good partner.

"They said that there was a premium on Billy's brother's sperm...You can understand my disappointment. ...No. More...That's more like it...None of your business. It will be better this time...I'm sure. I found out what he really likes...Anal sex...He will wear a rubber. He knows I don't like the mess...As you know, I'm familiar with all kinds of partialisms and fetishes...For the money. ...You can never have too much... Don't get mad, get even. ...It's not one of my favorite positions. ...Yes, I do prefer to be on top...In the middle of the night. On the boat. We're going over to Garrison Bite to be alone. If you want it fresh, be there before sunrise. If you want to watch, come early...Hate is a strong word. Disappointment. This hasn't been a good town for me....Don't worry, I'll fix him a couple of margaritas to relax him. Bring cash...If you want to know the truth, the Twins showed me that I prefer a woman...I don't want to drag this out. Garrison Bite. Our mast light will be on...I am...You can't insult me. Everything you say is true."

Eve hung up. She let out a long sigh and relaxed. She gave Harry a look of satisfaction. He was familiar with that look.

"He's nibbling at the bait," Eve said. "You could hear

269

the droll dripping from his lips when I mentioned anal sex. How long will it take to move the boat?"

"The channel is well marked," Harry said. "We can motor. That will save time. Maybe take a half an hour. We have plenty of time to do it or change our minds."

"Let's do it," Eve said.

"It's early," Harry said. "Let the tourists trade thin out a little before we do anything."

"Then we'll stay here with Velda," Eve said. "It will give her a chance to get some rest."

"She's going to want this gun when she wakes up," Harry said. "Let me see that .22."

Eve had her bag. The gun was in it. She gave it to Harry who opened the cylinder and looked down the barrel with the light behind it. He gave a nod and placed it on the blotter next to the .45.

"I've got a shotgun on the boat not even the cops could find," Harry said.

"Are you sure you can do this?" Eve asked and looked into his soul. It made him stop and think about the thousands of dead people he had seen and some he watched die. Now, he was planning on killing two people. He had seen Eve kill. The thought gave him confidence. She gave him strength.

"Yes," Harry said. "I'm sure."

Harry felt an anger inside that he hadn't felt in years. There was a vengeance in him. He could calm, center and meditate all he wanted, but it wouldn't go away. It was a primal instinct for survival tempered by hatred. It cut

270

through his self control. He moved with purpose lacking reason. Harry put it on automatic. What would be would be. It was out of his control. He only followed the path, he didn't build it.

"What was Billy's plan," Eve asked. "And what went wrong? How did he get hurt?"

Harry leaned back in the chair. The moment of truth had come so suddenly. He could tell that she was testing him to see if he measured up to the task at hand. He knew she wanted the truth.

"Billy wanted out," Harry started. "I told you how shitty his attitude toward life had become."

"Before White Rage died," Eve said.

"Yes, I guess I told you," Harry looked for the words. "It was simple enough. Billy figured he could get hit on the head and forget everything. He told me about it while we were sitting in an unmarked car surveying Needle Park. It was a place on the East Side where the junkies came to get their fix at the same time every day. Everybody knew about it. They spotted us. It didn't matter. They only had one thing on their minds. Junk. Heroin. Smack. Billy asks me which one do I want to arrest first, the one with the snot running out of his nose or the one puking in the garbage can. It wasn't the cops and robbers we played as kids. So we're sitting there figuring a way for Billy to get hit in the head without killing him."

"And not do any permanent damage," Eve said. "You didn't want to hurt him."

"Billy didn't care about pain. He was a tough kid.

271

The State Home was no picnic and the prep school was richer but could be just as tough on kids who didn't belong. Billy could take it. He knew that pain went away with time. He would get hit. Forget. And retire on a pension in Florida."

"What if he got slugged in an alley?" Eve asked. "You used to do it to others."

"No. We thought about that. The review board wouldn't buy it. You would need a witness. No, that couldn't be the way it happens. Then our answer comes driving up in a white *Cadillac*. This six foot two inch African Chief in full tribal dashiki robes gets out. He steps aside and the rats come to feed at the trough. Two guys in the back seat are handing out envelopes and collecting cash like the daily double window two minutes to post time. We knew who he was, but we couldn't touch him because he had beat the rap so many times, the department was scared of a harassment suit. This guy not only ran dope, he had a stable of teenage prostitutes working Time Square."

"Black girls?" Eve asked.

"Black, white, yellow. All young. All wasted," Harry said. "One time me and Billy were working undercover there, but we couldn't get one solicitation. We wondered what was wrong with us. Did we look gay? Inside this bar Billy finds a hooker and tells her we're cops. She says she knew. Billy wants to know how she spotted us. She looks at Billy and says to me: `Look at this guy. A guy like him can always get laid. He don't have to pay for it'."

"Was the Chief in anyway connected to the Don?"

Eve asked. "I mean the young boys, young girls?"

"Scum usually collects in one spot," Harry said. "Could have been. Didn't matter then. We were beat cops, not investigators. We were officers of the law and we were told to watch and not do shit. It really burned Billy. He felt frustrated and disillusioned."

"So how was the Chief your answer?" Eve got him back to the subject at hand.

"The plan," Harry said. "You want to know the plan. Billy figured that if he could get into a fight with this pimp. He could take a punch and take some satisfaction at the same time. The Chief was tough. He had once been a golden gloves contender. He could hit. Billy wasn't picking on any sissy. This guy was a bully. I won't bore you with the stories we heard about this guy from the girls. The kid hookers was enough to burn Billy."

"And the Chief was black," Eve said.

"He was black as the ace of spades," Harry said slowly. "That had something to do with it too."

"And what was your part in the plan?" Eve asked.

"I was backup. I was there to make sure that Billy won. Fair and square."

"What went wrong," Eve caught him looking at the guns.

"We followed the *Cadillac* until the Chief dropped off his brothers with the money. That pimp loved that car. And he wasn't afraid to be alone. He had more freedom on the streets than the people we were supposed to be protect-ing. He was the bad guy. We were the Law. Forget the

273

philosophies. To make a long story short, we pulled him over in an alley. And he comes out of the car swinging like he's fighting for his life. He caught Billy with the pension punch to the head right away. Boom. Billy got staggered. He dropped to the ground and the Chief comes with a kick. Billy caught his leg and brought him to the ground where he literally beat the shit out of him. It was a mess. Billy kept hitting him until his hands hurt and then he kicked him. I had to step in and pull Billy off of him. I had my back to the Chief when Billy saw the gun. He pushed me out of the way and took the bullet. I broke the mother fucker's fingers getting that gun out of his hand. The Chief was laying there in a heap across from Billy who was holding himself in with one bloody hand while he drew his gun with the other. He put the gun right up to the Chief's head. The Chief looked Billy right in the eye. He didn't flinch. He wasn't afraid. He had made his peace. Billy said to him, `no witnesses' and the Chief understood. He didn't blink. Billy blew his brains out."

"So you feel guilty and blame yourself for Billy getting shot," Eve said.

"I should have reacted sooner," Harry said. "The police report noted that I hadn't properly patted down the suspect. Who the hell thought that he would be stupid enough to carry a gun in New York."

"He could have gotten arrested."

"Yeah," Harry smirked. "Arrested. Instead he got dead. And Billy got hurt. I sat there with him in the blood and shit keeping him alive until the ambulance got there. I

274

was suspended for thirty days without pay. When I came back, Emergency Services had a new truck. They needed somebody with experience to work it. I got the job."

"And Billy got his pension."

"And a citation for bravery. The suits at headquarters threw a bag of coke in the back seat and I smashed a taillight."

"Probable cause to stop him. And the coke in plain sight."

"The Black newspaper did a feature about the Chief," Harry said. "Detailed all the times he helped his neighborhood. Also all the times he was arrested without conviction. It was a well balanced report. But it didn't mention Billy. Only that a police officer had been injured. The Chief had a big family and lots of friends. They were all at his funeral."

Harry stopped talking and Eve stopped the questioning. He saw his pain reflected in her face. The terrible irony, the horrific disaster. The crime.

"We better get going," Eve said. She wasn't going to push him. No cross examination. She seemed satisfied. "I'll go up and check on Velda. Pull the car around back."

"We could forget about the Don," Harry said and she looked at his eyes. He could take it. He didn't blink! "We could get the boat and keep going. Forget this place. There's nothing that compels us to kill him. Just the two of us, alone in the world."

"What about Velda?" Eve said.

Harry didn't have to answer. She knew the way to his

275

heart. Twenty years. Save the women and the children from the bad guys. Once he was the law of the land. Now he was the law of the jungle. It was instinctive. They would make sure that Velda survived. She didn't deserve to die. The Don didn't deserve to live. It was a judgement call. It was an easy decision to make. Eve looked away.

Harry watched her go into the stairwell with an easy grace and concentrated purpose. She could keep it together. She was some woman.

Through the opaque windows, it was hard to see what it was like outside. Harry opened the door and the humidity and heat hit him in the face almost as hard as the metal that cracked the bridge of his nose. Harry saw stars. He was stunned, but the pain soon set off alarms as if he had walked into a lamppost. The lamppost turned out to be the silencer on the end of a .22 mag., an assassins' gun. The gun was in the hand of the big guy who blocked the doorway and any view from the street. At his shoulder was the white haired Don, tan and smiling.

"You've been out to sea too long," the Don said. "We have Caller I.D. now. Mrs. Brown's Cookies. Welcome to the Twenty First Century."

The big guy came forward and moved Harry back into the office with the gun pressed at his heart. Harry retreated back to the desk where the .45 and the .22 lay on the blotter. Harry touched the bridge of his nose. It felt as if the skin was broken but it wasn't. His nose throbbed and his eyes hurt.

"Where is the bereaved widow?" the Don asked.

"We had a fight. She left me."

"And Velda?" the Don asked.

"She's dead," Harry said. "She should have stayed in the hospital."

"That looks like Velda's gun," the Don said to the big guy. "She must be dead or she'd have it on her. Two-timing Bitch. Laughing in my face whenever she saw me. She knew that when I thought I was communing with your magnificent brother, I was really rubbing that common black boy into my face and hair. Not that there's anything wrong with that. Some people prefer it. But not me. I just can't stand to be made a fool."

"Who told you about the sperm scam?" Harry asked.

"Wait a second," the Don said. "I'm the one with the gun. I ask the questions."

The Don stuck his hand into his pocket.

"Who paid for the contract on Adam Wise?" Harry asked.

The Don's hand came out of his pocket with the rubber ball he squeezed.

"That looks like the gun I gave Billy for...," the Don started.

Harry knew the sound as soon as the .45 roared and the Don's head was knocked back in a spray of red that took him back over a chair. The big guy got off two pops of his pistol toward the back door. The canon roared again and the big guy grabbed his chest. Another explosion and he was dead on the floor.

Eve came in the back door with a stainless .45 in her

277

hands.

"Velda had another gun," Eve said.

"You think I'm a one trick pony," Velda could be heard coming down the stairs. She came in wrapped in a brown sheet. She saw everything at a glance and grabbed the gun from Eve's hands.

"Both of you," Velda commanded. "Out the back fast. I'll handle this. They came to finish the job they started at the canal. I was ready for them."

Harry and Eve were at the end of the alley when they heard another shot and glass breaking. They walked hand in hand out into the commerce of the street. Eve had picked up her gun as they left and Harry felt it against him in her bag as he held her close.

"Velda's getting ready for the paraffin test for gun powder," Harry said. "Tying up loose ends."

"We better get some ice fast," Eve said looking at his face.

"A boat is a dangerous place to live," Harry had his story. "Accidents happen. Winch handle. Hurt like hell."

"I should have been up top helping you," Eve caught on fast.

CHAPTER THIRTEEN

When they got back to the boat, Eve bathed Harry with sea water, careful of his face where he held an ice pack. She rinsed him with warm water from the shower bag. Then she jumped overboard.

Eve came back on board, undressed and rinsed with the remainder of the water in the shower bag. She got a couple of caftans for them to wear. Then she brought out the bottle of tequila and a joint. Harry took a hit and handed it to her but she refused.

"Better not do that," Eve said. "I might be pregnant."

Harry took another drag and let it die out. He was watching Eve pour the liquor as she had done before. Her hand was steady.

"Drink this," Eve said handing him a double shot. "It'll put you to sleep."

"You know me pretty well," Harry said.

"I have an interest in you," Eve smiled.

"You know me well enough to give me a couple shots of tequila and a joint," Harry said. "It will put me out for hours. I'd sleep right through my watch."

"You're getting at something," Eve said. "What's bothering you?"

"Putting together some things that seem to fall into place in this puzzle." His voice was shaky. He took a deep breath. "You wound up with the gun that the Don gave Billy after your husband was killed. Nobody planted it in your underwear drawer."

Eve looked at him, started to speak, stopped and choked it back. She couldn't hold it. The truth wanted to get out.

"I called Billy when we stopped to dive for lobsters at Big Pine Key," Eve said. "Remember when I went ashore alone because I wanted butter and we were out."

"Somewhere along the way," Harry said. The brain cells that held that memory were dulled by the pot he smoked. Any desire to recall more was depressed by the booze.

"I told him when we would be in late that night. He said he wanted to meet me before sunrise on the jetty. Take the last of the high tide in and drift back out again when it turned. He didn't want you to know. I told him I could pull it off."

"You did. With ease."

"Billy had the gun with him," Eve said explaining. "I never knew it was Adam's. I never knew he owned a gun. I didn't lie about that, Harry."

"I believe you," Harry said. He took another shot. He knew he was going to need it.

"Billy was going to kill himself," Eve said. "He told how he killed Candy and his baby when he infected them. The guilt was more than he could handle."

"He didn't shoot himself," Harry said.

"He didn't want to hurt you," Eve raised her voice.

"He knew if he killed himself, you would feel that it was from what you did. But if it was a murder, you would feel better about yourself. You would want revenge. Billy knew you better than I did."

"So you helped him out," Harry said.

"I owed it to him," Eve explained. "After he kissed me goodbye, after I couldn't talk him out of it. After he told me of his pain. He handed me the gun. I don't know why I didn't throw it away. I took it with me and that's how it got here."

"After you shot him. After you killed Billy."

"Doctor assisted suicide. After what he thought he had done to Candy and the baby, Billy wanted to die. Being guilty for a loved one's pain. Not wanting to have to look at your work at what you've done. You understand that better than anybody, Harry."

"And Billy had arranged for the hit on your husband," Harry got ahead of her. "That's why he knew you would do it. That's why you owed him, isn't it?"

"I was Billy's angel of death," Eve said. "It's not a role I sought. I loved him. I loved Billy."

281

"You eliminated the one person who could implicate you in Adam's death," Harry controlled his tone. His anger was gone. He had no hate left. "Frisky could have tied you to Billy too, so you killed him."

"There's no proof of that," Eve said. "You're playing guessing games. You're acting like a cop."

"I could check into your bank account," Harry said. "See if there are any large withdrawals at that time."

"Is that what you want to do with your life? Come to a conclusion and then find evidence to back it up. You are a cop. Someone confesses to one crime and you try to pin every unsolved case on them. You told me how it's done, Harry. Are you going to put a bag of white powder ..."

"I was thinking out loud," Harry backed off. He had no evidence. He knew she was right.

"Well, then let me think out loud," Eve insisted. "I've known you and I've known Billy. I think you're the guy who wanted out. I think maybe you went up against the Chief. But he was a better athlete. All the pro teams are mostly black or Hispanic. They're taking over everything. Maybe the Chief was beating you. It was your `white rage' that brought it on. I could check the records and see when that Indian died. Check out your story. See if it was you up on that skyscraper. If there really was one. I could check the police report on Billy's accident. Maybe you were the one who killed the Chief. Maybe you were so willing to kill the Don because you did it before."

"So, that's what you think?"

"You loved Billy," Eve said. "Could you have killed

282

him? Do you want to think about the horror of his
future, his long slow death. The death of his beloved
Candy. The death of their child. At what point would
you give in? At what point would you want out?"

"We were bad for each other as kids," Harry said.
He wasn't interested in her questions or accusations.
"We were always getting one another into trouble.
Nothing big. Little stuff."

"Little boys, little problems," Eve said. "Big boys,
big problems."

"It didn't bother me that we hadn't seen each other
in ten years," Harry took another drink and another
toke. "For the first thirty we had been so close. Then we
found our separate paths. We were brothers and we
loved each other. If there is an after life, we'll be best
friends."

Harry closed his eyes and felt the world spinning
out of control around him. The tequila and the joint
were working. He could feel the sleep settling into his
system. The last thing he saw was Eve holding the .22
magnum.

When Harry awoke at the first light of dawn, Eve
was gone. The dinghy was still there. He checked her
cabin and all of her things were gone. She either swam
in or hitched a ride with the early morning crowd that
went ashore where they had jobs.

Harry shaved and put on fresh shorts and a shirt.
He found the letter from Billy with only his signature.
Harry knew what he had to do. His nose was swollen

purple and his eyes were black. He looked like hell. He
didn't feel much better. He put on sunglasses. It didn't
help his looks or his mood.

CHAPTER FOURTEEN

Harry rowed ashore and tied up at the Marina. There was an office supply store on the way to the police station and Harry borrowed a typewriter. He filled in the space above Billy's signature, putting the paper back in its original envelope. He wrote a check and mailed it in a separate envelope.

Harry was waiting outside the police station when Captain Art Adkins pulled up for a day's work. He looked haggard, as if he hadn't slept. It seems that there was a double homicide at Mrs. Brown's Cookie office.

"I got a letter from Billy," Harry told the tired cop who tried to hurry past him. Art Adkins stopped. Harry showed him the post mark.

"Has this got anything to do with two dead men," Captain Art Adkins asked. "That damned Velda. What a piece of work she is. Falling down drunk and she takes out

a professional killer and his boss. You know the Don.
Billy and I tried to nail him and couldn't. Then this old
broad takes care of it for us. And in self defense too. It's
hard to tell about people. What happened to your nose?"

"Winch handle," Harry said.

"You got to be crazy to live on a boat," Art Adkins
said. "So, you can help my case?"

"It's all in the letter," Harry said.

"Hearsay," Art Adkins said but took the envelope.

"The last testament of a dying man," Harry said.
"Best evidence. A grand jury would get to see it."

"Did it say who killed him?" Art Adkins asked.

"Yes," Harry said. "He also mentioned his work with
you and the photo you supplied."

"What photo?" Art Adkins started to go inside.

"The one taken after Billy and Candy split up," Harry
said.

"That's what Frisky told me," Adkins said. "He took
it and should know when."

"It really got Billy stirred up," Harry said. "Enough
to get involved. Enough to get him killed."

Captain Art Adkins wouldn't look Harry in the eye.
That revealed more than any words he could have mouthed.
Harry left him standing there with his mouth open but
nothing came out. They had both had enough of this case.
Harry walked away from it all.

As Harry walked the streets alone, he realized that he
was obligated to no one. No other human being counted on
him for anything. All his debts were paid. He felt free but

286

he also felt lonely. He walked the familiar path to Velda's office.

One of the store front windows was covered with plywood. The front door was blocked by a strip of crime scene tape. Harry went around to the alley and found the back door open. He could hear movement upstairs. He went up the steps and knocked on the door. Eve opened it.

"Hello," Harry said.

"Hello," Eve said to him and then called back over her shoulder. "It's Billy's brother. You can put down the gun."

Eve let him in. She wore cutoff shorts and a white blouse tied across her waist so that her naval showed. She was barefoot and her legs were a lovely tan. Harry followed her into the living room.

"I need a drink," Velda said coming out of the kitchen with a chrome plated .45 in her hand. She must have seen Harry staring at the gun. "A girl can't be too careful."

Velda's hair was combed out and fell well below her stitches concealing the wound. She wore a sheer cocoa colored robe that covered the rest of her injuries but still revealed her shapely figure. She had on lipstick and makeup that covered her facial bruises. Her heels clicked on the floor as she came toward him in her brown pumps.

"Can't a girl buy a drink around here?" Velda asked.

"I'll run down to the package store and pick up a bottle of brandy," Eve said going to the door where she had a pair of sandals. "I have money."

Eve went out and shut the door leaving Harry alone

287

with Velda.

"She's a good kid," Velda said.

"And a good shot," Harry added.

"She's no worse than any of us," Velda looked sideways at him.

"She killed Billy," Harry said.

"We're all killers," Velda said. "But who did we kill? We killed scum. We killed a plague, a virus that was destroying the good people of the world."

"You can justify it, you can rationalize, but it's still murder," Harry said.

"Don't play self righteous with me." Velda moved in on him. "I know you killed that pimp. Billy told me."

Harry couldn't move. Velda was up close to him and he could smell the cinnamon in her hair. Her eyes were dark and penetrating. She kissed him on the mouth and then walked away. The kiss of death.

"Did he tell you the whole story?" Harry said.

"The whole story," Velda said. "I was his wife. We had no secrets. Billy wanted to die. He wanted to die from the minute he took that bullet in the gut. He couldn't feel anything. He knew his legs were gone. He wanted to bleed to death in the street. He wanted to go out like a good cop in the line of duty. And you saved his life, Harry. The truth is that Billy never wanted to see you again."

Harry put his head in his hands and started to cry. Velda came back to him and put an arm around his shoulder until he stopped. He wiped his nose with a tissue she pulled from the pocket of her robe.

"The truth hurts," Velda said. "You can't run away from it."

"Velda," Harry finally spoke. "Why is it some people have it so easy and others like Billy and Candy have it so tough?"

"God only knows." Velda said.

Harry and Velda sat on each side of Eve drinking brandy from a bottle and smoking a joint. Eve abstained. She was feeling a little queazy. They were a sad lot. Then came the local news. Velda had brought a portable television out of the bedroom and set it on the floor by the fireplace. The first story was about her.

The videotape replay of her earlier performance made them laugh out loud. There she was in her hospital gown with the bloodstains on it. Her hair was a rat's nest that covered everything but her black eye. She told the reporter how she had gunned down the two hoods who came after her when they found out they hadn't killed her in the canal. Her language had to be bleeped several times and they cut away to the reporter when she opened the gown in back to show her wounds. She told the reporters that her husband Billy had been killed and maybe they thought she knew something.

"It probably had something to do with drugs," were Velda's last word to the reporter.

Then there was Captain Art Adkins refusal to comment on whether the gun found at Velda's was the same one used in other recent killings. Was it a gangland killing? Was this the beginning of a drug war?

"No comment," Captain Art Adkins said.

"Wait 'til they find the kiddie porn in the Don's house," Velda said. "They'll love that angle. This could go on for weeks."

"And what about all that sperm?" Eve asked.

"I think it's time to go sailing," Harry said.

"Not too far from an obstetrician," Eve burped but held it down.

"Do you want to come with us?" Harry asked Velda.

"I'd be like a mother-in-law on your honeymoon," Velda said. "No. I need to heal. I'm going to go on that Goddess Retreat in Maui that the Twins run. I still have time left on my six months since Billy. Nothing but safe sex for me for a while. I still have the ten grand from the sperm scam. And you've got the money Billy left you."

"Not anymore," Harry said. "I donated the whole three hundred thousand to Candy and Billy Jr. at the Pediatric AIDS Center."

"Well, aren't you the sport!" Velda said.

"Three hundred thousand," Eve said. "I thought that account showed a five hundred thousand balance."

"Hey," Harry said. "Nobody's perfect. I must have made a mistake."

"You're just like your brother," Velda said. "You're a rascal, Harry. You're just like Billy."

THE END

290

Printed in the United States
107814LV00002B/29/A